Copyright © 2024 by Melody Tyden

All rights reserved.

The characters and events portrayed in this book are fictitious. Any similarity to real persons, living or dead, is coincidental and not intended by the author.

No part of this book may be reproduced, or stored in a retrieval system, or transmitted in any form or by any means, electronic, mechanical, photocopying, recording, or otherwise, without express written permission of the publisher.

Cover design by: Melody Tyden

LOYALTY TEST

MELODY TYDEN

CONTENTS

Chapter One

~Jennifer~

The musician I'd been flirting with online for two days texted me back at 1:37 in the morning.

The message alert interrupted a particularly fun dream where Taylor Swift, Beyoncé and I were chilling on a girl's night. We were just about to get into the really juicy gossip when reality came crashing back in.

Groggily, I reached over to my bedside table and grabbed the phone to read his message.

> Just finished writing a new chorus for a song. Want me to play it for you?

Squinting at the screen in the darkness, I managed to type out a coherent reply.

> OMG, am I the first person who gets to hear it?

> You know it. I wrote it for you. Video chat?

With a groan, I sat up and grabbed my emergency supplies from next to the bed. Push-up bra, lip gloss, concealer under my eyes and a quick brush through my hair did the trick, and I hit record on my phone before hitting the call button.

"Fuck, you look gorgeous." A cigarette hung from his lips as he answered my call, his phone already set up so he could sit back with his guitar, the dim lighting working to his advantage. With his shoulder-length hair, dark stubble on his chin and bright blue eyes, he looked good and he knew it. "You'd look even better if I were there in bed with you."

The pout of my lips had been practiced in the mirror a hundred times before. "If your song's good enough, maybe you can be."

He flashed me a grin that could break hearts before beginning to strum on his guitar. The song wasn't half-bad, actually, but my eyes kept flicking up to the top of the screen, making sure I recorded every second.

"What do you think?" He grabbed a nearby beer bottle as soon as the song had finished, taking a long swig.

"I think..." I drew out the silence, batting my eyelashes a few times for good measure. "No song has ever turned me on so much. You said you're single, right?"

He grinned again, his eyes flashing away from the screen for just a second. "Absolutely. So, you wanna come over and hear it again in person? Or maybe we could just..."

He just said the magic words. With the ease of practice, I ended the call, stopped the recording, and blocked the asshole in a matter of seconds.

Fully awake by that point, I took screenshots of the texts and sent them along with the video recording to the woman who'd put me in touch with him in the first place.

The bastard's fiancée.

> I hate when things go this way, but you deserve to know the truth.

The message went to read immediately, as if she'd been waiting for it. I sat patiently in the stillness of my room, waiting for her reply in case she wanted to talk or needed a shoulder to cry on. Some women needed to be talked down from murder. Others just needed to know they weren't alone. I could never predict how someone would react when they found they'd fallen for a lying, cheating piece of shit.

However, when her response came, I could only describe it as stoic.

Thanks. It hurts, but I expected it. I guess the wedding's off.

That's your call.

I never gave any advice to the women who hired me to test their man's loyalty. I did my job and left it there. Only they would know the right path for them.

You want to know the worst part? That's not even a new song. He wrote it a year ago, and he said he wrote it for me.

That didn't seem like the worst part to me, but I could understand it must have stung.

You deserve better. And if you decide to end things, there are good men out there, I promise.

They were heavily outnumbered by the creeps and losers, in my experience, but I didn't add that part. No need to kick someone when they were down.

I hope so.

A defeated-looking emoji accompanied her reply.

Did you find one?

Pain tugged at my heart, just for a second, as I glanced at the empty space in my bed next to me.

Yeah, I found one. You will too. Good luck, Sarah.

Thanks, Jen.

I always left the door open for women to come back to me later on if they wanted to chat more, but they rarely did. Talking with me only reminded them of one of the most painful moments in their lives. I understood that.

Some men did pass my tests, but not as often as I would have liked, and pretty much never when I received a text from them at 1:37 am.

Nothing good ever came from texting a stranger after midnight.

After the interruption to my sleep, I woke up later than usual the next morning, but it didn't really make a difference to anyone other than me. My loyalty tests had become a full-time job, letting me work from home and set my own hours. On the one hand, it saddened me that so many women felt the need to use my services, but on the other hand, it paid the bills. All in all, I couldn't complain too much.

Bright California sunshine streamed in my kitchen window where I turned on my coffee maker and grabbed an apple off the counter before sitting down at the table with my laptop to get to work.

Meticulous records weren't optional in a business like mine. I had files on each man I approached, consisting of what his partner told me about him, links and screenshots from all his social media accounts, and the strategy I intended to use with him to see if he would be open to cheating. Once I made contact, I took screenshots of every single message before anything could be deleted, and recorded every phone call or video chat. My approach might *seem* improvisational, but a lot of work went into it before I ever made contact with the men in the first place, and even more effort went into documenting everything afterwards.

That morning, I updated the file on the musician from the night before, closing it out by updating my master spreadsheet with the outcome. *Fail* appeared in bright red letters, just one of many in a sea of red that made the few green *Pass* entries look out of place.

With that done, I took a look through the DMs on my bait profile, the one I used to message the men I tested. Nothing new had come in there since the night before, so I moved to the messages on my *other* profile, the one where women could request my services. There, the inbox had several new messages, as it always did.

With my cup of coffee in hand, I started going through them. By that point, I knew what to expect, with common phrases appearing over and over again.

> I never thought I would be in this situation.

> He says I'm being insecure, but I feel like something's not right.

> I'm probably being paranoid, but…

Excuses, gaslighting, and outright lying were frustratingly commonplace, and usually, when I went to the man's profile, more red flags appeared.

Shirtless pictures.

Photos of him with a car, or a bike, or something else meant to show off his wealth.

And most importantly: no pictures of the woman who contacted me in the first place.

Exceptions existed, but those staples were my bread and butter, and four of the five new messages that morning fit into that category.

The fifth one, however, looked a little different. After glancing at the man's profile, I went back to the initial message from his partner, a woman named Celine, and read it again, more carefully the second time.

> You probably hear this all the time, but I'm getting a bad feeling about my husband. He's a travel agent and he often goes on 'scouting trips' to check out hotels and cities to recommend to clients. During those trips, he has his phone off a lot. When he finally replies to me, he always says he had a poor

signal or some other excuse. At home, his phone buzzes with notifications all the time but I can never see who's messaging him. He never leaves it unattended. When I ask him, he says it's about work. He wants us to start a family, but I don't want to have a kid with someone who might be cheating on me. Can you help me find out for sure?

A lot of the hallmarks of cheating jumped out at me: the out-of-town trips, the unavailability, and hiding incoming messages certainly didn't sound good.

His social media accounts, however, looked clean. Along with a lot of travel pictures, which made sense given his job, I spotted his wife several times. They made a gorgeous couple, both tanned with long limbs, her with blonde-streaked hair and him with a dark, short cut, her eyes brown and his a vibrant blue. If they did have kids, those kids would be stunning. Romantic pictures of the two of them dotted his feeds, and his relationship status clearly stated 'married'.

Just because he didn't pretend to be single didn't mean he wouldn't cheat, though. He might have other accounts under other names, or he might simply be meeting up with women who weren't interested in anything long-term and didn't care about the literal or metaphorical ring on his finger.

They lived in San Francisco, not far away at all, which always made the approach a little easier. When I had to message men in the Midwest, for example, I had to be more creative about where I might know them from. With someone close to me on the west coast, I could spin it a lot of different ways.

With my initial checks out of the way, I sent a reply to the woman.

Hi Celine, I'm sorry to hear there might be trouble in your marriage, but that's what I'm here for. Here's a link to the packages I offer. If you're interested, choose the one that suits you best and send me any additional details you think might help me to make a good impression on him when I get in touch.

Her response came back quickly, while I worked through some of the profiles for the other messages.

> I don't see any packages where you meet him in person. Is that an option?

Just as quickly, I shot back a response.

> No, I don't do in-person meetings for my own safety. Most women agree that if their man offers to meet me, it means he would cheat with me too.

> Could you make an exception in this case? I really need to know if he'd go through with it.

> I'm sorry, but no. That's a hard limit for me. If it's necessary for you, then you'll need to find someone else.

Her response took a bit longer that time, but eventually, my phone buzzed again.

> I've heard you're the best, so I guess I'll have to trust you.

That managed to be both flattering and a bit insulting at the same time, but almost immediately afterwards, I got the confirmation that her payment had gone through.

The job had officially begun.

"Alright, Gabriel Carter," I muttered as I returned to his profile to start building my file on him. "Let's see what kind of woman would tempt you."

~Gabriel~

I gave my inbox one last glance at the end of the work day, making sure everything could wait for the morning before I shut my computer down. Despite having travel insurance, customers often got in touch with me directly if they encountered any problems during the trips I arranged for them, and although it added a bit of stress to my day, I didn't mind too much. My job was to make sure they had the best experience possible, and if I could do anything to help make that happen, I would.

As I stood up to grab my bag, my phone buzzed on my desk. Immediately, my heart beat a little faster, hope rising in my chest. Maybe Celine messaged me? She used to send me a text at the end of every day to see when I'd be home and say she'd missed me, but gradually, she stopped doing it. I couldn't even say for sure when the last time had been, and given the growing distance between us, I'd welcome that kind of small gesture to let me know she'd been thinking of me.

That hope only lasted as long as it took to pick up my phone, when I immediately saw the message didn't come from her. Someone I didn't know had messaged me, through my Instagram DMs, with the username 'sunnycali'.

> Hey, I'm sorry to reach out randomly, but I came across your Uzbekistan pictures. They're stunning! Could I ask you a couple of questions?

A little flush of pride swelled inside me. They *were* stunning photos, but I didn't have a very big following. Usually, a handful of my friends and family or former clients liked my travel pictures and that would be all. Though I didn't know why they'd reached a stranger, it made me feel good to know they had.

Not bothering to look at the person's profile before answering, I sent back a quick response.

> Ask away.

Out loud, I said goodnight to the others in the office and headed out onto the street to catch the bus home. With only one car, I normally took public transit so that Celine could have the car if she needed it during the day.

> I'll start with the big one first: I've been looking at doing a trip there, but I'm a woman travelling alone. How safe is it?

That question didn't have an easy answer, but I tried my best anyway.

> Well, I'm not a woman, so my experience won't really be comparable, but the locals I spoke to assured me that it's generally very safe. As long as you dress respectfully to the local culture and take reasonable precautions, it should be as safe as anywhere else.

She responded to my message with a laugh emoji before replying.

> I figured that you weren't a woman after I saw the picture of you on the beach in Turkey. Nice abs, by the way.

A wink emoji followed that statement, and I winced as I stepped onto the bus that stopped in front of me. Hopefully, this woman hadn't gotten the wrong idea about me. While I would be happy to chat about travel, it didn't extend any further than that.

It seemed best to nip any flirtation in the bud.

> I'm married, just so we're clear.

> Good for you? I just wanted to pay you a compliment.

Maybe I assumed too much? It *had* been a while since I flirted with anyone. I started to type out an apology, but she responded again before I could.

> I love a good beach pic.

A second later, a picture appeared in my messages of an absolutely gorgeous woman in a tiny bikini on a sun-kissed beach. Was that actually her? More curious than anything, I clicked onto her profile for the first time and saw that all the other photos matched the woman in the picture. A truly beautiful woman, and I'd be flattered by her compliment if I weren't already spoken for.

> Cancun?

She laugh-reacted again.

> You've got a good eye.

That still felt a little too flirty for me, even without any accompanying emoji, so I brought us back to her initial question.

> Well, I wouldn't dress like that in Uzbekistan, but if you're genuinely interested, I can do a bit more research for you. I'm actually a travel agent.

> Are you sure? I don't want to make work for you if I don't end up booking anything.

The constant start and stop of the bus in the city traffic slowed down my typing a little, but I still managed to fire off a response without any major typos.

> It would be good information for me to know. I'll get back to you in a day or two, and you can ask me any other questions you have then.

> Well, thanks. You're very kind. Your wife is a lucky woman.

> I'm the lucky one.

With that, I closed the chat, still feeling uncertain about whether or not she'd actually been hitting on me. It kind of felt that way, and as I slid my phone back into my pocket, I smiled. Celine would probably get a kick of that idea, so I would have to tell her about it over dinner. It would be nice to make her laugh again.

When I got to our house, though, the driveway sat empty, our car nowhere to be seen. Inside, I couldn't find anything to indicate where my wife had gone, so I sent her a text.

I'm home. Do you want me to start supper?

Lately, it seemed to put her on edge if I asked for her location directly, so I tried to ask in a more roundabout way when she would be home.

Lately, a lot of things seemed to put her on edge.

I'm over at Allie's and I'll eat here. Have whatever you like.

So much for telling her about my day. A twinge of annoyance plucked at my brain, but I did my best not to let it show.

Alright. Say hi to your sister for me. I love you.

I will.

I waited a few moments for any further reply, but none came.

With nothing else I needed to do, I made myself a sandwich and sat down in the living room to start looking at the online forums I used for travel questions for information about safety for independent women travellers in the former Soviet republics known as the 'Stans'.

It seemed a bit strange that someone as beautiful as the woman who messaged me would be travelling on her own, but maybe she simply preferred it. After all, Celine didn't like travelling with me. All the minor inconveniences made her irritable and we ended up at each other's throats. Maybe this woman's partner reacted the same, or maybe she didn't have one.

It really wasn't any of my business.

With a shake of my head, I got back on track, and soon, I had information from a few sources I trusted. I drafted my reply in my phone's notes, figuring I would wait until the next day to send it to her since I'd told her it would take me a day and something else might occur to me by the morning.

By the time I finished, it had passed eight o'clock, and Celine walked through the door twenty minutes later.

"How's Allie?" I asked as she walked into the kitchen, not bothering to stop and give me a kiss like she used to.

"So busy. Brad's away for work all week and she's struggling with the baby. I might stay overnight there tomorrow."

"Does she want to come and stay here?" I offered, not wanting to invite myself to Allie's house but also not really pleased about the prospect of another night away from Celine. We hadn't had a proper conversation in weeks. Sex, when it happened, felt obligatory rather than desired.

It felt like she'd started slipping away from me and I had no idea why. Somehow, I had to find a way to turn it around.

"All the baby's stuff is there," she answered me from the kitchen, plates clattering as she fixed herself something to eat. She must not have had a chance to eat at Allie's after all. "It'd be too much work to pack it all up and bring it over. It's just one night."

That time, it would only be one night, but all those 'one nights' added up to a lot. Even so, I kept my mouth shut, knowing that any perceived criticism would only make Celine defensive. With nothing else to say, I changed the subject. "Hey, guess what. I got a really random message today."

"I'm going to go have a bath," she cut me off, stepping into the living room at last to give me a quick peck. An unfamiliar scent clung to her clothes, which must have come from something at Allie's house. "You can tell me about it later, okay?"

Without giving me a chance to respond, she walked out of the room with her bowl of food. I flipped on the TV in an attempt to distract myself, and by the time the show finished and I headed to bed, Celine had already fallen fast asleep.

Chapter Two

"*Why* do men think that's attractive?" I groaned out loud as I opened my DMs to find yet another dick pic to add to my substantial collection. The shot, taken in a reclining position on some kind of chair, featured the man's hand wrapped around his hard cock, his jeans and white briefs pulled down just enough to get the shot, and the caption 'thinking of you' with a devil emoji. It came from one of the men I'd just started messaging that morning. Within twenty messages, he decided that sending me a picture of his rather unimpressive junk mattered more than his two-year relationship.

With a sigh, I took a screenshot and sent it to the woman who'd hired me to test him.

Recognize this?

Her reply only took a few seconds.

I'm going to twist that dick off him with my bare hands!

Once she confirmed she had all she needed, I blocked the guy, updated his file with the screenshots and the woman's replies, and completed another row on my master spreadsheet.

On a per-hour rate, that case made me a fair bit of money, but they weren't all that easy.

Like Gabriel Carter, for instance.

After our DM conversation that afternoon, I sent the initial screenshots to Celine.

Not only did he skip right over all the opportunities I gave him to flirt, he didn't make a single comment on the photo I sent. He quickly pointed out his married status *and* he called himself lucky to have his wife. Those kinds of sweet, heartwarming comments were few and far between in my day-to-day work.

However, when Celine's response came in later that evening, she didn't sound satisfied.

Although I didn't necessarily agree, she knew him better than I did.

No late-night texts came in that night, giving me a full night of uninterrupted sleep for a nice change. In the morning, I went for a jog through my neighbourhood to clear my head.

It only partially worked, though; Gabriel Carter kept popping up in my thoughts.

Some men looked like passes at first, saying all the right things because they knew their partner could access their phone. Eventually, they'd offer to connect with me on a different platform instead, one that didn't keep permanent records, and at that point, their tune changed dramatically. Maybe Gabriel would be the same, but Celine told me that he never let her see his phone in the first place, so why go to the trouble?

Over the year and a half that I'd been doing the tests, I'd developed a bit of a sixth sense as to how things would go right from the first interaction, and everything in my gut said Gabriel would be a pass. What convinced his wife that he wouldn't be? Something felt off, but I couldn't put my finger on anything concrete, and in the end, I could only do the job I'd been hired to do.

Back at home after a shower and breakfast, I started my work day, and several new messages were waiting for me, including some from Gabriel. After thinking about him earlier, I went to those ones first.

> Good morning. These are some first-hand accounts I found from other female travellers. I've removed names and identifying information, but they're all legit, I promise.

Following that were three texts of copy-and-pasted details from women who had been to Uzbekistan, and in the last text, Gabriel added a few more words of his own.

> If you decide you're interested, I'd be happy to help you plan out a trip. Absolutely no pressure to book it through me. I love helping people discover someplace a little out of the ordinary. Have a great day.

Not a single word sounded flirtatious. He didn't even seem to want to sell me anything. That gut feeling that told me Celine had nothing to worry about got even stronger.

However, since she said she wanted me to pursue it, I responded.

> Wow. This is so nice of you, thank you. And yes, absolutely, I'd love to chat with you about potential itineraries. Where are you based? Maybe I can come into your office?

I knew exactly where he worked, and as I already told Celine, I wouldn't meet him in person. By suggesting I would, though, it would make him more willing to accept my downgraded alternate offer instead. It almost always worked.

> I'm in San Francisco. I'm guessing from your username that you're in California too?

> Pasadena.

If he checked my profile, he'd figure that out easily enough. The fact that he didn't already know suggested he hadn't spent much time browsing through my pictures. Or pretended not to have.

> SF is a little too far for me, unfortunately. Maybe we could video chat instead? I want to see which places make your eyes light up.

He could have taken that slightly flirty comment and ran with it, but he didn't, sticking to business instead.

> Everything I recommend will be good, but sure, we can do video. I have time tomorrow afternoon if that works for you?

I dropped a pleading-eyes emoji with my next message.

> Nothing for today? You've got me all excited.

Three quarters of the men I messaged would have jumped on that innuendo, but Gabriel ignored it entirely.

> I could squeeze in some time over lunch, if you don't mind seeing me eat.

> Sounds perfect.

> I'll try to call around 12:30. Speak to you then.

That gave me a couple of hours, in between working on my other clients, to figure out how to tempt him, but I already had a feeling it would be easier said than done.

~Gabriel~

By the time I glanced at the clock after my busy morning, I only had ten minutes left until my scheduled video chat with the stranger from

Instagram. Luckily, I had a packed lunch that only took a minute to grab from the fridge. Celine had already left the house for her morning jog by the time I got up, so I ate breakfast alone. Though the potential new client and I wouldn't be in the same room, at least I wouldn't have to have lunch alone too.

Taking my laptop into the meeting room, I pulled up my files on Uzbekistan and placed the call at 12:30 precisely.

"Very punctual. I like that." The warm, teasing voice reached me before her video switched on, but a second later, the screen flickered to life and one of the most stunning women I'd ever seen smiled back at me.

The bikini picture honestly hadn't done her justice. Posed and practiced, it seemed slightly artificial despite being beautiful. The woman I saw on the screen, however, looked far more natural and inviting. Honey-coloured hair hung in soft waves over her shoulders, her slightly rounded cheeks were a sweet shade of pink that matched her full, glistening lips, and light hazel eyes stared straight into the camera, confident but somehow sweet.

For a moment, I almost forgot what she just said, but it came back to me a second later: she appreciated that I kept to schedule. "I'm not looking to waste your time," I assured her. "I'm Gabe, by the way."

"Jen. Thanks for talking to me, Gabe. It's always a bit of a crap shoot when you approach someone online. You never know who's going to be a creep."

I could only imagine the kind of comments she got. "Well, I'm sure you have way more people approaching you than I do, but let's get down to business. Tell me what made you want to go to Uzbekistan."

I took a bite of my sandwich as I finished speaking, hoping she would talk long enough that I could swallow before needing to say anything else.

A bright smile flashed across her face, her eyes never moving from me. "To be honest, there aren't many places I *don't* want to go. The world is an amazing place and I want to experience as much of it as I can. Don't you agree?"

"It's kind of my job to agree," I pointed out with my hand over my mouth, and the speakers of my laptop vibrated with her laugh. I never really knew what sultry meant before, but if I had to choose one word to describe her laugh, that would be it: deep and rich and warm. *Sultry.* "But yes, I absolutely agree. You can learn an awful lot by travelling, both about the places you go and about yourself too. Travel is amazing, you won't get any argument from me there. But why Uzbekistan in particular?"

She took a deep breath, her chest rising just enough to give me a glimpse of her cleavage at the bottom of the screen. Even though I didn't intentionally look, her low-cut shirt made it hard to miss. "I've always found the Silk Road history fascinating, along with the architecture. As you probably already guessed, I'm a sucker for the Instagram-ready backgrounds."

Her self-deprecating laugh suggested she didn't take herself too seriously, even though a lot of people probably followed her just to see her looking pretty in pretty places.

"I'm most interested in visiting the cities, like Tashkent and Samarkand," she added. "They're probably easiest to get around."

"Those are both great destinations, and I would add Bukhara or Khiva to that list too. Both, if you can, depending on how much time you have. Would you travel by train?"

"Probably, if you think it's safe? How did you go between cities?"

"I took the train and it felt safe to me, but if you want to do an overnight one, I would pay the extra to get a private room."

We spoke for almost twenty minutes without a pause while I polished off my lunch. It didn't feel anywhere near that long; only when I glanced down at my phone did I realize exactly how much time had passed. "I'm sorry to cut this short, but I've got a client coming in just a few minutes and I need to make sure I'm ready for them."

"Where are they going?" Jen asked. Her curiosity seemed genuine. Not once in the whole conversation had she glanced away or looked uninterested.

"Spain. A little less exotic, but still exciting."

Her warm laugh filled the room again. "I have a feeling you could make anything sound exciting. Do you ever provide companion travel services for your clients?"

The idea of travelling with the woman in front of me, who seemed to get just as much joy out of exploring and experiencing things as I did, appealed to me far more than it should have, especially when she ran her tongue over her lips to wet them. She didn't mean for that to look as seductive as it did, I felt sure. "No, I only make the arrangements from here, but I'm always available by phone if anything goes wrong and they need some help."

"So, your wife is the only lucky woman who gets to travel with you?"

For a second time, she called Celine lucky, and something about the way she said it made it feel like we were in danger of slipping into more flirty territory. That, combined with the fact that my client would be there any minute, led me to wrap the conversation up. "I really do need to run, but you know how to reach me if you have more questions."

"Could we talk again another time?" she asked. "You said you had some time tomorrow? Or if you don't mind, we could talk outside of work hours? It would be easier for me, actually."

As much as I would like to continue our conversation, the idea also made me slightly uneasy. Maybe if I spoke to Celine about it first, it would feel more above-board. "I'll check my schedule and get back to you. Have a good day, Jen."

"You too, Gabe. Thank you for your time." She blew me a kiss just before signing off, and I exhaled slowly, trying to push down the weird guilt I felt. If I had met a woman like her before Celine, I would have jumped at the chance to spend more time with her, but thinking that way didn't do me any good. I loved my wife, and if I didn't feel as connected to her as I once had, the responsibility came down to me to fix it.

Maybe that night would be a good time to start.

~Jennifer~

My younger sister let herself into my house as she always did, like a hurricane blowing in, walking straight into my kitchen to peer over my shoulder at the pot on the stove. "What are we having?"

Since I'd been expecting her, I didn't even look up. "Chicken caccia-tore."

"Mom's recipe?" she asked, dipping a finger into the pot before I could swat her hand away.

"Naturally. Go make yourself useful and set the table."

"Damn, that's good. Why does yours always taste better than mine?" she groaned, licking her finger and eyeing the pot again.

"Because I actually follow the recipe. And if you put that finger back in my sauce, I'll throw the whole thing out and you can order pizza from down the street instead."

With a shudder, Eda backed off, going to wash her hands before grabbing the dishes from my cupboards. "How is that place still open? The pizza is terrible."

"I'm convinced it's a front for money laundering or something. No one is ever there but they're still in business."

No matter how long it had been since my sister and I saw each other, we always jumped right back into conversation as if there hadn't been any break at all. She lived down in Los Angeles, pursuing her dream of being a set designer for the movies, close enough to see each other regularly but just far enough away that we had to make an effort. At least twice a month, we'd have supper together, gossiping about her life and mine, usually at my house since she still shared an apartment with two roommates. Our parents had retired up in Washington, so aside from major holidays, she was the only family I saw regularly.

Unlike my parents, Eda also knew all about my loyalty test business and she loved to hear the details of my latest jobs. That week, she dove straight in as we sat down with the food and the wine. "So, how many new dicks have you seen this week?"

I grabbed one of the rolls I'd warmed in the oven as I dug into my food. "Only three. It's been a slow week."

"Business slowing down, or the guys are being less gross?"

"Definitely no slow-down in business," I assured her. "And still plenty of fails too. They're just doing it in other ways rather than literally exposing themselves."

"God, men are such pigs," my perpetually-single sister declared, taking a swig of her wine. "Matt excluded, of course."

"Of course." She always made that exception. Even four years after my fiancé died, she still wouldn't group him in with the rest of the gender. He'd been the big brother she never had, and she missed him almost as much as I did. "I might actually be working on a pass, though. It's still ongoing, but it's looking good."

Her eyebrows shot up. "Ooh, so they *do* exist?"

"They do, I promise. But this one is a bit weird."

I left it there as I took another bite of my supper, trying to decide how to explain the situation with Gabriel. After my call with him earlier, during which I got so caught up in our conversation that I actually forgot to try to flirt with him until the very end, I sent another message to his wife.

> We spoke for twenty minutes and he made no attempt to hit on me. Didn't comment on my appearance. When I offered to speak with him outside of work, it seemed to make him un-

> comfortable. I'm not saying it's impossible that he's cheating, but he doesn't seem to be interested in doing it with me.

Occasionally, the men I tested were in a 'committed affair', as I put it. They cheated, yes, but only with one person. They weren't just looking for *any* woman, so in those cases, my tests weren't of much use.

Or maybe he wasn't cheating at all. That felt a lot more likely to me. Celine thought otherwise.

> He must be suspicious. I'll give him some space so he has time to talk to you without me knowing. Keep trying.

At some point, I would run out of excuses to keep contacting him, but she'd chosen one of my most expensive packages, so I couldn't stop the job without a good reason to. As much as I trusted my gut that he would still turn out to be a pass, I would have to try again.

With Eda's prompting, I told her a bit about my interactions with Gabriel. "A hot travel agent? Sounds perfect for you," she teased me, and her eyes widened as I glanced down at my plate for a second. "Oh my God, you're blushing! You like him, don't you?"

"He's married."

"Maybe not for long," she snorted.

"Eda! I don't date cheaters, *especially* not ones that I helped to catch."

She let it go and we moved on to talking about her life instead of mine. She told me all about designing her current set and the latest dating exploits of all the women in her apartment, but apparently, Gabriel lingered in her mind the same way he'd been hanging around mine, because she asked me about him again before she left that evening. "What's the name of this travel-agent guy?"

"You know I can't share that with you." My clients paid for discretion as part of my services.

"I have good friends who work in the theatre scene in San Francisco. They might know him or his wife," she insisted. "You never know. It's a small world. I promise I won't say why I'm asking, but it might be helpful to know what kind of reputation they both have. *Please* let me help.

Your job has provided me with so many hours of entertainment, it's the least I could do."

If it were any other client, I would have said no, but I couldn't entirely get rid of that feeling that something important to this case sat just out of my reach. Though I still didn't feel great about it, I gave in. "Alright, but listen: under *no* circumstances are you to mention me or the fact that he might be cheating. Are we clear?"

"I get it," she promised me, crossing her fingers over her heart just like she'd done since we were kids. "It'll be completely anonymous. Maybe one of my friends is cheating with him!"

She looked so delighted at that prospect that I had to laugh, which set her off too. Her familiar warm embrace before she left made me feel even lighter.

"Maybe you should book yourself a trip with this travel agent before you expose him," she added as she headed out the door. "You're supposed to be travelling, remember? It's what Matt wanted."

"I know." Those had been his instructions, but I couldn't imagine doing it without him. "Maybe I will."

She knew as well as I did that I didn't mean it, but she let that one go too, blowing me a kiss before closing the door behind her. The silence that lingered after her departure, the calm after the storm, always felt more profound than before, and in those moments, I missed Matt most of all.

Before I could get too upset, though, my phone buzzed in my pocket, and I pulled it out, grateful for the distraction.

To my surprise, the message came from Gabe.

Chapter Three

My sister answered my call in the middle of shouting directions at a colleague. "That's the wrong cue, it's coming in too early! Number forty-seven. Four-seven. Yeah. Hello?"

I couldn't be sure she had switched to talking to me, but I answered anyway. "Monica?"

"Hey, Gabe. Sorry, you caught me at a bad time."

"I know it's tech, and I'm sorry." My sister worked as a lighting designer in the theatre, and just before a show opened, technical rehearsals consumed her from dawn until dusk.

"If you know, then it must be important. What's going on?"

Hopefully, she would agree that my reason for calling warranted interrupting her day. "I just need a woman's opinion. Which would appeal to Celine more: a romantic dinner, a massage, or a walk on the beach?"

Monica groaned into the other end of the line. "Seriously? Don't you have any other women in your life you could ask?"

"None that know Celine as well as you do. I won't keep you. Answer the question and I'll be out of your hair."

"Why does it sound like you're apologizing for something?" she asked suspiciously. "What did you do?"

"Nothing. At least, I don't think I did." It would explain the change in her, but no matter how much I racked my brain, I couldn't come up with any transgression I might have committed. "I just want to do something special for her. That's all."

"Well, *you* should know your wife best," Monica pointed out. "What do you think she'd like?"

Honestly, I had no idea. The things we used to do together didn't seem to excite her anymore. At that exact moment, I felt like I could better predict what Jen, the woman I spoke to earlier that day, would like. "Please just answer the question."

She probably would have argued with me more if she didn't really need to get going. "Well, she's a picky eater, so I'd say dinner would be tricky, and the thought of you having your hands on her gives me the creeps, so I'll go with the beach walk."

I pressed a frustrated hand to my forehead. "Helpful as always."

"And yet, you keep calling me. Good luck, Gabe. Gotta run; the director's ready. Start again from twenty-six?"

She'd already gone back to work by the time the phone disconnected, and a heavy sigh deflated my shoulders as I looked around the empty kitchen. Monica and Celine never really got along as I hoped they would. Though they tolerated each other for my sake, their strong personalities clashed with each other. It didn't help that Celine had once overheard Monica wondering if Celine would feel the same about me without our parents' money, and she appreciated being called a gold digger about as much as any woman would. On the surface, they'd moved on, but I knew that unresolved feelings still lingered on both sides.

Keeping in mind their differences, I decided that if Monica suggested the beach, I probably *shouldn't* go with that one. Instead, I decided to set things up for a massage. With scented oils and candles, I turned our room into a mini-spa with a fluffy towel on the bed for her to lay on, while warming up a few finger foods that I could feed to her while she relaxed.

I actually felt pretty damn proud of myself as I surveyed the finished scene, until the phone buzzed in my pocket.

Sorry, I'm still at Allie's. I'm going to stay here again tonight with Brad still away. Enjoy the peace and quiet.

My eyes flitted from the screen back up at the preparation I'd just finished, and my stomach sank with the realization that it had all been for nothing.

Fuck.

She said the day before that it would just be one night, and I took her at her word. More fool me, apparently.

What could I do? *Demand* that she come home? That would only upset her, and maybe Allie really did need her. Getting upset wouldn't help with my larger goal of reconnecting with her, so I'd have to put my hurt feelings aside and approach it differently.

If she wouldn't come to me, maybe I could go to her instead.

After blowing out the candles and putting everything away, I called a taxi to take me to the upscale grocery store that Celine liked. She would have preferred to shop there exclusively but our budget didn't allow it. As a treat, I picked out a few pastries and asked the taxi to drop me off at Allie's house next.

I couldn't see our car in Allie's driveway, but the open windows suggested people were at home, so I went up and knocked. Celine's younger sister opened the door to me, her baby strapped to her chest, and her eyes registered her surprise as she took me in.

"Gabe! What are you doing here?"

"Celine said you needed some help, so I came to help too. Don't worry, I brought treats."

Allie licked her lips when I held up the box of baked goods. "How did you know the secret password?"

Taking the box from my hand, she stepped aside to let me in as I bent down to say hello to my nephew. "Where *is* Celine?" I asked, glancing into the empty living room to my right.

"She ran out to get a few things for me, actually," Allie explained. "With traffic, she might be a while. Let me send her a text and see where she is."

Walking to the kitchen, Allie tapped away on her phone while I trailed after her, noting the immaculate cleanliness of the house. I couldn't see any signs of Allie's apparent struggle to keep up with things with Brad away, nor any sign of Celine's presence. Usually, she had a couple of different coffee cups on the go and would leave them strewn around wherever she happened to put them down. It had become a running joke between us to see if I caught them all before I ran the dishwasher at night.

At Allie's house, I didn't see any.

Though I didn't know exactly what it meant, something seemed off, and that feeling got even stronger when Allie put her phone down and looked up at me with a forced smile. "As I thought, she's stuck in traffic. It might be a while. You're welcome to stay and watch TV here if you want."

"I don't want to intrude. I came to help, but it seems to me that you have things under control."

Her eyes slid away from mine and my feeling of unease got even stronger. Though I couldn't remember even deciding to ask, I heard the words coming out of my mouth anyway.

"Can I see that message Celine just sent you?"

Allie's eyes darted down to her phone for a second and she reached out to pull it closer to herself. "What? Why?"

"Because I'd like to see it."

I didn't see a need to explain myself any further than that, and when Allie hesitated again, I had my answer. Something on her phone was worth hiding, but she didn't owe me those answers. My wife did.

"Wait," Allie called out after me as I headed back to the door. "It's not what you think."

"What do I think?" I asked, daring her to say the words out loud that I wouldn't even admit to myself. I *couldn't*, but the seed of doubt had been planted, and I couldn't deny that, just like Allie couldn't bring herself to answer my question. "Goodnight, Allie."

The taxi had already left so I had to call another one, and by the time I reached the dark house again, my thoughts were threatening to drive me crazy.

I needed a distraction, *any* distraction, and though I could think of a million reasons why it wouldn't be the best idea, I found myself texting Jen, the woman I'd spoken to earlier.

You said speaking in the evenings is better for you, and it turns out I'm free tonight. Do you want to continue our conversation?

~Jennifer~

After how uncomfortable Gabriel seemed about the idea of speaking to me outside of work, his offer to do just that took me by surprise. Maybe I'd been wrong about him. It felt like this would be the conversation where I'd find out for sure, so I set the scene as well as I could, quickly changing into a skimpy bathing suit and going to sit out in my backyard. I could claim to be sunbathing while offering him a little visual temptation.

When I had everything ready, I texted him back.

Absolutely! I'll give you a call.

After hitting record on my phone, I placed the video call, and a moment later, Gabe's handsome face filled my screen. He sat in a comfortable-looking living room, with a large framed wedding portrait on the wall behind him.

That really didn't suggest a guy looking to cheat on his wife, nor did the way he winced at the sight of me. "I don't want to interrupt if you're in the middle of something."

"I'm just enjoying the sunshine," I said, offering him a flirty, inviting smile, but he could barely look at me. His eyes kept darting to the side, and I got the distinct feeling he would hang up if I didn't make a change.

So much for the direct approach.

"It's getting cooler, though. Let me grab a cover-up."

Placing the phone in its holder, I angled it so he'd have a perfect view of my ass as I walked away to grab one of the caftans I kept handy. The low, wide neckline still exposed a good amount of cleavage, but a lot less than the bikini did, and by the time I sat back down, he looked relieved.

If this guy was a cheater, I might have to consider a new profession because I couldn't get anywhere with him at all.

I wouldn't give up though, not as long as Celine had me on the clock.

"All alone tonight?" I asked sweetly once I'd picked the phone back up.

Gabe's lips tightened, just for a second. "Yeah. What about you?"

"Just me here. You're lucky I had anything on when you called. Sometimes, I walk around naked when there's no one around."

Gabe's blue eyes looked away again. "Maybe we should talk later."

Fuck. He looked on the verge of hanging up with me, so I'd either have to dial it right back or go all in.

I decided on the latter. Eventually, I had to make a move or we'd just end up chatting about travel forever.

"I'm sorry. I'm really not very good at flirting." Putting myself down almost always worked to encourage men to compliment me in return, but Gabe only tensed further, so I kept talking. "I know you're married. You said so, and I can see your wedding picture behind you. But some people have open relationships, or are at a different place in their marriage, and I just wanted to let you know that if you're at all interested, I am too. It doesn't have to be anything long-term. One night would be fine with me."

Gabe glanced back over his shoulder at the large picture on the wall, as if he'd forgotten it hung there. When he turned back, he exhaled deeply before replying. "I'm sorry if anything I did gave you the wrong idea but I'm not looking for anything sexual. At all. You're very attractive, but I'm not that guy, so if that's the only reason you got in touch with me..."

"It isn't," I quickly countered. "And please, don't apologize. I thought it might be possible, but I didn't mean to insult you. I suppose you've never even been tempted?"

I didn't know what the odds were that he'd confess any previous cheating to me even if he'd done it, but I might as well ask while we were on the subject.

"No. This really isn't the conversation I want to be having, not tonight, so I'm going to..."

He reached for the phone as if to end the call, so I quickly blurted out the first thing that came into my head. "Why not tonight?"

His hand hovered in front of the screen. "What?"

"You said 'not tonight'. What's different about tonight?"

Slowly, the hand lowered, revealing his face to me again, and the uncertainty and confusion in his eyes seemed genuine. I leaned forward, as if I could somehow get closer to him that way.

"I shouldn't talk about this with you. Not after what you just said."

The words were so quiet, I had to turn up the volume to catch them all. "Forget about what I just said. I took a shot, but you're not interested, and I respect that. Honestly, I do," I added when he seemed unconvinced. "Like I said, I'm not very good at flirting. I know that. I come on too strong."

"And you flirt with married men," he pointed out, a little of his regular charm coming back. "That might be part of the problem."

An almost-real grin flashed across my face. "It's not usually my go-to move. I thought I felt something between us, but I read it wrong, and that's fine. If there's something you need to talk about, you've already got me here, and I've literally got nothing better to do. Talking to me has to be better than sitting in an empty room, isn't it? Please say yes."

My plea at the end made him smile, and he sat back completely, his intention of hanging up forgotten for the time being. "You're really easy to talk to, Jen. That's not the issue."

"What's the issue, then?" I pulled the top of my caftan tighter together to try to make him even more comfortable.

His mouth opened and closed a few times as he debated how to begin, before he sighed. "This really isn't your problem."

"Probably not, but sometimes, it's easier to share a problem with a complete stranger. I can give you my unbiased view."

I honestly had no idea where he might be going with all of this, but since this would probably be the last time we spoke, I didn't necessarily want it to end just yet. Once we hung up, I would be telling his wife that he passed and close the job, but first, I could be a sympathetic ear for him as a thank you after wasting so much of his time.

"This is going to sound crazy," he warned me. "And it probably is, but I don't know what else to think right now."

He'd started to sound a lot like the women who messaged me on a daily basis, so I answered him the same way I answered them. "If it's bothering you, it's not crazy. You just need to see the situation clearly, so why don't you tell me about it?"

Gabe exhaled through his nose in a short, huffing sound. "It's ironic, since you were just talking about cheating and I... well, I'm starting to think that my wife might be cheating on me."

Thanks to years of experience, I kept a neutral expression, betraying nothing of how I felt, but inside, my mind raced in confusion. What the hell? Was this some kind of ploy to get my sympathy? But why would he lie if not to sleep with me? I just flat-out offered that and he turned me down, so it didn't seem likely he'd try to manipulate me now.

I had no idea what to think.

"What makes you think so?" I asked as calmly as I could.

He described a situation very much like many of the stories I'd heard from my clients before. The gradual distance growing between them, spending less time at home, even staying away overnight.

"She told me she's been staying with her sister, but I think her sister might be covering for her based on what happened today." Gabe's shoulders slumped after he finished recounting the whole story. "Or it's all in my head and I'm making myself crazy over nothing. What do you think?"

I thought Celine had some explaining to do, but I needed more information before I exposed my actual purpose in making contact with him. Maybe a reasonable explanation *did* exist for all of this, and I asked him to consider that possibility too. "Is there any other scenario besides her cheating that would explain everything you've noticed?"

He thought about it for several seconds, his brow creased as he worked his imagination. "I suppose she might be working on something secret as a surprise for me? That's not really her style, but I guess it's possible." With a sigh, he dropped his head into his hands. "I need to talk to her, don't I?"

"That would probably be for the best. Open communication usually solves an awful lot of problems."

Another sigh followed, but he nodded too. "You're right. I'm going to go and figure out what to say and how to say it. I'm sorry for dumping all of this on you."

"I'm the one who should be apologizing. Hitting on you was questionable at best in the first place, and knowing that you had all this on your mind only makes it worse. I'm sorry, Gabe."

"It's alright," he assured me, and even though it wasn't, I believed he meant it. He really did seem like a genuinely nice guy, an extremely rare commodity in my life as of late. "I'm sorry we didn't get to talk about travel."

I smiled at his attempt to lighten the mood, and Eda's words came back to me about needing to travel more. Maybe she had a point. "Well, I'm not ready to commit to Uzbekistan yet but I could do with a weekend getaway and I've been thinking about Napa Valley. That's practically your backyard, so you must know all the secret spots. If you're looking for a distraction, you could send me some ideas."

What the hell? I shouldn't be making plans to be in touch with him again, not after he passed my test and especially not with the strange situation with Celine. But the words came out anyway, and a bit of light sparked in Gabe's eyes again.

"I can definitely do that. I have a lot of discounts with places up there so I can get you a great deal if you want to book. When are you thinking?"

"This weekend?" I kept digging a deeper hole for myself, for no good reason at all.

"Okay, let me see what I can do. Thanks again for listening, Jen. Have a good night."

I managed to keep my mouth shut that time and simply wave while he hung up, but as soon as his face disappeared from the screen, I let my head fall back with a loud groan. This job had gotten way more complicated than it should, and the smart thing for me to do would be to back away from it entirely.

I could almost convince myself that I would do it.

~Gabriel~

Almost the same moment I hung up with Jennifer, the front door opened, and I quickly shoved my phone into my pocket and rubbed a hand down my face to get my bearings before I stood up. Talking with Jen had been helpful, but the person I really needed to talk to walked into the living room a moment later, her forehead creased in concern as she dropped her handbag onto the chair and folded her arms over her chest.

"What's going on? Allie said you came over, acted really weird, and left before I got back."

I answered Celine's question with one of my own. "Where were you?"

"When you went to Allie's? I went down to the organic market to pick up that vegan cheese spread she likes so much, and to the drugstore to get some more diapers and wipes for the baby. Didn't she tell you that?"

Celine's tone didn't sound defensive so much as angry as she gave her very detailed answer, and it threw me off. Based on the suspicions that had crept into my mind, I expected her to look guilty, but instead, she stood there looking me straight in the eye, demanding an explanation for *my* behaviour.

"She did tell me that, but she also sent you a message that she wouldn't let me see," I pointed out.

"When has she ever shown you her messages? Why should she? What a weird thing to ask her to do. I've been over there trying to help her cope with everything, and you went in and upset her for no reason."

In the face of her anger, I tried to grab hold of that feeling I had earlier, that uneasy certainty that things weren't as they seemed. "She seemed to be coping just fine to me. The house looked spotless. There weren't even any of your coffee cups lying around."

Celine let out a snort of disbelief. "*That's* the reason you wanted to see her phone? Because I cleaned up my coffee cups before I went out instead of leaving them for my postpartum sister to deal with? That's pretty weak, Gabe."

She sure made it sound that way, and I tried to remember what else had seemed odd to me. Nothing concrete, just a feeling I got from the way the house looked and the way Allie acted, but I couldn't say any of that to Celine. It would only make things worse.

Still, I wasn't ready to completely give in yet either. "Maybe I overreacted, but you've hardly been around lately. You say that we're going to talk and then you disappear again and come home with a weird smell on you..."

"A weird smell?" Celine repeated, enunciating each word slowly, her face scrunched up tight. "Do you mean Brad's cologne that I sprayed on myself after the baby threw up on me? I didn't realize you were keeping track of my *scent*. This possessive side of you is not a turn-on. And if we're not talking, it's only because you're on your phone all the time, or travelling somewhere that I can't reach you."

She brought that up every time we had any kind of argument, and it frustrated me every single time. "Some countries don't have reliable roaming. I've explained this to you. And what do you mean that I'm on my phone all the time? When you're here, you have my full attention. You're just never here."

"Oh, really? You're never doing anything on your phone? So, you wouldn't have any problem with me looking through your phone right now?"

As she held out her hand for it, my stomach dropped.

Even though the DM conversations with Jen were completely inno-cent, if Celine took one look at Jen's profile, she would jump to the worst conclusions.

Frozen by indecision, I hesitated a moment too long, and Celine let out a huff. "That's what I thought. You freak the fuck out at Allie for not showing you her phone, and you won't even let me look at yours. I'm going back to Allie's to reassure my sister that she didn't do anything wrong. I don't even want to look at you right now."

With that, she turned on her heel, grabbed the bag from the chair, and headed back out the door, her long hair flipping over her shoulder as she rounded the corner in one final *fuck you.*

In the silence that followed the door slamming, I sank back down onto the couch beneath our wedding picture. We'd had fights before, but never like that. She never just walked out without talking things through, and I knew deep down that going after her wouldn't make things any better. For better or worse, we both needed some space to calm down before we spoke again.

Would she really cheat on me? She had an answer for everything, but something still felt off. I couldn't think of any other reason for the change in her. It had come on so gradually that I hadn't noticed just how far the cracks between us had grown, but I barely recognized the woman who just yelled at me.

Maybe I should have let her see the messages when she asked. I'd always intended to tell her about them, she just never gave me the chance, and now, they felt like something dirty even though they weren't.

Or had I messed up just by answering Jen in the first place?

Now that I knew she actually *had* been flirting with me, the smart thing to do would be to cut off all contact, at least until Celine and I got past whatever the hell was going on between us.

First, though, I'd promised to help her arrange a trip.

Desperately needing a distraction, I placed a call to my favourite boutique inn in Napa Valley to see if they had any availability for the weekend.

"Hey, Gabe, nice to hear from you." The owner, Manuel, appreciated the business I'd sent his way over the years, and I appreciated how well he treated the clients I sent him. It made for a mutually beneficial friendship. "You're in luck! I just had two cancellations for this weekend, a family group that can't make it. I intended to advertise on our social media that they're available but I can reserve one for your client instead, if you like?"

I didn't know how serious Jen had been about making the trip, but if I didn't take it, the opportunity would disappear. "Let's do it. Put it under my name for now, and I'll send you the client's information tomorrow."

If she didn't take it, maybe I could use it, either with Celine if we patched things up before then, or by myself if I needed a getaway. At that point, I had no idea which way it might go.

"All booked," Manuel confirmed. "I'll speak to you tomorrow."

Despite the late hour, I sent one last text.

I reserved a room at the Four Winds for you. Here's their website. If you want the room, please call them directly to confirm. I'm going to be offline for a few days, I need to take some time to sort things out in my personal life.

With that taken care of, I headed to bed alone.

Chapter Four

~Jennifer~

When my eyes opened the next morning, the uneasiness from my conversation with Gabriel the night before still lingered in the back of my mind. After we spoke, I turned my phone off for the rest of the evening, needing to disconnect and think things through before I made contact with Celine again.

In all my time doing loyalty tests, I'd never come across a situation like this. Someone was lying to me. Either Celine or Gabriel wanted to cover their tracks, and though I strongly felt Gabe had told me the truth, I had to accept the fact that I might be biased simply because I liked him. I'd flirted with hundreds of men online and never felt the simple connection I did with him, like we could actually be friends. He felt genuine to me, sincere and open, and if it was all an act, he'd done a damn good job of it.

Celine's behaviour seemed more suspicious. Thinking back to the way she tried to insist that I meet with Gabriel in person made me wonder what she'd been trying to achieve. Did she want to provoke him into cheating to cover up her own affair? That seemed like a lot of trouble to go to, and for what purpose? If she wanted to get a divorce, she could just get one. People got divorced for all kinds of reasons, and it sounded like Gabe hadn't even had any suspicions until the last couple of days, *after* Celine hired me.

Something didn't quite add up. A piece of the puzzle remained missing, and I couldn't do much about it other than hope that Eda's inquiries turned up something useful.

With a sigh, I rolled over and grabbed my phone, looking for a message from my sister. She hadn't been in touch, but I did have a message from Gabe that came in the night before and my chest tightened as I read it. I could almost feel his pain as he said he would be unavailable for the next few days. Did I really understand him that well, or could I be projecting my own feelings onto him?

I'd never doubted my instincts in my job this way, and I didn't like it. I also had a message from Celine.

> Do you have any updates? I asked my husband straight out to show me his phone last night and he refused. I'm certain he's hiding something.

Again, pressure squeezed in my chest. So, they *did* talk after our call. Did he confront her with his suspicions? Did she try to use me against him, even though the flirting had been entirely one-sided? Or was he leading me on, presenting one face to me and another to her? Uncertainty clawed at my stomach, and I closed the message without replying, still needing more time to decide what to do.

In the meantime, despite his own problems, Gabe had still managed to make arrangements for me in Napa Valley for the weekend. The name Four Winds meant nothing to me, but when I pulled up the hotel's website, a soft sigh slipped through my lips. It looked *perfect*. Just the right amount of luxury without being ostentatious, a gorgeous estate with rooms that I could already tell I wouldn't want to leave.

Everything about it appealed to me, and the fact that Gabe made that connection only reinforced the idea that we understood each other on a fundamental level.

As soon as I saw the place, I knew that whether or not I'd actually intended to follow through when I asked Gabe for recommendations, I wanted to go. Everything seemed to be conspiring to tell me I needed this break.

Since he said I should call to confirm the reservation, I dialed the number right away, not wanting to miss the opportunity.

"Good morning, Four Winds Napa," a cheery woman's voice greeted me. "How can I help you?"

"Good morning. My name is Jennifer Bradshaw. I believe you have a room on hold for me for this weekend, starting tomorrow, and I'm calling to confirm the reservation."

"Absolutely, I can take care of that for you." Nails clacked against keys in the background as she looked up the information on her computer, and a moment later, she let out a puzzled hum.

She didn't say more than that, so I asked for clarification. "Is there a problem?"

"I'm not seeing you here," she admitted. "We only have twelve rooms and there's no Jennifer at all."

I couldn't think of any reason Gabriel would have given me false information, so I opened my mouth to ask her to look for his name instead when she offered an alternative.

"As it happens, though, we have a last-minute cancellation on one of the rooms. I can book you in right now if you like."

"Sure, that would be great." Whatever the mix-up had been, I wouldn't worry about it if they still had room for me.

After giving her all my details and credit card information, we hung up and I got out of bed, feeling more ready to tackle the rest of the day's work with the prospect of a short holiday to look forward to.

Several hours of flirting later, I got a text from Eda.

I should be a private detective! You won't believe all the dirt I got.

How can I believe it if you don't tell me what it is?

Calling you now.

A few seconds later, the phone rang, and I accepted the video chat to see my sister sitting in her apartment with a glass of wine and a smug smile on her face. "You owe me for this big time."

"Save your self-congratulation until the end. Tell me what you've got."

She began with a litany of who knew who and how she made contact with people in the San Francisco theatre scene, but I quickly lost track of the trail until she got to the end of it. "...and it turns out Betty is working on a show right now with Monica Carter."

"Carter?" I repeated curiously, picking up on the name immediately. "A relative?"

"His sister!" Eda announced gleefully. "And when they had a break today during the tech rehearsal, Betty let me call her to complain about the nightmare sister-in-law I invented, and she roped Monica in to give me advice. She did not hold back! That woman spilled *everything.*"

"You still haven't told me *any*thing," I reminded her, rolling my eyes at her enthusiasm even though my own curiosity had been fully piqued.

Finally, she dove in. "So, Gabriel and Celine have been married for two years. They were together for two years before that, and Monica said she heard rumours during that time that Celine started seeing someone else, but she never had any proof so she didn't say anything to her brother about it."

Not an awful lot to go on, but it did interest me, especially since I hadn't said anything to Eda yet about the conversation I had with Gabe the night before. She had no way of knowing about his suspicions of Celine cheating.

"Anyway, they got married, and Celine stopped trying. She stopped working, stopped wanting to travel with Gabriel or spend any time with his family. Monica said she's barely seen her in the last year. She's totally mooching off him and not putting in any effort. Gabriel says they've been trying to get pregnant, but Monica thinks Celine is secretly taking birth control."

Again, as interesting as that might be, and as much as it made my heart hurt for Gabe, it didn't really help me at all. "What does that have to do with her hiring me?"

"I'm getting to that!" Eda took a long sip of her wine, drawing out the suspense while my toes tapped impatiently against the floor. "I asked Monica if she thought Celine might be using her brother for his money, and she said probably, but not his 'current' money."

My eyebrows drew together. "What does that mean?"

"Exactly what I wanted to know. Apparently, he's got a great big payment coming from his grandparent's estate. It pays out to both Gabriel and Monica when they've been married for three years or when they turn 30, whichever happens first."

"So, she thinks Celine's sticking around for the money," I guessed. "But why would Celine hire me?"

"Because..." Eda paused for dramatic effect, her face nearly splitting with her grin of anticipation. "Under normal circumstances, inheritances aren't included in assets if they split up. However, according to the terms of the trust fund, if they get divorced because he cheated, she's entitled to half, no matter what. It's literally a condition of the fund! Guess Grandma and Grandpa didn't like cheaters much. Can't say I blame them."

I let out a long breath as I put the pieces together. "So, she needs to prove he's cheating before he figures out that *she* is and files for divorce himself."

"Exactly." She literally patted herself on the back before prompting me to join in the praise. "You can thank me now."

"You did good." Not only did she get closer to Gabe than I ever imagined she would, she'd just slid the missing puzzle piece into place.

Gabe's wife wanted to trap him into giving away half his inheritance and intended to use me to do it.

Just one big question remained: how the hell was I going to break that to him?

~Gabriel~

Celine didn't come home that night. Not that I expected her to by that point, but the pang of disappointment hit me anyway when I woke up and found the bed beside me untouched. She hadn't texted or called either, and I headed out for work that morning feeling completely off-balance.

Did I overreact? Did she? Everything seemed muddled, and the way Jen kept popping back into my thoughts didn't help things. I was a married man, for fuck's sake. Why the hell was I thinking about her so much? My guilt made me doubt myself even more, and by the end of the day, I hadn't moved any closer to figuring out what to do next.

With my sister still busy with tech rehearsals and none of my male friends the kind I could dump this kind of heavy situation on, I had no one to turn to for advice. The only person besides my sister that I felt comfortable talking to that way? Jen. Which was *insane*. I barely knew her, and she openly hit on me despite knowing about my wife. And yet, I couldn't shake the feeling deep in my gut that she would understand.

I'd turned off notifications on Instagram so I wouldn't be tempted to see if she messaged me, but as I wrapped up work for the day, I decided to at least find out if she booked the room I'd reserved for her.

Manuel answered again when I called, and after greeting him, I got right to the point. "I'm just wondering if my client got in touch to take the room?"

He took a look on their computer system, humming to himself as he did. "No, it doesn't look like they did. It's still in your name and unconfirmed."

Huh. Maybe Jen hadn't liked the look of the place after all. Maybe I didn't know her as well as I felt I did.

Since I couldn't ask her the reason without breaking my self-imposed communication ban, I decided to move on instead. "In that case, would it be okay if I took it?"

It would mean spending money I didn't have, but a change of scene might be exactly what I needed. What Celine and I *both* needed.

"Of course!" Manuel sounded genuinely delighted at the idea. "I will cover the room and dinner on your first night here. After all the business you've sent our way over the years, it will be our pleasure to have you."

My shoulders sagged in relief that I wouldn't have to scramble to cover the cost. "That's very kind. Thank you."

After promising Manuel I would seek him out when I arrived, I sent a text to my wife.

> Things got a little heated last night. We still need to talk properly. How does a weekend in Napa Valley sound? Just the two of us, no distractions.

Usually, she would jump at the idea of a photogenic trip that didn't involve too much travel time, posting details on her social media that made it look like we lived much more lavishly than we did.

However, it seemed she still hadn't forgiven me, based on her reply a couple of hours later.

> You've got to be kidding. I don't want to go anywhere with you after yesterday. Did you actually book something without asking me? How are we paying for that?

Perhaps I'd have to call Manuel back and cancel. Taking a deep breath, I tried to be flexible.

> We don't have to go anywhere. We could talk here. When are you coming home?

> Brad's work trip has been extended to Monday. I'm staying at Allie's.

Nothing in her reply suggested a willingness to talk, or even to see me. Celine could hold a grudge like nobody else I'd ever known. I'd seen it from the outside several times, but it appeared I'd earned myself one by showing too much interest in her whereabouts.

I could have argued. I could have gone back to Allie's and forced her to talk to me, but I couldn't muster the energy or the enthusiasm. Getting out of town, even on my own, sounded like the best course of action, and Napa Valley would be as good a place as any to contemplate my future.

With Celine still using our car, I found the cheapest rental I could and headed out of town after work on Friday. The sun sparkled across the bay as I drove over the Golden Gate Bridge, the water shining with the promise of some of the peace and relaxation I'd been missing all week. Gradually, the landscape around me shifted, the coast giving way to the rolling hills and vineyards of Napa Valley. With every mile putting more distance between me and my problems, the tension in my body lessened and the ache in my stomach grew a little less painful.

Maybe I wouldn't solve anything that weekend, but I could forget about my troubles for a while and simply enjoy the adventure of being somewhere different. Travel had always been my greatest joy, even when it came to being a local tourist.

The Four Winds sat in a small vineyard along a rural road, far from any traffic or bustle of people. A few cars already dotted the parking lot behind the hotel, but no activity could be seen as I got out of the car and stretched my legs after the hour and a half drive. My stomach rumbled, reminding me that I hadn't eaten much yet that day. I hadn't felt like it, and I knew that the hotel's excellent restaurant would put everything else to shame anyway. At least I'd be hungry for it, and as I grabbed my duffel bag from the passenger seat, I already felt a bit better.

Another car meandered down the road towards the hotel as I climbed the steps, probably belonging to another arriving guest, so I stepped inside to complete my check-in, not wanting to delay anyone else.

"Ah, Mr Carter," the woman at the desk exclaimed when I gave my name. "Manuel had to run out for a while but he'll be back later. He wants to say hello."

"I'll make sure I see him," I promised. "Which room am I in?"

"The Chardonnet room on the first floor," the woman confirmed. "There's a wonderful view from the bay window in there. If you need anything for your stay, just let us know."

Since I didn't have to provide any payment information, the whole process went fairly quickly, and she handed me the key just as the door behind me opened, letting the next guest in.

I turned around, ready to give the newcomer a friendly smile before I headed to my room, but the expression quickly fell off my face as I got a look at the beautiful blonde woman standing there, gazing up at me with stunned surprise that seemed to match my own.

"Jen?"

~Jennifer~

Shit.

Staring at Gabe's face in the lobby of the Four Winds hotel, my mind went completely blank while panic rose in my chest. What was he doing there? Did he come to see me? Had I been set up?

The drive to Napa Valley took most of the day. I left mid-morning, after the morning rush hour cleared, thankful for the ability to work in my car by connecting my phone to the car's computer. I would still need to document everything later on, but at least I wouldn't be completely out of touch. The dedication paid off when I got yet another dick pic from one of my current jobs, and I pulled over to send it to the guy's girlfriend while I took a lunch break.

Aside from that, I thought about Gabe. What to tell him and *how* to tell him were at the forefront of my thoughts, but I couldn't entirely get rid of the echo of the things Eda had said to me either.

You like him.

He might not be married for long.

Those thoughts were *not* helpful. I didn't want to break up his marriage so that he'd be single. I only wanted the best for him, which would be to know the truth about his wife.

However, as I imagined how it might play out, I couldn't see a happy ending. From years of experience, I knew that being the bearer of bad news usually meant the end of my interactions with the person in question. If I laid it all on the line for him, that would be the last I heard from him, I could pretty much guarantee it. He wouldn't take kindly to the fact that I'd done nothing but lie to him since the moment I made contact.

Unless...

Unless I didn't tell him that part right away? Did he need to know Celine hired me in order for me to tell him the rest?

I knew all kinds of tricks about how to catch cheating partners. I could help him prove Celine's infidelity without revealing my role, providing some support for him during a painful time, and afterwards, I could tell him the rest of it. Maybe by then, he'd be willing to weigh my initial deception against my subsequent helpfulness. If he didn't forgive me at that point... well, I'd have to live with that, but at least I could give myself a fighting chance of maintaining a friendship with him afterwards.

I'd pretty much decided on that approach when I stepped into the Four Winds and saw the man himself standing in front of me.

"What... what are you doing here?" I stuttered, glancing around for any sign that we were being watched. What that would prove, I couldn't guess, but it felt too unlikely to be a coincidence.

Gabe's stunning blue eyes followed my gaze into each empty corner before he turned back to me. "What are *you* doing here? The hotel told me you didn't call to take the reservation."

As the conversation with the hotel receptionist replayed in my memory, the wheels of my brain started to work again. "Did you have the reservation under your name or mine?"

"My name." His brow remained furrowed a second longer until his expression suddenly cleared, understanding dawning on him just as it had for me. "I didn't tell you that."

"You didn't. When I called, they couldn't find anything under my name, but they had a room free, so I took it."

"When they told me you hadn't booked it, I decided to use the room myself," he explained, a grimace pulling at his lips. "I'm sorry, I didn't mean to intrude on your vacation."

"It's not your fault. I should have told you I booked it, but you said..."

"... I'd be taking a few days off," he finished for me, shaking his head as a quick smile flashed across his face. "Well, I fucked that up."

His blunt assessment made me laugh, my body relaxing at the realization that the whole thing came down to a simple mix-up and not a set-up at all.

"I don't need to stay," Gabe added, turning and handing his room key back to the receptionist, who'd been trying very hard not to eavesdrop on our conversation despite being able to hear every word. "You travelled a lot farther than I did. I can come back another time."

"Don't be silly." I stepped forward to take the key from the woman and put it back in Gabe's hand, noting his wedding ring still wrapped around his ring finger. "It's not like we're sharing a room. I'm sure we can go the whole weekend without seeing each other if we really try."

Truth be told, I didn't want that at all. I wanted to tell him the secrets eating away at me, but his tense posture suggested any move in the wrong direction would send him back to his car and back to the city, so I did my best to set him at ease.

Luckily, my smile drew his out again, and his eyes showed only gratitude as he stepped back, holding up the key in his hand with a flourish. He really was attractive when he smiled. "Alright. Have a good stay, then."

"You too."

He disappeared up the large staircase to the left of the reception desk carrying a small duffel bag in his hand while I watched him go, barely realizing I kept staring until the woman behind the desk cleared her throat.

"Well, I'm guessing you're Jennifer Bradshaw, then. I'm Tara, the woman you spoke to on the phone."

She offered me a sheepish shrug at her own role in the mix-up, and I quickly waved my hand to brush away any concerns. "Nice to meet you, and don't worry for a second. An honest mistake on all sides, and I'm sure we'll both enjoy ourselves in the end."

That didn't come out exactly as I meant it, but she didn't act as though I said anything odd. She moved on to checking me in while I took a deep breath, trying to calm my racing heart. As I told Celine during our first interaction, I'd never met any of the men I tested in person, mostly for my own safety, but Gabe didn't really count. He wouldn't be inappropriate with me, and we wouldn't even have to see each other if we didn't want to. The hotel might be small, but with different schedules and interests, we could avoid each other without even trying.

Once Tara gave me all the information about dinner and breakfast times and all the services the hotel offered, she handed over my key and I headed up the staircase, following in Gabe's footsteps. The hotel had four rooms on the ground floor and eight rooms on the first, where mine and Gabe's both seemed to be. Rather than being numbered, each bore the name of a different kind of wine, a nice touch since we were in the heart of wine country. I found the Chianti room in the corner on the left of the large landing at the top of the stairs, and as soon as I stepped inside, I let my bag drop, sighing in contentment.

It looked even better than it did on the website. A large bay window protruded from one wall, giving a near-panoramic view over the vineyards outside. The room itself had been decorated in hues of orange and red, drawing inspiration from the Tuscany region of Italy where Chianti originated. Besides the king-sized bed, a small sitting area in one corner sat next to an electric fireplace, and inside the ensuite bathroom, a deep soaker tub took up half the room, everything sleek and clean and utterly inviting.

I had only just arrived and already, I didn't want to leave.

Unfortunately, I still had work to do. After unpacking, I updated my files with the progress I made in the car. Gabe's file still sat there, unfinished, but after staring at it for a few seconds longer than necessary, I closed the laptop lid and took out my phone instead, taking some photos of myself in the beautiful room to add to my bait profile. I'd post them once I got home, once no one could track me down there. I couldn't be too careful, and no one had ever found me in real life before.

Not until Gabe.

My stomach began to grumble as I took a few photos in front of the fire, and I glanced at my watch to see it had already passed seven o'clock. It would be getting late to head into town for food, especially since I didn't know where to go, but the receptionist said the hotel restaurant had availability. Maybe that night, I could eat in the hotel for the sake of convenience, and the rest of the weekend, I'd make other arrangements.

When I went down to ask about a table, however, Tara rushed out when I rang the bell and gave her apologies. "We actually had a group come in and fill up all the tables that weren't already reserved."

"That's okay, I can just do room service." The thought of eating in my beautiful room appealed to me quite a lot, actually. "Do you have a menu?"

Tara's lips twisted in a grimace. "I'm so sorry, but we're short-staffed. I'm actually helping out in there as well as working the desk. We can't offer room service tonight."

It seemed I would have to go into town after all, despite the protests of my stomach that had only grown louder since I got downstairs and smelled the incredible aromas wafting out from the open dining room door at the end of the hall behind the reception desk.

Getting upset about it wouldn't do me any good though, so I shrugged. "Well, that's my own fault for not making plans earlier. Can you recommend anywhere good that won't get me back too late?"

As she started listing off places, pulling out a map of the local area to show me where they were, the stairs behind me creaked, and like a sixth sense, I knew without looking who it would be.

"Heading out tonight?" Gabe asked, his voice light and almost tentative, too polite to simply ignore me entirely, as he could have.

"The dining room's full," Tara explained before I could answer. "We're trying to find a good alternative."

"You wanted to eat here?" Gabe's blue eyes met mine as he stepped up to the counter next to me. His cologne smelled much better than it had any right to, working its way through my body in a way that nearly made me shiver.

"I did, but we can't always get what we want."

Where the fuck did that come from? The words slipped out of my mouth before I thought them through, before I said them to the man I had literally asked to cheat with me, and his eyebrows shot towards his hairline.

"Don't worry about me," I added, gathering up the information Tara had given me. "I'll figure something out. Have a good night."

Only a few steps from the door, Gabe's voice stopped me. "Jen, wait. I have a table reserved for tonight. You can have it."

Was this guy for real? Every bone in my body cried yes, and I refused to take advantage of him. "I'm not making you go out instead of me. You're the one with a reservation."

He shrugged as he gestured towards the open dining room door. "Well, the table does have two chairs. Would you like to join me?"

Chapter Five

~Gabriel~

Hiding in my room didn't work.

After leaving Jen at reception, I went upstairs and turned on the TV to pass the time, hoping if I waited long enough, I wouldn't run into her again that evening. The desire I felt to spend time with her, to find out what she thought of the hotel and what she planned to do that weekend, along with a dozen other harmless, innocent questions, wouldn't have worried me if it weren't quite so strong. Removing the source of the temptation seemed like the best course of action; if I didn't see her, I couldn't give into it.

But after waiting an hour, I headed back downstairs to find her at the reception desk, and I had to accept my fate. For whatever reason, the universe seemed to be pushing us together, and I reminded myself that I had more self-control than my earlier actions suggested. We could have a nice, friendly dinner without it meaning anything more than that.

Laughter and chatter filled the warm, cozy dining room as the receptionist showed the two of us to the table that had been reserved for me. Nestled in a small alcove, it gave the illusion of some privacy while looking out over the rolling hills that surrounded the small hotel.

It would be rather romantic, if the situation were a little different.

"Thank you, Tara," Jen said before the woman hurried off to take care of her next task, and though it was a little thing, I couldn't help thinking that Celine never bothered to learn the names of the staff when we went out anywhere.

Those kinds of comparisons wouldn't help my state of mind, so I cleared my throat as I pulled the chilled wine that had been left on the table from its bucket. "The owner is treating me tonight. Want to help me take advantage of it?"

Jen smiled as she held out her glass. "I never say no to free wine."

After I poured some for both of us, we both took a sip. The fruity white, crisp and refreshing, seemed to help us both relax. Jen's tongue darted out to swipe a stray drop from her bottom lip as she set her glass down, and I couldn't tell if she'd done it on purpose or not, but I found it sexy either way.

Focus, Gabriel.

"How was your drive?" I asked to steer us back into friendly, neutral territory.

Her shoulders lifted in an elegant shrug. "Fine. You?"

"Fine." That didn't work to stimulate conversation, so I tried the weather next. "The forecast looks good for the weekend."

"It does," she agreed, a smile starting to form on her lips. "If you ask me what I'm planning to do for the weekend, I might head into town tonight and eat alone after all."

That had, in fact, been the next question on the tip of my tongue. "What's wrong with asking that?"

"You're acting like we don't know each other at all."

"We barely do," I pointed out. "All you know about me is that I'm a travel agent going through some personal issues, and all I know about you is…"

The words died in my throat, nothing that wanted to come out being close to appropriate. *You're beautiful and you wanted to sleep with me.*

"Is what?" Jen prompted, leaning forward onto the table to hear me better over the chatter of the other diners. The movement pushed her breasts together, accentuating her already significant cleavage.

Desperately, I scrambled for something, *anything*, to say. "You like to travel and you're a good listener."

I pulled the wine glass back to my lips, filling my mouth so I wouldn't have to speak again.

Jen shrugged again, her body still leaned towards me. "Friendships have been founded on less. But if we want to know each other better, this is the perfect opportunity. Why don't you tell me something about yourself?"

"Like what?"

"Like... what's the first trip you remember going on as a kid?"

The tension in my muscles relaxed, tension I hadn't even fully noticed until it disappeared. That question, I could answer. "My family travelled quite a lot. My mother came from Greece, and her parents, my grand-parents, still lived there when I was young. I remember going to visit them."

"What do you remember about it?" Her eyes never left me, as if she'd never heard anything more fascinating than the words coming out of my mouth, just the same as when we were on the video call together.

A smile tugged at my lips as I let my mind wander back to those early memories. "I remember the blue of the sea. It's different from the California ocean, clear and calm. The land felt dusty and old, the houses all faded from decades or even centuries in the sun. My grandmother would let me stick my finger in the honey while she baked, and I remember its warm sweetness, the taste lingering on my tongue for hours."

"That sounds idyllic." The words, along with her warm smile, encouraged me to keep going.

"I enjoyed it, but more than that, it showed me how life can be different somewhere else but just as real. We're all just people living our lives, no matter where those lives take place. The neighbourhood kids I played with there were just like my friends at home, even though they spoke a different language. I think those early trips gave me an ease with travelling that a lot of people don't have so young."

"I can understand that. Do you think..."

Whatever she wanted to ask got cut off as Tara returned to our table to take our orders. By the time she moved on, I decided to turn the tables and get her answer to the same question. "What about you? What's your first travel memory?"

The light faded from her eyes just a bit, enough that it felt like someone had turned down the temperature, the warmth that had filled my body cooling just a touch.

"I didn't travel as a child. In fact, the farthest we ever went as kids was to Disneyland."

My eyebrows drew together. "Do you mean in Florida?"

She would know the difference between Disneyland and Disney World, I felt certain, and she quickly confirmed she did.

"No, I mean the one thirty miles from where we lived. My parents owned a store and their lives revolved around it. They pretty much never took a day off, at least not at the same time. Holidays weren't something we did growing up. But in university, I met Matt."

The sweet smile that flashed across her face made me smile too, unable to stop myself even if I'd wanted to.

"He wanted to see the world, and he wanted me to see it with him. We made a good start."

"What happened to him?" I probably shouldn't have asked so bluntly, but the mix of pain and happiness in her eyes captivated me. I needed to know. She loved the guy; I would have sworn to it.

Jen's lips tightened, and I thought for a moment that she would refuse to answer. She would be well within her rights to do so. Like I said, we hardly knew each other.

But something seemed to change her mind, and inhaling deeply, she pushed the words out.

"He died on his 25th birthday, on his way to the party I threw for him."

"Fuck." From her profile and the conversations we'd had to that point, I never would have guessed at something that painful in her past. We all had pieces of ourselves we kept hidden, regrets and roads not taken, but hers felt particularly heavy. "I'm sorry."

She flashed another smile my way, tight and pained. "Life doesn't always turn out the way we think it will."

No, it certainly didn't. I could relate to that, and as if she could read my thoughts, Jen turned the conversation back to me once again.

"On that note, did you speak to your wife the other night? What did you find out?"

~Jennifer~

Talking about Matt didn't come easily to me. Normally, I didn't talk about him at all, especially not with anyone I flirted with for work. His part of my life belonged to me alone, and I guarded the memories jealously. Possessively. Talking about them seemed to dilute them somehow, so I never did, not even with Eda who'd known and loved him.

And yet, something made me speak the words to Gabe. Maybe I wanted to open up to him so that he'd open up to me in return. Maybe something in his nature assured me he would respond in a sensitive way, treating the revelation with the gravitas it deserved.

Whatever the reason, I said the words out loud, but before he could ask any follow-up questions, I seized the opportunity and brought the conversation to the topic I'd been dying to ask him about ever since we sat down.

The issue of Celine's potential infidelity had been hanging above us like a cloud, there but not acknowledged, and although I didn't know how Gabe would react, I had to bring it up.

His shoulders tensed, his grip around his wine glass tightening. "We talked but I didn't learn much. All I really know for sure is that she's angry with me for being suspicious."

My jaw clenched on his behalf. A classic narcissist move: make the person with valid concerns feel like they're the ones acting strangely, so the narcissist can play the victim. I'd seen it so many times coming from the men I tested once their partners confronted them with the evidence I provided, and from what Eda helped me piece together about Celine, it made perfect sense that she would behave that way too.

And Gabe, the genuinely nice man that he was, actually felt bad about it. I could see it in the downturn of his lips and the way his eyes dropped to the table as he said the words.

Maybe I could have held back what I wanted to say if he left it there, but his next words were too much for me to bear.

"Maybe I'm deflecting my guilt over chatting with you onto her, and seeing something that's not really there."

"You have *nothing* to feel guilty about," I blurted out, the words coming out stronger than intended. "*I* came onto *you*, and you did nothing to encourage it. Don't let her gaslight you into thinking this is your fault in any way."

Gabe's eyes snapped back up to mine, looking startled by the sharp edge to my tone. "What do you mean?"

Swallowing my indignation, I tried to answer more calmly. "If she's cheating and doesn't want you to know, she might try to spin things around and put the blame on you. But surely, as her husband, you have the right to ask about her change in behaviour. If anyone's deflecting, it's her. That's what I've seen in other situations, anyway."

Gabe's head cocked to the side. "Are you a psychologist or something?"

"In a way." My work *did* involve delving deep into the male psyche, so technically, I didn't lie. "I work with people going through problems in their relationships, and I see a lot of this kind of thing. I can't say for sure that's what Celine is doing, but it feels that way to me from the outside looking in."

Slowly, Gabe nodded, rolling the idea around in his head. "She does have a way of twisting things to her advantage," he admitted. "Nothing is ever her fault. It's actually kind of impressive if you don't…"

He trailed off there, his eyes dropping again as his brow furrowed, and I leaned forward even further, trying to see his face. "If you don't what?"

Although he didn't answer my question, he did look back up at me, his eyes cooler than before. "How do you know her name?"

"What?" My heart began to thump heavily as I realized my mistake, but I asked him to clarify his question anyway to try to buy myself some time to come up with an excuse.

He confirmed that the question meant exactly what I feared it did. "I never told you my wife's name. How do you know it?"

I couldn't think of a single good reason I would know it other than the truth, except maybe that I'd been stalking him, neither of which would go over very well. More than that, I wasn't ready to come clean just yet, especially not when we were getting to the heart of the matter.

Wincing internally, I lied. "You did tell me, the other night when we were talking about her. I remember thinking what a pretty name it is."

His eyebrows knitted even closer together. "I don't remember saying it."

I shrugged as casually as I could. "Sometimes, things just slip out. You were pretty distracted."

The wariness in his gaze lasted another few seconds before it melted away, his shoulders slumping again. "I guess so. Sorry. I didn't mean to accuse you of anything, I just… I feel like I'm going crazy. Things are shifting so fast and I have no idea why."

Guilt surged through me as he accepted my version of events rather than what he knew to be the truth. I'd just done exactly what I'd accused Celine of, and he could be too nice for his own good. No wonder Celine thought she could get away with setting him up.

Not wanting to keep the deception up any longer than I had to, I got straight to the point. "Let's say, for the sake of argument, that she's cheating. Is there any reason she wouldn't just leave you to be with the other guy? What's keeping her with you and lying to you?"

As Gabe leaned back, thinking it over, I held my breath, hoping he'd reach the same conclusion Monica already had, and fast. I would rather he figured it out on his own instead of me having to tell him, and once he did, we could move on to proving the theory.

After that, I'd find a way to tell him the whole truth, and hope that we could still be friends afterwards.

~Gabriel~

If I let myself think about it too long, the fact that I was sitting in a rather romantic restaurant in a beautiful hotel, talking about the potential of my wife cheating on me with the woman who had approached me out of the blue to hit on me, I probably would have reached the conclusion that I'd lost my mind.

So, I didn't think about it. Instead, I tried to focus on what Jennifer asked me: if Celine was cheating, why would she be trying to convince me otherwise?

"It really doesn't fit in with Celine's personality," I answered, saying the words out loud to try to help me sort through all the conflicting ideas in my head. "Usually, she's pretty upfront about what she wants. She even told me when and where to propose to her."

Jen's eyebrows shot up as she took a sip of her wine. "Were you planning to propose?"

"Yes?" The word came out as a question, and I winced. "I mean, I'd been thinking about it. I had the ring, but things didn't seem quite right at the time. She seemed distracted, like she had somewhere more interesting to be than with me. A lot like now, actually."

I hadn't really made that connection before, but there had been one other time when I wondered if Celine might be seeing someone else, back when we were dating. She'd been secretive and distant, and for a couple of weeks, I thought we might break up. Honestly, I even thought it might be for the best. But suddenly, things shifted, and she suggested we go on a trip together, something she knew I'd jump on. We went to Paris, which she said would be a perfect place to propose. I did, she said yes, and things were better after that.

Things were good.

Until a few months ago.

"Let's back up a little further," Jen suggested. "How did you two meet?"

It had been a while since I told anyone that story, and a smile crossed my face at the thought of it. "Well, before I became a travel agent, I worked as a flight attendant."

"Really?" Jen's eyes filled with curiosity again. "That must have been interesting."

"That's one word for it. I loved the travel, but the customer service part had its ups and downs."

Jen nodded sympathetically. "I bet. Long flights don't always bring out the best in people. Was Celine one of your passengers?"

"That's right. We were on a flight from New York to San Francisco and she had a panic attack mid-flight. My colleagues were able to cover for me while I sat with her to help her calm down. She told me she also lived in the city and we exchanged numbers. Things grew from there." The memories of those early days of our relationship and the uncertainty of what it might turn into sent a nostalgic warmth through my body. "When it started to get more serious, my work schedule became an issue, so I found a job with a travel agency instead. I still got to travel, but not every week."

Our food arrived, and we took a break from the conversation to dig in, both of us exclaiming over how good everything looked and tasted. As we settled into the meal, Jennifer resumed her gentle questioning.

"What does Celine do for work?"

The question, though completely innocent, made me wince again because I knew how it sounded. "She worked as a receptionist when I met her, but after we got married, she decided to become a homemaker. Totally her choice, I'm not one to conform to gender-prescribed roles or anything like that."

Jen laughed at my disavowal. "I believe you. I don't think you're holding her captive inside the house."

"Hardly."

As her smile faded, she leaned in again. "If this is too nosy, tell me to butt out, but are you guys financially secure enough that she doesn't need to work? San Francisco is an expensive place to live, and I don't know how much travel agents make."

It *was* a pretty nosy question, but everything about her seemed sincere, like she really just wanted to help, so I answered her honestly. "We're surviving, but we're not rich by any means."

"So, she's not staying with you for your bank account?" she teased.

I smiled back, taking the joke in good humour. "I doubt it."

As soon as the words left my mouth, however, another thought crossed my mind, something I hadn't thought about for a while. Although we were just making ends meet for the time being, we were due to get the inheritance from my grandparents within the next year. I'd been planning to use it to help support our family, when we had one, and set aside some savings. Celine had talked about getting a new house and a new car.

Would *that* be enough to make her stay even if she'd fallen out of love with me? I couldn't be certain, but the doubt settled heavily into my chest, a weight bearing down on my heart that made it a little harder to breathe.

"What's wrong?" Jen asked, picking up on the change in me even though I hadn't said a word.

I gave her a smile, hoping she wouldn't notice its tightness. "I'm just ready to talk about something else, if you don't mind."

As helpful as she'd been, I didn't feel entirely comfortable telling her about the inheritance. Maybe because she would read something into it that I couldn't be sure about. Maybe because people always got a little bit funny at the mention of *that* much money.

At the end of the day, she remained a stranger, and the situation between me and Celine was about as personal as something could get.

"Why don't you tell me about your job?" I suggested as a new subject of conversation. "You know what I do, but I don't have a clue about your work other than that you deal with relationships in trouble."

Jen nodded as she leaned back in her seat, putting her fork down and picking up her wine glass. "That's pretty much it. I offer support to people, usually women, who think they're being cheated on."

That seemed awfully ironic, considering the way she'd approached me, and she gave me a sheepish shrug before I could point it out.

"I know what you're thinking, and you're right. But through my work, I've learned that people have all sorts of arrangements, and that some people's definition of monogamy is a lot more fluid than other people. I don't judge. It's just when those ideas between the people in a relationship don't line up that there's going to be trouble."

I supposed I could understand that, and I appreciated that once I made it completely clear that I wouldn't be cheating, she backed off. That night, she didn't seem to be hitting on me at all, and talking to her felt far more comfortable than I would have imagined it could. "What kind of support do you offer these people?"

"All kinds," she replied vaguely. "But mostly, I help them get proof of the infidelity, and I could do the same for you, Gabe. If you want me to."

My heart rate immediately notched up, adrenaline pumping through my body. Was I ready to truly admit to myself that Celine might be cheating? Did I want to face the proof of it?

It wouldn't be easy, but living in willful ignorance didn't sound a lot better. Even though I might regret it, I found myself nodding at the beautiful woman across the table. "As long as it's discreet, that might not be a bad idea. One way or the other, I'd like to know. What exactly would we have to do?"

Chapter Six

~Jennifer~

The hotel's restaurant outdid themselves with our meal, but I could barely concentrate on the delicious food as the conversation with Gabriel honed in on the offer I wanted to make him. Finally, we got to the heart of the matter, and when he said he wanted to know, I exhaled in relief.

"There are a couple of things we could do, but in this case, I think hiring a private investigator will be the most useful. I have some connections and I'm sure I could find someone who can start work this weekend. Maybe even tonight."

Gabe's eyebrows shot up. "Really?"

I shrugged, trying to play it off. He didn't need to know that my laptop up in my room contained a massive spreadsheet of contacts and resources, not just in California but across the country, that I could provide to my clients if they wanted more proof than what I got for them. "Like I said, it's part of my job."

He nodded slowly, his jaw ticking as he thought it over. "How much does it cost?"

"I'll cover it. It's the least I can do for making you uncomfortable earlier."

Again, I left a lot of things unsaid in blank spaces between the lines. With no income of her own, Celine must have already used his money to pay me in the first place, so it seemed poetic that it would be used to catch her in the act instead.

How did she have access to that much money without him knowing, I wondered? How many other things had she hidden from him?

"I can't accept that," Gabe tried to protest, but I didn't let him go any farther than that.

"You can, and you will. A lot of these people owe me favours for sending business their way anyway. I won't have to pay full price."

The white lie seemed to make him feel better as he nodded slowly again. He had a habit of doing that, I'd noticed, as if the gentle motion of his head helped the thoughts to settle inside his brain. I found it rather endearing.

"I guess they'll need to know where to find her?" he asked next. "Addresses, car info, stuff like that?"

"All of that," I agreed. "We can go to my room and make the call together."

His shoulders tensed at the mention of my room, letting me know he still didn't entirely trust me. Not wanting to come on too strong, I offered an alternative.

"We can use one of the hotel's common rooms if you're more comfortable with that, but it would be more public."

"It would be better in private," Gabe had to agree.

"Then we'll take care of it right after supper, and you can have the rest of the evening to yourself."

I didn't want to give him a chance to change his mind, so as soon as our meal ended, I led him up to my room. It had been a long time since I spent any time in a hotel room with a man, but a completely platonic visit like this didn't count.

"Make yourself at home," I offered once we were inside. I'd left my laptop on the bed, so I picked it up and headed over to the seating area, sitting in one of the armchairs with my back to the wall so Gabe couldn't see my screen. I didn't want to risk him accidentally getting a glimpse at something he shouldn't while I pulled up my list of San Francisco-based PIs.

Gabe took a seat on the sofa, not right next to me but the next spot over, and he glanced around us while I tapped away on my keyboard. "This is a great room. I haven't been in this one before."

"It is," I agreed warmly, shooting a smile at him over the top of my laptop lid. "You were right about the hotel. It's been great so far."

"You haven't had much of a chance to relax yet, though," he pointed out.

"Maybe not, but it'll put my mind at ease to know that you're going to get the answers you deserve."

From my list, I found the top-rated guy on my list and gave him a call, but it went to voicemail. The second guy answered, but already had a full caseload that weekend. The third choice, a woman named Sarah, sounded like our best chance when she said she could begin that night.

"I've heard great things about you, Jen," she said when I finished introducing myself and put her on speaker phone. "Are you branching out into real-world investigations?"

"Just in this one case," I replied, my eyes darting to Gabe, hoping he wouldn't read too much into her words. "I've got the client right here, I'll let you speak to him directly."

Placing the phone down on the coffee table in front of Gabe, I sat back while Sarah went over some basic details with him: his home address, his car information, the usual places where Celine might go.

"She's been staying with her sister on and off for the past week," Gabe explained, and his mouth twisted with the next words. "Or at least, that's what she told me. When I went over to see her, she'd gone out. If she's cheating, I have a feeling her sister's aware of it."

I honestly couldn't imagine how that made Gabe feel. If Eda ever cheated on her husband and I found out, I wouldn't hesitate to tell him. Well, first, I'd demand that *she* told him, and if she refused, then I'd do it myself. She would do the same for my partner too. I couldn't understand the mentality of protecting a person doing something so blatantly wrong, even if they were family.

Maybe Celine had promised her sister part of the payout? Maybe they were just as rotten as each other?

"I'll start there," Sarah promised. "Where else might she be?"

Gabe listed off Celine's favourite stores and coffee shops, parks and movie theaters, all the places she might spend her time. He knew so much about her. A lot of men wouldn't be able to list any of the places their wives went on their own, but he had a whole laundry list of places Sarah could try.

"Does she know you're out of town for the weekend?" I asked when they had finished going through all of Sarah's questions.

"Yeah, I texted her before I left, in case she needed me."

Of course he did. "In that case, Sarah, I'd start at their house."

With him out of the way, Celine might get bold enough to bring her lover into her own space, and Sarah clearly agreed it would be possible. "That'll be stop number one," she promised. "I'll update you as soon as I have any news."

After thanking her, we hung up and the room fell silent as I placed the closed laptop and my phone down on the floor beside the chair, out of the way.

"I never thought I'd be doing this." Gabriel's lips pressed together as he stared out the window in front of him. The sun had almost set and shadows shrouded the world outside. "I thought we'd be together forever."

"You don't know anything for sure yet," I reminded him gently. If and when he got his proof, there would be time for anger and sadness. Until then, speculating would only be a waste of emotion. "Try to relax tonight and take your mind off it. Watch a movie, read a book."

He nodded as if he agreed, but a moment later, he turned those deep blue eyes of his to me. "Would it be okay if I stayed here a bit longer? Just to talk?"

"Yeah. Sure." My answer came out a little too quickly, and I couldn't even say why. Luckily, he didn't seem to notice, or he pretended not to. "What would you like to talk about?"

~Gabriel~

I should have gone back to my room, but the prospect of being alone with my thoughts after hiring a private investigator to follow my wife filled me with dread. Although I could have tried to turn on the TV or find a book in the hotel's small library downstairs, it wouldn't stop my mind from wandering. I needed something more immediate to distract me, and the woman in front of me seemed to do a good job at it.

With Jen around, things didn't feel quite so hopeless.

"Well, we both like to talk about travel," I reminded her, shifting in my seat so that my body turned towards her a little more. "Tell me your worst travel story."

A laugh bubbled out of her, making a ridiculously appealing sound. "You get points for creativity. People usually ask for the good ones."

"Everyone's got good travel stories. Real travellers have bad ones."

"True," she agreed before leaning back in her seat and tucking her legs up to the side, looking completely at ease and comfortable. She wore a cream sweater and tan pants that evening, casual and not at all as blatantly sexy as the things she'd worn when we video chatted in the past. She still looked gorgeous, but in a way I found much more inviting and less intimidating than her appearance on our calls. "I'm not sure if I can think of any that were purely bad."

"That's a lie if I've ever heard one," I blurted out, but she only laughed at my challenge.

"It isn't. I guess I'm a bit of a hopeless optimist. Things might not turn out the way I anticipated, but that doesn't make them a disaster. Like this one time, my phone died during the night in Berlin and Matt and I missed our express train to Copenhagen the next morning by two minutes. Two minutes!"

She threw up her hands in disbelief, and I couldn't help but smile. "German trains are horribly punctual."

"Annoyingly so," she agreed, grinning back at me. Her smile lit up her whole face, making her eyes sparkle. "So, we had to rebook onto three separate trains that took ten hours to get there instead of four."

"Ouch." The wince that crossed my face came less from the idea of ten hours on a train than it did from imagining the meltdown that Celine would have had in a similar situation. She would have found a way to blame me for it and pouted until I made it up to her somehow, probably by buying her something. A hollow ache of anxiety churned in my stomach at the mere idea of it.

I had a feeling Jen's reaction would have been quite different, and she immediately proved me right. "We were disappointed at first, but you can't change the past, you can only make the present as enjoyable as possible."

"And how did you do that?"

The sparkle in her hazel eyes grew even stronger. "We filmed our own murder mystery on the train."

"What?" I hadn't expected that at all, and my burst of laughter made her giggle.

"Why not? We had our cameras and we had the time. Some of the other passengers got in on it too once they realized what we were doing. Even the conductor guest-starred in a scene. It's a masterpiece, I assure you."

"I'm sure." That actually sounded like a blast. I'd never travelled with anyone who would have done something like that. "I'd love to see it sometime."

Her smile faltered, just a touch. "I haven't watched it in ages, but I should dig it out sometime. See if it holds up."

Fuck. Despite the brave face she put on, I could see the way the light in her eyes dimmed when I suggested it. She'd probably been avoiding it after her boyfriend died, but I hadn't thought about that before opening my mouth.

"What about you?" she asked before I could apologize for my insensitivity. "What's your worst travel story?"

"I'm not convinced yours counts as a bad one at all," I pointed out.

Jen shrugged. "I warned you."

She had, so I let it go and tried to think of which experience to share with her. We were talking about this to avoid me overthinking about Celine, so I didn't want to bring up anything that featured her, though there were several memories that would qualify. Instead, I tried to focus on something closer to what Jen had described: a situation that could have ruined a trip but turned into a pleasant memory instead.

"Well, I've got a train story of my own. I was in Russia, on a small rural train by myself. We stopped in one small town and we didn't start going again. We sat there for half an hour before the conductor made an announcement, but naturally, he spoke in Russian and I had no idea what he said. Everyone else got off the train so I did too, and tried to find someone on the platform who spoke English. No one did."

Jen leaned forward, giving me her full attention as she always did. "What did you do?"

"I hadn't quite figured out a plan yet when these two grandmothers came out of the little cafe in the station and linked their arms through mine, chattering at me in Russian. Though we couldn't communicate one bit, they took me to a nearby house, fed me, let me sleep in the guest room, and took me back to the train station the next morning. They put me on a train, and sure enough, it took me exactly where I wanted to go. I tried to give them money but they refused to take it. They just patted my cheeks, and one of them slapped me on the ass when I got on the train."

Jen's eyes had begun to twinkle again. "That's amazing, but very trusting on your part. What if they'd been trying to kidnap you? They might have tied you up in their basement!"

"Honestly, getting married off to one of their granddaughters worried me more," I admitted.

Her bright laugh filled the room. "Would that have been the end of the world?"

"I suppose I would have learned Russian eventually."

We traded a few more stories, and a few more after that. Her sense of adventure and her good humour shone through every word, and she never once looked bored or that she'd rather be anywhere other than in our conversation.

When I finally glanced down at my watch, I swore in surprise. "Fuck, it's after midnight. I didn't mean to keep you so long."

"Is it?" She seemed equally surprised as she reached down to grab her phone off the floor. Messages filled her home screen, I noticed, when she tapped on the screen to wake it up. Apparently, she had a lot of people vying for her attention.

And yet, she'd chosen to spend the whole evening with me.

It made me feel rather special.

"I'll let you get some sleep. Sorry," I apologized again as I got to my feet. My muscles and my bladder both protested at the movement after hours of being stationary. Honestly, I couldn't believe so much time had passed. It felt like minutes.

"I would have kicked you out if I wanted to get rid of you," she told me firmly. "I really enjoyed talking to you, Gabe."

"I enjoyed it too."

Other words lingered on the tip of my tongue, wanting to invite her to join me for breakfast or to explore the region with me the next day, but that would be completely inappropriate. She came there for a break, not to see me, not to mention the not-so-small fact that I was still a married man.

So why the hell did this feel so much like the end of a date?

"Have a good night," I blurted out, and turning away, I rushed out of the room before any other words could find their way out of my mouth.

Time to go to bed.

~Jennifer~

The door closed behind Gabriel with a soft click and I exhaled in both relief and disappointment. I enjoyed the evening with him a lot. Too much, really, given the situation, and it frustrated me that I felt more attracted to him than I'd felt to anyone in a long time. And I *shouldn't*, because after all the heartache I dealt with on a daily basis, I never wanted to be the cause of it by going after a taken man.

But *was* he taken, when Celine already seemed to have one foot out the door?

I didn't even know *what* to feel anymore.

What I *did* know was that I had a string of messages that needed a reply from some of my other jobs, so despite the late hour, it didn't look like sleeping would be in my near future.

I started with the guy who messaged me the most, his texts getting more and more agitated when I didn't reply.

> Did you miss me? ;) Sorry, I had a friend come over with a crisis. She needed my full attention but I'm all yours now.

A normal, empathetic human being might have asked about my friend, but this particular jerk had other priorities.

> 2 late. Got myself some other pussy tonight.

With that charming remark, he sent me a picture of himself with his hand down another woman's shirt as she grinned drunkenly at the camera.

A grin that definitely did *not* belong to his girlfriend.

It seemed this trash would take himself out with very little help from me, so I sent the picture and a screenshot of his borderline-harassing messages to the girlfriend in question.

I'd barely started responding to the next guy on my list when another message popped up. Assuming it came from the woman I just messaged, I swiped it out of the way, but at the last second, I caught a glimpse of Gabe's name.

Frowning, I exited my message and went in search of his text. What would he be messaging me about after we just spent the whole evening together?

> Hey. You're probably asleep, but I just wanted to say thanks for… well, all of it, I guess. Helping me with the PI and helping me to keep my mind off it. I left before saying thank you properly, so… thanks. Good night. Or morning, if you don't see this until you wake up. Either way. Gabe

My cheeks ached from the wide smile that spread across them as I read his rambling message. Flustered Gabe was absolutely adorable, but what did his rambling mean? Could it be a sign that he felt more attracted to me than he let himself show, just the same as I felt towards him?

My eyes glanced up at the time on my phone: 12:37.

I shouldn't reply. I should wait until the morning and pretend I really had been sleeping, like he assumed. Nothing good ever came from texting a stranger after midnight: I *knew* that, and yet, I typed out a reply anyway.

> You don't need to thank me. I told you I wanted a break from my day-to-day, and tonight definitely gave me that. Now get off your phone and go to sleep!

> I will. Good night. Again.

Still smiling, I went back to my other message. That man also hadn't gone to sleep yet, and after a few minutes of flirting, he asked for a photo.

It only took me a minute to pull off the sweater I'd been wearing and put on my lace-trimmed nightgown instead, ensuring my breasts were displayed to their best advantage before taking a picture of myself in bed.

At the last second before I hit send, I realized the name of the hotel could be seen on the folder on my bedside table, and I quickly exited the text and went into my photos to edit it out. Although I'd broken my cardinal rule by spending time with Gabe in person, I had no desire to make it easy for anyone else to find me.

Satisfied the location would now be anonymous, I sent it straight from the photos app and went back to my messages while I waited for a reply. The girlfriend from the first guy of the night had come back to me and confirmed that the photo of her man and the random woman were enough for her to call things off with him. My work done there, I blocked him. That would be another one I could cross off my list in the morning.

After finishing all of that, the guy I sent the photo to hadn't replied yet, which I found odd. However, when I clicked into our text thread to see if I'd missed something, the picture didn't appear. It didn't look like I sent it. My brow furrowed in confusion as I returned to my list of conversations, where it only took a second to realize my mistake.

I sent the photo to Gabe instead.

Fuck.

How the hell did that happen? I had *never* mixed up conversations before. I must have been distracted, I had no other excuse, though really, it was unacceptable.

I'd spent half the evening convincing Gabe I had given up on trying to seduce him, only to send him a deliberately provocative picture of myself in bed after he wished me a good night. If I didn't say something, he would think it had all been a lie, or that I had some kind of split personality. The Jekyll and Hyde of online seductresses.

But what other options did I have? If I told him I meant to send it to someone else, that would sound even worse.

I had a rational explanation for all of it, but the idea of having to explain myself felt overwhelming, especially when we still didn't have any concrete answers about Celine.

Desperately, I chewed on my lip, trying to decide on a course of action which wouldn't paint me as a complete lunatic, a compulsive liar, or both, when a reply came through.

> You don't have to try so hard to get my attention, Jen. You've got it, believe me. Have a good night.

Chapter Seven

~Gabriel~

It had been so late by the time I finally fell asleep that when I woke up, the sun already streamed brightly into my hotel room. I grabbed my phone to check the time, and it opened to the last thing I looked at the night before: that incredible photo of Jen in her bed.

Just like it had the night before, my body immediately responded to the image, and with a groan, I turned the phone off again.

Why had she sent it? She offered no explanation, no message to accompany it, and so I'd been completely unprepared for both the picture and my reaction to it.

Sure, I'd seen more seductive images on her Instagram, but that had been before we spent the evening together. After having dinner with her and talking with her late into the night, she felt much more real to me, and therefore the picture felt more intimate, especially since I knew mere feet separated us when she took it.

Completely inappropriate? Absolutely.

And yet, I couldn't tear my eyes away from it.

Something drew me to her, something I couldn't fully explain, but no matter how gorgeous or kind or funny she might be, the fact remained that I still had a wife at home. A wife who might be cheating on me, yes, but who also might not be. Innocent until proven guilty, right? Maybe Celine was just going through something she didn't feel comfortable confiding in me about, and there I was, staring at a sexy photo of another woman I'd just spent the evening with.

And even if she *was* cheating, it didn't give me carte blanche to do the same thing.

Even looking at Jen's photo for as long as I did made me feel dirty, and uncomfortable, and more than a little guilty.

Trying to ignore the heat flowing through my veins, I typed a message and deleted it, and typed a new reply about five times. I didn't want to encourage Jen any more than I already had, but neither did I want her to feel bad about feeling a connection with me when I felt it too. The first reply sounded too harsh, the next too flirty, and so on until I finally decided on the response I ultimately sent. She didn't reply before I went to sleep, and that morning, she still hadn't sent anything else.

The whole thing confused me, but I couldn't fixate on it. Until I had some answers about Celine and what that meant for our marriage, I shouldn't be thinking about Jen at all, in any capacity.

"Gabriel!"

Manuel greeted me as soon as I set foot on the main floor after getting ready for the day. He came out from behind the desk, and when I held out my hand, he ignored it, wrapping me into a strong hug instead.

"I'm sorry I missed you yesterday, I got held up."

"It's not a problem," I gasped, trying to get my breath back after he squeezed it out of me. "Thank you for the wonderful dinner."

"My pleasure. And I hear you had a lovely companion. Did you bring your beautiful wife with you?"

My stomach twisted, though I couldn't even say for sure which part of what he said bothered me. "No. Just a friend. I'm here alone."

His disappointed expression suggested he'd been excited to meet her. "Maybe next time, then. You're always welcome."

We chatted for a few more minutes, my eyes constantly flicking to the staircase, wondering if Jen might come down the stairs and what she would say if we ran into each other. However, she didn't appear, and I convinced myself to see it as a good thing while I made my way out to my car to get my day started properly.

Whenever I travelled these days, I couldn't completely divorce myself from thoughts of work, so I decided to head to the contemporary arts centre to see what the current exhibitions were like. Having first-hand experience of attractions helped me decide which clients might also enjoy them. The sculpture park and wildlife preserve offered plenty of opportunity to walk off some of my anxious energy, and by the time I finished my visit, I felt a little calmer than before.

I had also worked up an appetite, and the Oxbow Public Market was the obvious choice for lunch. Local producers sold almost every kind of food imaginable at its stalls, and the patio offered a shaded, comfortable place to enjoy whatever I decided to pick up.

Waiting in line at the cheese stall, I spotted her.

Jen had her back to me, but her cascading honey-coloured hair would have stood out anywhere. She chatted with the stall's owner, her sparkling laugh ringing out as he said something amusing. My feet seemed to root me to the spot as I debated whether to stay and let her see me or go and pretend I hadn't seen her. How did we keep ending up in the same places?

Before I could decide, she turned around with her purchase and spotted me. Uncertainty flickered across her face, but only for a moment before she walked over sporting a smile.

"Are you stalking me, or am I stalking you?"

Honestly, I couldn't be sure. "Seems like we have similar tastes."

I meant the cheese, but the sentence came out flirtier than I intended.

Jen's smile tightened as she leaned closer to me. "Well, since you're here, I owe you an apology for sending that photo last night. I love the room so much and was messing around taking pictures to see if I could find a good angle, and somehow, I sent it to you. I feel like such an idiot."

That made a lot of sense, actually. More than any other scenario I'd come up with, and I exhaled in relief. "Okay. Good. I mean, don't get me wrong, the photo looked great but it felt a little..."

"Out of line? Aggressive? Psychotic?" she supplied, her face squeezing into an adorable grimace. "You can say it."

"Out of character, actually. You're quite different online from how you are in person."

"Yeah. I get that a lot." She gave me another tight smile before holding up the bag in her hand. "Well, I'm going to finish picking out my lunch. I won't disturb you anymore."

Based on her explanation, I didn't want her to feel bad over a silly mistake. "You're not disturbing me. I'm here for lunch too, and it makes more sense to eat together rather than at separate tables, pretending we don't know each other."

"I suppose," she agreed, though she didn't sound fully convinced. "Only if you're sure you don't mind."

"I'm sure. Let me grab something here and we can check out the rest of the market together."

So much for avoiding her, but as we walked through the market together, exploring the different stalls and chatting to the people who worked there, getting along just as well as we always seemed to, I couldn't bring myself to be too upset about the way things had turned out.

~Jennifer~

"There's no way. You'll choke!"

My eyes went wide as Gabriel lifted a massive chunk of cheese to his mouth. It looked taller than his jaw could stretch, and he just asked me if I thought he could eat it in one bite, claiming to have learned a technique while travelling in northern Africa that would help him survive such a ridiculously foolish attempt.

"And you won't even enjoy it. That's high-quality cheese right there," I added, hoping that might discourage him, and it seemed to work better than my fears over his choking did.

He hesitated, his eyes flicking between the cheese and me. "Will you believe me that I *could* do it?"

"Fine. Yes. Just don't make me do the Heimlich on you." I shook my head at his grin while he broke off a much more reasonably-sized piece and popped it into his mouth. "Why do men always think shoving a lot of something down their throat is impressive? Women in general have more experience with that anyway."

He almost choked despite my precautions. After coughing a couple of times, he took a swig of the non-alcoholic wine I'd picked out for the two of us to share. "I can't decide if you're trying to save my life or trying to kill me."

"Why does it have to be one or the other?"

Somehow, we'd been sitting out on the patio for over an hour and a half after wandering the market together for thirty minutes before that. Time seemed to fly while talking to him, and neither of us appeared to be in a hurry to move on with our day. Thankfully, when we bumped into each other, he accepted my excuse about the photo I sent him the night before, dispelling any potential awkwardness before it had a chance to take root.

He really did try to see the best in people.

Just as that thought crossed my mind, my phone chimed loudly in my pocket. I'd put it on silent except for messages from two people: my sister, and Sarah, the private investigator. When I pulled it out, Sarah's name stared back at me.

"What is it?" Gabe asked, clearly reading something in my face that I didn't quite manage to hide.

"I got a message from Sarah," I answered truthfully. "I haven't opened it yet, though. Do you want to know what she says?"

The lighthearted camaraderie between us seemed to evaporate as he swallowed hard, as if the cheese had gotten stuck somewhere on the way down. "Sure. No point in putting it off, I guess."

I read it out loud so we were both getting the information at the same time.

> Checking in to let you know I'm still on the job but nothing to report so far. Found her car at her sister's house last night. She left around noon and went back to her own house. No sign of anyone else there. I'll stick close by and let you know if anything changes.

I blew a breath out as I took that in, trying to ignore any disappointment that might try to push its way into my heart. Looking up, I gave Gabe a forced smile. "Well, that's good news."

"It is," he agreed, though his expression didn't match his words. He looked almost as conflicted as I felt. "Maybe it's all in my head."

"She's not expecting you back for another twenty-four hours at least," I reminded him. "Let's not jump to any conclusions, good or bad, just yet."

"I suppose that's smart." Looking around us, Gabe seemed to realize just how much time had passed. "The afternoon's going to be gone if we stay much longer, and I'm sure you have other things you'd like to do. I keep monopolizing your time."

"Only because I let you." I gave him another smile, warmer that time, but I could tell our moment of connection had ended. His mind had returned to his wife, and I had to respect that. "Will you be stalking me again for supper?"

He laughed as he got to his feet. "I guess we'll have to wait and see. Enjoy the rest of your day, Jen."

"You too." I watched him walk away, noticing how a few other women glanced his way as he passed them, while Gabe remained oblivious to the attention. In almost every way, he provided a vivid contrast to the men I interacted with on a daily basis.

I hadn't made any firm plans for the afternoon, but over lunch, Gabe told me about the arts centre he visited that morning, so I headed there next. In the sculpture park, I sat beneath the sunshine in the fresh air and answered a few messages on my phone. Although I'd given myself the weekend off from taking on new clients, I had to keep a few embers burning on some of my tests-in-progress.

After sending a few messages, I put the phone down beside me and let my mind wander. What would Gabe think when I told him the truth about my job? Would he find it dishonest, or would he see how I helped people? I couldn't be sure how he'd react, but I knew that I had to come clean with him before long. As soon as the situation with Celine settled, I would bite the bullet and confess it all.

Perhaps I wouldn't have to wait too much longer. While still sitting there, another text from Sarah came in.

> We've got some activity. Sending pics now.

For the first time, I got an inkling of what the women I worked for must feel when they waited for me to get back to them. Pictures began to come through one-by-one of a car pulling into the driveway of what must be Gabe's house and a man getting out, glancing around before heading up the front step. When Celine opened the door for him, they seemed to embrace before going inside.

Given everything I knew, nothing I saw surprised me, and after sending Sarah a quick thanks and asking her to stay put to see how long he stayed, I sent Gabe a text.

> Looks like I might be interested in stalking you for dinner tonight after all. How about room service in my room at the hotel?

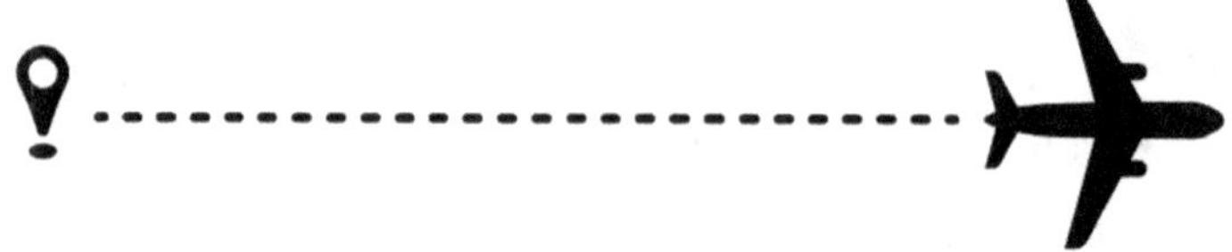

~Gabriel~

I stared at Jennifer's message for a long time, trying to decide if it marked another of her flip-flop changes of character between her online persona and her in-person self, or whether she had a legitimate reason for asking to see me that evening.

Luckily, a second message came in before I needed to make that determination myself.

> There's something I need to show you.

Though she didn't say any more than that, I could guess what she meant: the investigator must have sent her something about Celine. Uneasiness churned in my stomach, the bitter sting of my wife's potential unfaithfulness mingling with the undeniable desire I felt for the woman who had just invited me to her room for the second night in a row.

Pretending my attraction to Jen didn't exist would be unwise. It needed to be acknowledged so it could be controlled. I had no intention of acting on those feelings, so I needed to be aware of them to avoid doing anything stupid.

As for the 'thing' Jen had to show me, it must have been bad news. If it weren't, she would have just told me, like she did at lunch. Thinking about how it would affect me, she suggested meeting more privately, and I appreciated the consideration.

Her thoughtfulness tipped the scales for me.

> Sure. Message me when you're back and I'll come over.

Try as I might to enjoy the winery tour I joined before her message came in, my thoughts were anywhere but on the grapes in front of me, and I skipped out before the tastings to head back to the hotel. At the desk, I confirmed the restaurant was fully staffed that evening and that room service wouldn't be a problem.

"Do you want to order something now?" the man at the desk asked.

"No, thanks. I'm... I'm waiting for someone."

The stammered response made it sound like a lie, but although he gave me a slightly confused look, the man said nothing else and I quickly retreated up the stairs. Seconds felt like hours as I waited in my room for another message from Jen. Thankfully, she didn't make me wait too long.

> I'm back. Come over whenever you're ready.

I could have pretended I hadn't been waiting, but that seemed silly. She must have known I'd be desperate to know what she'd learned, and sure enough, when she opened the door for me a minute later, she didn't look at all surprised to see me there.

"Come on in. I already placed an order for food, I hope that's okay?"

"You ordered for me?" It surprised me, but I didn't mind. Celine never would have gone to the trouble.

"Based on what you ate last night and at lunch, I feel pretty sure you'll like it," she promised. "Besides, I didn't want to waste time since we both know why you're here."

We sat back down in the same spot where we'd chatted the night before, but this time, rather than sitting in the armchair, Jen sat on the sofa next to me.

"This is what I received today."

She handed the phone to me so I could read the message from the investigator myself. It came in just before she texted me that afternoon, so I certainly couldn't complain she'd held anything back from me. My stomach flipped as I forced myself to open the photos.

The first one didn't show much, just a car I didn't recognize pulling into my driveway. In the next one, a man got out of the driver's side, but the camera saw him from the back, I couldn't make out any of his features. A moment later, he must have turned back to look at the street, because the next photo showed his face on full display, looking almost directly at the camera, and I let out a muttered curse.

"Are you fucking serious?"

Jen leaned in closer to peer at the photo before her warm hazel eyes looked up at me. "Do you know him?"

"Yeah." My heart thumped a hard, steady rhythm in my chest as I stared at the photo. "His name is Isaac. I work with him."

Jen's chest rose with her inhale. "At the travel agency?"

"Yeah. This is... this can't... this doesn't make any sense." Getting a full sentence out became a struggle as I flipped through the other photos of him going up to the door, Celine opening the door to him, a smile on her face that I hadn't seen in quite a while, her arms going around his shoulders and his around her waist before they went inside.

It didn't seem real. I didn't know how it could be.

"They barely know each other."

Obviously, that must not be true, and Jen gently pointed that out. "It seems they do."

My mind spinning, I cast back in my memory for any time the two of them would have spent together. Speaking out loud, I tried to put the pieces together. "He joined the agency last fall. They would have met at the company's Christmas party. She came into the office a couple of times in January to see me, but that's..."

I trailed off, the situation becoming clearer to me with each passing second. Celine *never* came to the office to see me, but in January, she did. Both times, I had important clients there, meetings I had mentioned to her in advance. She assured me she didn't mind waiting, which, now that I thought about it, should have been a red flag too. Both times, I came out of my meeting to find her at my desk, scrolling on her phone. I assumed she spent the whole time there.

Perhaps she hadn't. Perhaps she'd come for an entirely different reason.

My mouth dried up as my imagination took over, months of clandestine meetings, all behind my back. In April, Isaac had been booked on a scouting trip to the Seychelles. At the last minute, he had to pull out, and he offered the trip to me instead. I asked Celine if she wanted to go with me, assuming a trip to the island paradise would yield the kind of photos she'd love to share, but the length of the flight put her off. She stayed home, and so did Isaac, while I spent a week on the other side of the world.

How many other things had I missed?

"Is he still there?" I managed to croak out.

Immediately, Jen got to her feet and poured me a glass of water. It helped with the dryness, but not with the nausea roiling around my stomach.

I gulped it down anyway.

"He's still there," she answered when my glass had been emptied. "We don't know what he's doing there, though. The pictures don't prove much."

Maybe not, but nothing else made sense. Any doubts I might have had were completely swept away when I saw the man's face. The way she'd been pulling away from me seemed obvious, along with the way she kept picking fights.

She'd been done with me for a while. I just hadn't noticed it.

"You could go home and confront them," Jen suggested. The words came out quieter than usual, as if she were a lion tamer trying to soothe a distressed animal. "She wouldn't need to know about the investigator. You could say you simply decided to come home early and see what she has to say."

I supposed I could. In just over an hour, I could be standing outside that door, ready to surprise them both, but the thought sent an icy chill through my body that made the nausea even worse. "I thought you just ordered supper," I reminded her weakly.

"Don't worry about me. You need to do what's best for *you*. If there's ever a time to be selfish in your life, Gabe, this is it."

I tried to imagine walking in on them, but I suspected that somehow, no matter how much in the wrong she might be, Celine would find a way to make it my fault. Avoiding confrontation seemed easier. Maybe that made me weak, but I honestly didn't know what to think or feel at that moment.

"Is that what you would do? Try to catch them in the act?"

Jen didn't answer me directly, giving me a more general response instead. "Some people need to see it with their own eyes. Others require less proof; they just feel it. Neither is right or wrong. You know how you feel, so seeing this, based on everything that's been going on between you, is that enough for you to know how you want to proceed? Or do you need more?"

Did I know how I wanted to proceed?

Maybe a chance still existed, however small, that Celine wasn't actually cheating. Maybe Isaac had another reason for being at my house for hours without me there. But when I thought about the way our relationship had deteriorated over the past few months, the feeling I'd gotten when I went to Allie's and didn't find Celine there, and the fact that, at the very least, she'd been hiding being friends with Isaac from me, it all added up to one thing.

My wife and the woman I thought I married were two different people.

Maybe she'd never been the woman I loved at all.

Seeing her in bed with Isaac wouldn't change that. It might cement it, but I didn't require it to make the decision that I knew I needed to make, the one that I had already made, whether I'd been ready to admit it to myself before then or not.

I didn't want to be married to Celine anymore.

Chapter Eight

~Jennifer~

It broke my heart to sit there and watch Gabe come to terms with the end of his marriage.

The fact that he'd decided to end it wasn't in doubt for me even though he hadn't said anything out loud. I'd sat on the other end of the video chat with enough women to know the signs: the disbelief, the pain, and the acceptance, all of which flashed across his open, expressive face in exactly that order.

He didn't deserve this. He would also be better off without her, I didn't doubt that, but it didn't make the pain any easier for him to take at the moment the foundation cracked and left a gaping hole beneath him where there had previously been solid ground.

"I don't want to see her," he finally said, his voice barely louder than a whisper. "Not tonight."

"Then you don't have to." Just like with the women I helped, I would back up whichever choice he decided to make. The 'right' decision varied from person to person, and only he knew what felt right to him. "You can stay here or you can go back to your room, or anything else you want to do. I meant it when I said not to worry about me."

His nod suggested he believed me, but he opted to stay anyway. "I don't think I want to be alone either."

"That's fine. Supper will be here soon and some food might do you good. How about a drink?"

"Yes, please."

Even heartbroken, he couldn't help being polite. With a heavy heart of my own, I grabbed one of the wine bottles I'd picked up that day and used the hotel's corkscrew to open it up. Two glasses poured, I returned to the sofa and handed one to him. He downed half the glass in one gulp.

"Do you want to talk about it?" I asked. Again, everyone dealt with things differently. Some people wanted to hash things out and figure out what went wrong while others didn't want to think about it at all until the situation had a chance to fully sink in.

"No," he answered quickly before scrunching up his nose. "Yes? Maybe. I don't know. You're already way more involved than you want to be, I'm sure."

"Stop. Worrying. About. Me." I said each word as a complete sentence, poking my finger into his shoulder with the final one. "What do *you* want to talk about?"

He tried to smile at my gentle teasing, but it looked closer to a grimace as he stared down at his wine glass. His five o'clock shadow ran along his jaw, looking stronger in profile, and for a brief second, my fingers itched to trace the line of it. "Would you mind if I ask you for a woman's perspective?"

"On what?"

His grimace grew stronger as he glanced over at me. "On why she would cheat. I mean, I don't expect you to know the specifics about why she's unhappy in our marriage, but if she's so unhappy that she wants to be with someone else, why wouldn't she just tell me so?"

My heart beat faster as I tried to keep my expression neutral. I'd wondered the same thing, and I got my answer through my sister and his. Could I help him come to the same conclusion I'd already reached?

"Well, why do you think she married you in the first place?" I started.

His eyes drifted away from me again as he searched his memory for the answer. "She said she loved how supportive and caring I am." He gave a shrug, as if it embarrassed him to say it out loud, even though it didn't surprise me at all. "And the sex was really good. Sorry if that's too much information."

"It's fine, don't apologize." I had a feeling he *would* be good in bed, based on that supportive and caring nature of his. I could imagine he wouldn't consider his job done until his partner had been fully satisfied.

Trying to ignore the heat that spread through my body at that thought, I shifted my position, angling myself towards him more as I took a drink of my wine and did my best to keep us on track.

"Have any of those things changed to make her unsatisfied, do you think?"

Bless him, he honestly considered it even though I could have told him he hadn't done anything wrong. Thankfully, he came to the same conclusion on his own. "I really don't think so. I have to travel sometimes, but I always invite her to come with me and call her when I'm away to make sure things are okay. I didn't notice anything changing until she started to pull away."

A knock at the door interrupted us, and I brought the room service cart inside, bringing our meals over to the sofa so we could continue our conversation while we ate. Gabe thanked me as I handed him the seafood linguine I'd ordered for him.

"This looks fantastic. Celine probably would have ordered me whatever *she* wanted."

He glanced over at my salad with thinly-veiled disgust, and I laughed. "Too much wine and cheese today, I need to be a little bit good. But I saved room for dessert, don't worry."

Those words sounded dirtier than I meant them. I literally *had* ordered dessert for us, but my tone somehow shifted, and Gabe's gaze dropped to my lips, just for a fraction of a second, before he turned back to his plate and shoved a forkful of pasta into his mouth.

I cleared my throat as I speared some leaves on my plate. "Celine doesn't know what you like?"

Gabe nearly choked as he swallowed, and I tried not to groan. Why did everything sound like an innuendo all of a sudden?

"You said she would have ordered you the same meal that she had," I reminded him before I could make things worse.

"Right. I said that." He shook his head as if trying to shake out the dirtier thoughts that had started to fill the air between us. "She doesn't really pay attention to things like that, I guess."

"Things like what you like to eat? When you've been together for four years?"

He started to shrug again before a look of confusion crossed his face. "I don't remember telling you how long we were together."

Fuck. He hadn't, and Celine hadn't either. That bit of information came from Eda's snooping.

Maybe the time had come to tell him about Celine hiring me, at least. I'd wanted to wait until he put the whole picture together, but he just gave me the perfect opportunity.

I opened my mouth to respond, but before I could get any words out, Gabe shook his head. "You're distracting, I guess. I forget too many things when I'm around you."

His eyes met mine for a brief moment before he dropped them again, but the heat in that eye contact nearly took my breath away. It all but confirmed for me that the connection I felt between us wasn't one-sided. He felt something too, even if he shouldn't.

"I don't know why she doesn't notice those kinds of things," he continued, completely unaware of my swirling doubts and emotions. "Monica says she's just selfish, there's nothing more to it than that."

"Monica?" I knew he meant his sister, but he definitely hadn't mentioned her to me before, so I played dumb that time.

"My sister. She never really liked Celine." He let out a huffed, rueful ghost of a laugh. "Maybe I should have listened to her more than I did."

He took another drink of his wine while I tried to find an avenue that would lead us to talking about his inheritance. If I could get him down that road, then there'd be nothing left to stop me from telling him the full truth about my part in all of it.

Focusing on his family might get us there, so I gave that a try. "Are you close with your sister?"

"Yeah, pretty close. She's great." For the first time since he came into the room, he almost smiled.

"It's just the two of you?"

"Yeah. Not only in our immediate family, but the extended family too. Both my parents were only children."

No cousins meant his grandparents' inheritance went straight to him and Monica. We were getting closer. "You must have been spoiled by your grandparents," I teased lightly.

That same attempt at a smile appeared again. "We were. Still are, really. My mom's parents, the ones from Greece, moved here to retire."

They were still alive, then. "What about your dad's parents?"

Any hint of a smile vanished. "They passed away a couple of years ago, but they're still doing their best to spoil us."

We were so close to where we needed to get, I could almost reach out and touch it.

I kept my tone as innocent as possible while I took another bite of my salad. "What does that mean? Did they leave you a lot of money?"

"Kind of. They thought that young, single people wasted money on stupid things, so they put a clause in their will that we wouldn't get it right away."

I mustered up a laugh even though my heart had begun to pound. *Come on, Gabe. Make the connection.*

"They sound pretty smart," I said out loud.

"They were," he agreed. "We don't get anything until we turn thirty or we're married for..."

He trailed off, his fork frozen halfway to his mouth, and I held my breath as I waited for him to finish that sentence.

~Gabriel~

There were days in the San Francisco bay when the fog got so thick, the city seemed to be floating in a cloud. The Golden Gate bridge disappeared and people on one side of the street could barely see people on the other. Sidewalks you'd walked down your whole life could seem unfamiliar, the path ahead unclear and mysterious.

Then, out of the blue, the sun came out, the fog lifted and everything seemed brighter and clearer than it ever had before.

That almost described how I felt at that moment.

The fog that had been obscuring my understanding of why Celine would cheat on me but stay married to me suddenly cleared, and I could see the whole picture as sharply as looking across the bay on a sunny, cloudless day.

How could I have been so completely blind when the answer had been right there all along?

"Gabe?" Jen's voice seemed to come from far away even though she still sat right beside me. Blinking slowly, I tried to pull myself back to the present, back to the hotel room where we were still finishing our meal. "Are you okay?"

"Yeah, I'm... I..."

Words failed me as I put my plate down and reached for my wine glass, draining the rest of it in one gulp. I wanted to laugh and cry at the same time, giddy with understanding and crushed by the realization of exactly how little the woman I once loved actually thought of me.

"What is it?" Jen asked, putting a comforting hand on my knee, as if she knew I needed something to ground me in the moment before my thoughts flew away again, pulling me along with them.

My words came out flat and cold, but at least they came. "My grandparent's estate. I get my share of it either when I turn thirty or when I've been married for three years."

She leaned a little closer. "And you've been married for two?"

"That's right. If we get divorced before that, Celine's entitled to her fair share of our assets, but not any of the inheritance. That must be why she's staying with me even though she clearly doesn't want to. For the money."

The thought struck me as so ridiculous, so base and uncaring, that I had to laugh. It didn't sound much like a laugh, though. The noise that came out of me was harsh and pained, and Jen's hand squeezed my knee in sympathy.

"Money can make people do crazy things. It's not the same thing, obviously, but before Matt died, he changed his life insurance to make me the beneficiary. He didn't tell me he'd done it. It came as a complete surprise when his father settled his estate, and it turned out to be quite a lot since he'd been young and healthy and no one expected him to die."

We'd been talking so much about me that it took me a second to refocus. Despite the whirling, careening thoughts in my head, I did my best to give her my full attention, the way she always did for me. "That was thoughtful of him."

"It was." Despite her words, her lips twisted into a grimace. "Unfortunately, his father didn't agree. He was furious that I would get it when we weren't even married yet."

It must have just been my distracted state, but that didn't make any sense to me. "That's hardly your fault. Not your fault that you weren't married and not your fault that he made you the beneficiary."

"You sound like my sister." Her quick smile let me know she meant that as a compliment. "It sucked, though. Rather than supporting each other through our grief, I got cut off by his family. Even when I offered to share the payout with them, the damage had been done. None of his family speak to me anymore. Either they're still upset at how things played out or, in the case of his sisters, I think they're just embarrassed. I lost not only my fiancé but my almost in-laws as well. Money brings out the worst in people sometimes."

I couldn't argue with that when I felt the brunt of it myself, but through my own self-pity, empathy for her surfaced. "I'm sorry you had to go through that."

Jen leaned into me a little more, nudging me with her elbow. "I'm supposed to be comforting you, not the other way around. I just wanted to show that sometimes money changes people. They do things you never thought they'd do, especially if it's a lot of money."

"We're talking about a lot," I admitted. "That's exactly why my grandparents put the restrictions on it that they did. I guess they knew that it would attract the wrong type of people. In fact..."

I trailed off again as another thought occurred to me, one that turned my stomach even more than the first.

"Gabe?" Jen's face had gotten closer to mine, and when I looked over at her, her hazel eyes seemed kinder and warmer and more appealing than ever before.

"Sorry, I don't mean to keep zoning out on you. Something else just occurred to me."

"What is it?"

Swallowing down my nausea, I tried to explain. "Before we got married, Celine and I almost broke up. She started to pull away, a lot like she's doing now, and I thought maybe the relationship had run its course. It felt like the end. But things turned around: she became more attentive, more present, and then she told me I should propose, as I already told you. When she turns on her full charm, she's awfully hard to resist."

I always figured that explained why Monica didn't like Celine much, because Celine had never tried to make my sister like her. When she tried, *really* tried, she could win over just about anyone, and I fell for it, again and again.

"And?" Jen prompted, still waiting for the punchline.

"It all happened around the time my grandparents died. I didn't tell Celine about the inheritance or the conditions but the lawyers sent some of the paperwork to my house and she opened it before I got home. She claimed she'd done it in error, that she'd been expecting something else, and that as soon as she realized what it actually pertained to, she put it back without reading it. But shortly after that, her charm offensive began, which ended in our marriage."

Jen put it all together much quicker than I had. "So, she found out how much money you were getting and decided to stay with you."

The seasick feeling in my stomach got worse. "I think she must have. Fuck. You must think I'm such an idiot."

I dropped my head into my hands, and Jen's hand moved from my knee to my back, rubbing in warm, soothing circles. "I don't think that at all. You trusted her and she took advantage of that. It doesn't make you stupid. It doesn't make you anything, but it makes *her* an ass."

The blunt assessment made me smile beneath my hands, in spite of everything. "I guess I should be thankful that she cheated, in the long run. Or grateful that I found out about it, at least. After three years, she could have gone on a huge spending spree and I would have been none the wiser. I guess I have you to thank for that."

Raising my head, I turned to look at Jen, finding her only inches away from me. We both froze there, her eyes as wide as mine were at the unexpected proximity, our lips only a breath apart. It would be so, so easy to lean forward, just a tiny bit, and show her exactly how much I appreciated the way she'd opened my eyes.

Not only did she help me uncover Celine's lie and confront my feelings about our relationship, but she reminded me what spending time with someone could feel like when that person was actually a good match for me and not just pretending to be.

She gave me just a hint of what a relationship with someone like her would be like, and I wanted that more than I'd ever wanted anything before. In just a couple of weeks, I felt more comfortable with her than I did with Celine, but with all the excitement of a new attraction too. The best of both worlds, and I wanted more.

I wanted more with *her*.

"Gabe." She whispered my name, her gaze dropping to my lips for just a second before returning to my eyes. "I have to tell you something."

Normally, I would have let her speak, but the wine and the emotional turmoil and all the built-up feelings overwhelmed me, so instead, I did what I knew I shouldn't. What I'd been trying not to do ever since we found ourselves at the same hotel.

I leaned forward, closing the tiny gap between us, and I kissed her.

~Jennifer~

My sister and I had developed a shorthand code for when she asked how my dates went since Matt. There hadn't been that many, but I forced myself to try dating every now and then, and when I spoke to Eda afterwards, she always asked me two questions: 'did you kiss?' and 'was Matt there?'

No matter how the evening had gone to that point, when my date kissed me, my mind immediately went to my former fiancé and how the kiss compared to the way it used to feel when Matt kissed me.

Up to that point, I had to answer 'yes' to the second question every time she asked me. Matt had always been there in the back of my mind as soon as another man's lips touched mine.

When Gabe kissed me, it didn't happen, and I didn't even realize it until later.

When it happened, I didn't think about Matt at all.

The kiss took me completely by surprise. Maybe that partly explained why Matt was nowhere to be found. Since I hadn't expected it, I didn't try to clear my mind, which usually only made me think of the very thing I tried to avoid remembering. I had been entirely focused on comforting Gabe, my heart breaking for him more with every new realization he made, until he suddenly lifted his head and we found ourselves face-to-face, hardly a breath's distance between us.

Something in the air shifted. His pupils dilated and my body tensed, and when I glanced down at his lips, I wondered what they would feel like against mine.

But I didn't think of Matt.

Instead, I thought about how I still needed to tell him about Celine hiring me, how we should get everything out in the open before anything happened between us, because it suddenly felt very possible that it *might* happen.

More than that, I wanted it to.

But before I could tell him, he kissed me, and everything else faded away.

Soft lips with a hint of wine lingering in their taste. A gentle hand that reached up to my cheek, featherlight but somehow still warm. The deep, earthy scent of his cologne and the caress of his breath against my skin. Those sensations consumed me, leaving no room for thought at all. For a wonderful, blissful handful of moments, I could simply *feel*, and it felt better than anything had for a long, long time.

Until reality came crashing back in, and I remembered that the man kissing me still didn't know how I'd ended up in his life in the first place.

It must have hit Gabe at almost the exact same second it hit me because we both pulled away from each other, both of us gasping for air, his lips parted and red and his blue eyes wide and panicked.

"Fuck. I'm so sorry, Jen. I shouldn't have... I didn't mean to... fuck."

He sprang to his feet, burying his head in his hands again while I called out after him. "I know you didn't plan that. It's okay."

"No, it's not." Lowering his hands, his tormented eyes met mine. "I'm married. No matter how I feel or what might happen next, at this moment, I still have a wife, and this makes me no better than she is."

I couldn't let him believe that, especially since he still didn't know the full story. Beating himself up any more than he already had would be unfair. "There are things you still don't know about her. What I wanted to tell you is…"

Again, he cut me off, this time not with a kiss, but a forceful shake of his head. "I should go. I think I need to be alone after all."

"Wait, Gabe, please. This is important."

I got to my feet too, reaching for him, but he pulled back as if my touch might scald him. "Please, Jen. I'm not angry with you, not at all. I just need to get out of here. I'm sorry."

With that, he headed for the door, and I exhaled in frustration as it clicked shut behind him. Clearly, he was in no state to hear what I had to tell him. It would upset him too, rightfully, and it would be better if he were in a good frame of mind to begin with.

To distract myself from my own spiraling thoughts, I cleaned up the remains of our meal, poured myself a glass of wine and tried to watch TV. It didn't work. My mind kept wandering and so did my eyes, drifting over to the door as I hoped for a knock from Gabe.

Should I go to his room? What if he refused to open the door? Should I text him what I had to say? That last idea felt completely wrong since a text could never cover all the context I needed to provide.

At a loss, I called Eda for advice.

"Hey! How's Napa?"

Her voice came through the speaker so loudly, I had to hold the phone away from my ear. That, combined with the way she popped the 'p' in Napa told me all I needed to know: my little sister was drunk.

"Where are *you*?" I asked, trying to keep the amusement out of my voice. Though we often enjoyed a glass of wine together, it had been a long time since I'd seen her overindulge.

"At a birthday party," she giggled. "Don't ask me whose birthday it is because I don't know."

Clearly, my timing sucked that night in more ways than one. No useful advice would be coming from my sister in her current state. "Alright, you have fun. I'll catch up with you later."

"Wait!" Her cry reached me just before I could end the call, and I could hear the background noise getting quieter as she moved to a different location. "Why did you call?"

"It's not important. We can catch up later."

"Jennifer." She said my name so much like my mother did when I got in trouble that I had to laugh. "Whenever you say it's not important, it's important. I'm tipsy but I can still talk. What's going on?"

I still had my doubts about the validity of her advice that evening, but with no other real alternatives, I gave in. "It's about Gabe," I admitted, lowering my voice as if someone might overhear me. "He's here. At the same hotel as me."

"What?!" Eda's shriek didn't match my volume in any way. "Did he go there to see you? Did you invite him?"

"No, and no. It's just a mix-up, but we've been spending some time together, and he kissed me, but he still doesn't know who I am and I..."

"Whoa, whoa, whoa, back up. He *kissed* you?"

Hopefully, she'd moved to a completely different room or everyone at the party must have heard that. "Will you lower your voice, please?"

"I will not calm down," she said, even though I'd said nothing about being calm. "Was it good? Did you like it?"

She paused, but not long enough for me to answer before adding her usual question.

"Was Matt there?"

It didn't hit me until that moment that he hadn't been, not at all, and my chest both ached and felt lighter at the same time with the realization. Even in the aftermath, my thoughts had been so focused on Gabe, Matt hadn't even crossed my mind. "No. He wasn't."

Eda let out a loud breath directly into the phone. "Wow."

"Yeah."

The best thing about my relationship with my sister was that no further words were needed. We both knew the significance of my answer.

"Where is he now, then?" she asked after a moment's silence.

It was my turn to sigh. "He felt guilty about kissing me when he's still married, and he left. I don't know if I should go after him or give him some space. Should I text him something? Wait until the morning? I don't know what to do."

Even through the phone, even through her drunkenness, I could practically see the smile on my sister's face. "Do you have any idea how long it's been since I've heard you like this? You're the queen of flirting! People literally pay you to do it, and you're stressing like a teenage girl over whether you should send a text."

"Because it's not real when I do it for other people," I pointed out.

Like it or not, what I felt for Gabe had begun to feel *very* real.

"Okay, here's what you're going to do," Eda told me, taking charge once her initial shock wore off. "Send him a text. Tell him you still want to talk to him, you're available, but leave it up to him. If he doesn't come back tonight, show up at his door with coffee in the morning. He'll have calmed down by then and you can tell him everything."

Even drunk, she made sense, and since I had no better plan, I accepted hers. "Alright, I will. Have fun at your party. I love you."

"Love you too," she replied with a loud, wet air kiss. "Can't wait to meet this guy!"

"That's a very long way away," I tried to protest, but she hung up before I could be sure she heard me.

It took me almost twenty minutes to compose a text I felt satisfied with, open and friendly without being flirty, and after I sent it, I stayed up for another two hours, waiting for a reply or a knock at my door, but neither came. Eventually, I had to accept we wouldn't be talking that evening, and I'd have to move to Eda's plan B.

After getting ready in the morning, I made two cups of coffee in my room and with my heart pounding at both the memory of Gabe's kiss and the confession I needed to make, I made my way down the hall to Gabe's room.

However, when I got there, the door sat open, and inside, a housekeeper stripped the sheets off the bed. She caught sight of me as I stood in the doorway, confused and lost, and gave me a smile. "Can I help you, ma'am?"

"The man staying here..." I started, trailing off there because I didn't know exactly what to ask.

I didn't need to say more than that, anyway. She filled in the blanks for me. "He checked out first thing this morning."

Chapter Nine

~Gabriel~

I didn't sleep at all that night. While I tossed and turned in the comfortable hotel bed, my mind veered from memory to memory, looking for an answer to how my life got so completely out of control.

Did Celine ever love me at all? As I sifted back through all the memories of our life together, I thought she must have. Nobody could be that good an actress for that many years. When did love turn to indifference, and ultimately to dislike? She must have disliked me by that point, because I couldn't imagine treating anyone I cared about the way she'd treated me over the last few months.

Mixed in with those thoughts and memories were thoughts of Jen and what it would be like to be with someone like her instead. Someone who genuinely had my best interests at heart, someone who listened and cared. Someone like the person I thought I found in Celine, until I had someone to compare her to.

A rush of guilt accompanied each thought of Jen, knowing that I kissed her. What the hell had I been thinking? It had been a stupid, stupid thing to do.

Worst of all, I enjoyed it.

I wanted to do it again.

But that couldn't happen so long as things remained up in the air with Celine, so long as each moment with Jen was tied up with Celine.

I needed to do this right. Before I could do anything else with Jen, before I could even talk to her about what happened, I needed to speak to my wife.

So, first thing in the morning, before the sun rose, I packed up, checked out, and got in the rental car to head back to San Francisco.

Dozens of different scenarios about how our confrontation might play out ran through my mind as I sped along the empty early-morning highway. Maybe Isaac would still be at my house. *In my bed.* Maybe he wouldn't. Maybe Celine wouldn't be there either, and I'd need to go track her down. Maybe she'd confess or maybe she wouldn't. Maybe she'd be angry or she'd be sad.

Maybe, maybe, maybe.

The word drummed in time with the beating of my heart, drowning out everything else as I pulled into our street and parked the rental car outside my house. The driveway sat empty with no sign of Isaac's car that had been parked there in the photos that the private investigator sent. With the garage door closed, I couldn't tell if Celine's car, *our* car, was inside or not. I would have to go into the house and see if she was home.

Silence greeted me as I opened the front door, but that didn't mean much. Even with the drive from Napa, it hadn't hit eight o'clock yet. Celine never got up before nine if she could help it.

Sure enough, I found her fast asleep in our bed, the other side looking undisturbed, as if she'd been there alone all night. While I had the time to myself, I looked around the rest of the house, looking for any sign of Isaac being there, but nothing looked out of place. Little slivers of doubt began to work their way beneath the certainty I'd felt when I saw the photos in the first place, but it didn't really matter, I reminded myself. Whether they slept together or not wasn't the issue, or at least not the *only* issue. I came there to end things, and I intended to follow through.

"Celine." Standing in the doorway, I called her name to wake her up, not wanting to put it off any longer.

She stirred slowly, her tan, toned arms stretching out lazily as she let out a low hum, a sound that used to drive me crazy.

That morning, it didn't affect me at all.

"Gabe?" She blinked over at me through her bleary, barely-open eyelids. "I didn't expect you back so soon."

The way she said that, or maybe just the fact that those words were the first thing out of her mouth, struck me as odd. Almost as if she *did* expect it, but why she would have, I couldn't guess. "I thought you were staying at Allie's all weekend."

"Brad came home early." She pulled herself up in the bed, the covers falling back to reveal her pale orange nightie, my favourite one. That felt deliberate too, though I couldn't say why. "I'm glad you're here, though. We need to talk."

We certainly did, and I wanted to say my piece before she had a chance to spin things to suit herself. "I'll go first, and I'm going to be blunt. This isn't working anymore. You're obviously unhappy, and I am too. Taking some time away this weekend really helped me to see things clearly."

Her lips twisted into something close to a sneer. "I bet it did."

What did *that* mean? Her statement threw me for a second, but convincing myself she just wanted to get under my skin, I kept going. "I know that you had Isaac here this weekend."

Surprise flashed in her eyes, but only for a second. As quickly as possible, she covered it back up with disdain.

"I don't know how long you've been seeing each other, and frankly, I don't care. I don't see the point of either of us being unhappy. If you wanted to work on this, to fight for it, that would be one thing, but you seem to have given up on us a long time ago."

"What are you saying?" she asked, getting to her feet and crossing her arms beneath her breasts, pushing them together in a calculated gesture I'd seen her do a hundred times before. Usually, I fell for it, but not that time. My eyes remained fixed on her face and the unattractive sneer that curled her lips and wrinkled her nose. "You want a divorce?"

The word made me wince, even though I did want it. I never thought I'd be the kind of guy who ended up divorced, but half the population seemed to. Turned out I fell into that half.

With that in mind, I forced the words out. "Yeah. I think we should get a divorce."

The moment of truth had arrived, and out of all the reactions I'd imagined on the long drive home, I never anticipated what actually happened. Her eyes brightened and the sneer on her face transitioned into a smile instead. She looked almost happy for the first time in weeks. "Fine. As long as you give me what I'm owed, I'll make this easy for you."

Blinking in surprise, I tried to reconcile her response with what I'd concluded with Jen the night before. If Celine had married me for my inheritance and stayed with me for the same reason, why would she give in so easily at this stage? What had I missed?

"It's in both our interests to keep this civil and simple," I pointed out cautiously.

"Of course. You give me half of everything, including your grandparent's estate, and you'll never have to see me again."

Again, she took me completely by surprise. She knew the terms of my inheritance as well as I did, and those terms clearly stated that we had to be married for three years before she became entitled to any of it. "The estate isn't part of our assets."

"Except for the clause about what happens if you cheat on me," she amended, her tone turning sugary sweet on the surface, with a poisonous undertone beneath. "And if you want to talk about people we spent the weekend with, Gabe, maybe we should start with *you*."

My heart began to pound even harder than it had anytime that morning as the memory of Jen's soft, sweet lips against mine flashed through my head. Celine didn't know about that, though. She *couldn't*, and even if she did, a kiss didn't count as adultery in a court of law.

"What are you getting at?" I asked. Before I said anything she could twist, I needed to know what she already knew.

Still with that too-sunny smile, she turned around to grab her phone off the bedside table. "Let's see if this sounds familiar to you: 'I know you're feeling guilty about what happened. I won't tell you that you shouldn't, but we still need to talk about Celine. If you feel up to it, *when* you feel up to it, please come back to my room. I'll be here.'"

Word-for-word, she read Jen's last text to me, the one she sent the night before that I hadn't responded to yet, and all the warmth seemed to drain from my body, replaced with an icy chill that froze my heart in my chest.

"How... how do you have that?" I managed to whisper.

"Oh, I have them all," she said, showing me the screen as she scrolled through pages of text messages between me and Jen. "I had my suspicions before but I could never find anything. You must have deleted the messages off your phone whenever you met up with women on your overseas trips."

"What?" It had begun to feel like I'd stumbled into a house of mirrors. Everything seemed distorted, nothing where it should be. I had no idea what she meant.

Celine didn't answer my question, but she kept talking. "So, I found this woman online. I hired her to hit on you."

She turned the phone back around to open another app before showing it to me again. An Instagram profile stared back at me with Jen's face on it, but not the profile she'd messaged me from.

Loyalty tests, the biography at the top read. *Get the proof you need.*

All the air left me and my throat closed up, making it almost impossible to breathe. "You... hired... her?"

That couldn't be true. It couldn't be.

And yet...

Flashes came back to me, things that Jen had said about how she helped women deal with cheating partners. Did she mean this? Had she been telling me the truth while doing the same thing with me?

Could she really have been playing me the entire time?

My heart cried 'no'.

My mind didn't know what to think.

"That's right. She sent me copies of every message you exchanged. Put it all together and it's pretty damning, Gabe. Like this one, for example. 'You don't have to try so hard to get my attention, Jen. You've got it, believe me.' This whole thing, plus the testimony of the hotel staff confirming you were both at the same hotel all weekend should be convincing enough for a judge, I'd wager."

Hearing my own words in the context of Celine's narrative sent a wave of nausea through me. "I didn't... we didn't sleep together."

Celine merely smiled. "Honestly, it doesn't matter if you did or not. It looks like you did, and that's enough. We could spend a lot of money taking this to court, and I will fight you for every penny I can, or you could simply hand over half of everything to me now and we can both walk away with a clean start."

"You mean you can walk away with Isaac?" I asked, trying to regain *any* control over the conversation. While I may have hidden Jen from her, she wasn't blameless.

It didn't work. Celine didn't even flinch that time. "Legally, the only thing that matters is your fidelity, or lack of it. That's the clause that counts, and all of this makes for pretty compelling reading."

She held up her phone again, taunting me with Jen's face smiling at me from her profile, and if I thought I felt stupid before for letting Celine use me, it hadn't even begun to scratch the surface of how dumb I felt now.

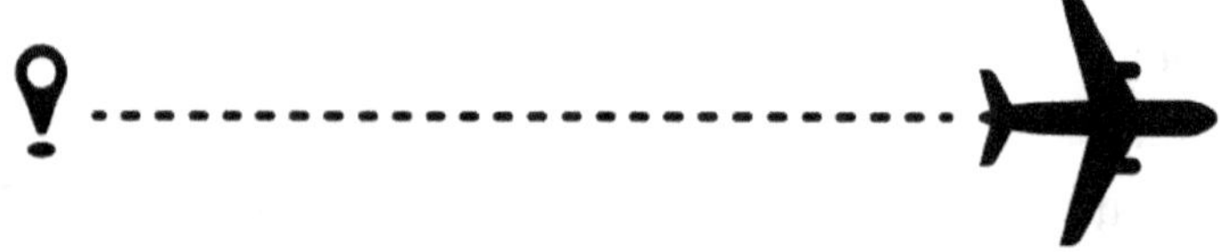

~Jennifer~

The text I sent to Gabe after finding his hotel room empty that morning went unanswered.

Where are you? Are you okay?

Despite checking my phone every five minutes, no reply came. He didn't even read it.

The private investigator's latest update didn't add much to what we already knew. She said Isaac left Gabe's house just after midnight, alone, and satisfied that Celine had gone to bed, Sarah also headed home to get some much-needed sleep. I told her to take the day off and I'd let her know if Gabe wanted anything else from her once I had a chance to connect with him.

After a while, I checked at the hotel reception to see if Gabe had left a message for me there, but he hadn't. He simply vanished, and a hot, heavy lump of anxiety sat in my stomach as I tried to figure out what it all meant. Did he really feel so guilty about kissing me that he would completely cut me off? It didn't seem in character for him to ghost anyone, especially after the connection we both felt, but I couldn't come up with any other reason for his radio silence unless something truly awful had happened to him. After Matt, I refused to let my mind go too far down that road.

Eventually, I had to check out and begin the long drive back to Pasadena.

Though I tried to work on the drive home, my heart wasn't in it, and I fumbled a test that should have been a sure thing. The guy turned suspicious when I accidentally referenced something he hadn't told me directly, and before I could reply, he blocked me.

Shit. Based on all the other signs I picked up from him, he had been well on the way to exposing himself as a cheat, and I blew it. I'd have to refund that client with my apologies since I had no one to blame but myself. Not wanting to screw up any more cases, I didn't attempt to do any further work.

My stomach had just started to grumble when I turned onto my street close to supper time, and when I saw a figure sitting on my front step, for just a moment, I thought it might be Gabe. Even though that made no sense, even though I'd never told him where I lived, my heart beat a little faster and my tongue ran over my lips in anticipation.

As I drew closer, however, I realized the person had a much more feminine and familiar form than the missing Gabriel Carter.

"Did you get so drunk last night you forgot what day it is?" I teased Eda as I got out of my car. "You were here for dinner earlier this week."

"Nice to see you too," she teased back, coming over to give me a hug. "I was on my way home from the weekend, and you were sort of on the way, so I came to get all the juicy details in person."

"On the way from where?" After grabbing my overnight bag from the car, I let us both into the house and we headed to the kitchen.

Her answer made my feet skid against the hardwood floor for a second. "San Francisco."

Trying to cover up my surprise, I kept going and pulled a bottle of wine that I'd picked up at the Oxbow Public Market out of my bag. "What were you doing there?"

Eda slid into one of the chairs at my kitchen island, inspecting the wine bottle while I dug out some glasses for us. "After talking with my friend Betty the other night when I did that recon work for you, we realized it had been way too long since we hung out, so I went up for the weekend. That's why you caught me at some random person's birthday party when you called last night."

I had been wondering about that, but with Eda working in the entertainment industry in LA, far stranger things had happened. "That sounds like fun. Did you have a good time?"

Eda shot me a pointed look. "Are you seriously going to ask me about *my* weekend when the last time we spoke, you'd just been kissed by a married man? I need an update!"

With a heavy sigh, I opened the wine and poured out our glasses. "I don't really have one. I did what you suggested and he never wrote me back. This morning, he checked out of the hotel before I went to see him. He hasn't responded to my message from last night or the one I sent this morning. I have no idea what's going on."

Her brows knit together, but only for a moment before she pulled out her phone and began to type.

"What are you doing?" I asked warily.

Her airy reply was just about the last thing I expected her to say. "Texting Monica to see where her brother is."

"What?" I tried to grab the phone, but I got there too late. With a smug smile, she turned the screen to show me the message had already been sent.

"Don't worry, I haven't blown your cover. I got to meet her this weekend while Betty and I were hanging out. She's pretty cool, and she loves her brother, which makes me even more predisposed to like him than before."

My fingers rubbed against my forehead as I tried to process all of that. "You met her in person? And you talked about Gabe?"

"Yeah, but don't worry, I didn't mention you at all. I did have to invent new details about my nightmare sister-in-law, though. She's going to be disappointed when you and Gabe get married and I have to admit my brother doesn't exist."

Her grin let me know she wanted to rile me up, so I took a deep breath and didn't take the bait. "We're not getting married. He's still married right now, you might remember."

"But not for long, surely," she prodded, and though I hoped that would be the case, with no communication from Gabe, I had no idea. Had Celine somehow managed to convince him to give her another chance? What was going on with him?

Eda's phone buzzed with a text, and her grin got even bigger as she looked back up at me.

"It's Monica. Do you want to know what she said?"

I could try to play it cool, or I could give in to my curiosity, and the second impulse won out. "Tell me."

Her eyes scanned the text briefly before she read it out to me, and her smile faded from her face. With it, my stomach dropped too.

"What? What does it say?"

"It's not bad," she assured me quickly. "Apparently, he got in touch earlier today and asked if she could recommend a divorce lawyer. That's good news, right?"

I wanted to agree, but there had to be more to it judging by Eda's expression. "What else does it say?"

Her lips tightened before she looked back down at the screen and answered. "She says he seemed really distant and unhappy and he wouldn't tell her anything else about what was going on. Since then, he's been ignoring her calls." Her eyes returned to me. "Seems like it's not just you he's hiding from."

That made me feel a little better, actually, because it meant he wasn't just avoiding me out of guilt over our kiss. And I knew he'd gotten home safely, which lifted another weight off my mind. But what happened to make him withdraw so much not just from me but from his sister too?

With no other ideas, I pulled out my own phone and messaged Celine directly.

> There's nothing more I can do. He passed the test. I'm closing the file.

It only took a minute for her reply to come in.

> I got everything I needed. Thank you for your help.

~Gabriel~

Monica always had a knack of connecting with people as soon as she met them. Open and friendly, she had no problem letting people into her life, sharing details I would have considered too intimate to tell all but my closest confidants. She had circles of friends who had circles of friends, each one of whom would do almost anything for her, so when I needed to consult with a divorce lawyer, it made sense to go to my sister first. She would either know someone or she would find someone for me, no questions asked.

Well, *one* question asked, I supposed. When I made the request, her breath caught and she limited herself to two simple words: "What happened?"

I couldn't go into it all with her at that point. Celine's infidelity, Jen's betrayal, and my own gullibility combined to leave me feeling ashamed and bruised. "I don't want to talk about it," I managed to say. "Not now."

Something in my tone must have told her I meant it because she didn't push. "Alright. Let me see what I can do."

As usual, what Monica could do exceeded most people's best efforts. By mid-afternoon, she had the name of a top family law lawyer who could meet me with me first thing Monday morning. She left me the details in a voicemail message when I didn't pick up the phone, and when she tried to call me a few more times, I turned my phone off, not in the mood to talk to anyone. Celine had already left, taking a suitcase full of her belongings that didn't take her very long to pack, making me wonder if she'd been planning her departure for a while. I didn't bother to ask her where she would be spending the night since she'd probably lie to me anyway. I didn't trust a word coming out of her mouth.

She set me up. Whether or not she actually believed I cheated on her before, I couldn't prove, but I knew she would put on a show in front of the lawyers and any judge involved. All I knew for certain was that she'd decided to prove my infidelity, whether she believed in it or not, and she hired a woman who couldn't have been better suited to test me.

No wonder things with Jen felt so easy, so natural. None of it had been real, and the loss of her, the loss of the woman I thought I'd been getting to know and even starting to develop feelings for, stung nearly as much as the loss of my wife of two years.

At least with Celine, I had some warning. Jen's treason came out of nowhere.

Sleep refused to come that night. I tossed and turned for hours in the guest room, not wanting to sleep in the bed Celine and I had shared. Eventually, I dozed off out of sheer exhaustion into a fitful sleep, drifting in and out of consciousness, short and unsatisfying.

In the morning, I called my boss to say I'd had some personal issues come up that I needed to deal with. Since I never missed work if I could help it, she took me at my word. I would have been too tired to do any good anyway, not to mention I needed to meet with the lawyer, and I had to decide what to do when I saw Isaac again. Not only had Celine destroyed the comfort of my home, she'd made my workplace awkward too.

"Mr Carter. I'm Vicky Fairbanks." The lawyer's greeting and firm handshake gave the impression of strength and efficiency, two things that I didn't feel at all that morning. Around forty, she wore a suit that looked professional but not too expensive, her blonde hair cut short and her blue eyes piercing as she looked at me directly once we were seated in her sleek, elegant office. "What can I do for you?"

Over the next hour, I laid out my relationship with Celine, the inheritance from my grandparents, and the events of the last two weeks.

"I've heard of these kinds of services," she said when I told her about Jen's business, or at least as much as I'd been able to glean about it. "This is the first time I've had one involved in one of my cases though."

"There's that much of a market for it?" I didn't know why, but it hadn't occurred to me that Jen would have been doing the same thing with multiple men, and the thought turned my stomach even more. Did she laugh with them like she had with me? Did she kiss them too? How far would she have been willing to go?

"I'm afraid so," Vicky answered. "There are a lot of scummy men out there."

I couldn't be sure whether or not she included me in that assessment. "I didn't sleep with her."

"I believe you," she assured me. "Your wife has a point, though, that the messages don't look good. If we were relying on them alone, we might be in trouble. Thankfully, we don't have to rely only on them."

It relieved me to hear her say it, though I didn't know for sure what she meant. "What other kind of proof can I give?"

"Eyewitness testimony," came her reply. "We need to get your loyalty tester's side of the story. If she backs you up, you've got a much stronger case."

"She's on Celine's side, though," I pointed out. "She sent her all those messages. Why would she tell the truth?"

"Why did she help you arrange the PI to watch your wife?" Vicky countered. "And you said she had no idea you'd be at the hotel, right? Something doesn't add up, and I think we should talk to her and find out what it is. Do you still have her contact information?"

The thought of getting in touch with Jen filled me with dread, but I would have to do it. If it meant the difference between Celine making off with the money she'd married me for or not, I would do whatever it took to stop her.

Reluctantly, I pulled out my phone and started scrolling through my messages, but it didn't take long to notice a problem.

"They're not here."

"What aren't?" Vicky asked, glancing up from the notes she'd been scribbling.

"All the messages Jen and I sent each other. Every single one. It's all been deleted."

How was that possible? I'd been pretty out of it during the long, sleepless night, but surely, I didn't sleepwalk to my phone, delete those messages, and *only* those messages?

Vicky didn't seem fazed. "Were you texting each other? We can get records from your phone company of the number."

"No, we only messaged through Instagram."

She first approached me that way and we never bothered switching platforms.

Some kind of understanding seemed to settle over Vicky's face, but I remained firmly in the dark until she asked another question. "Does your wife know your account password?"

She must. She must have gone in and deleted the entire chat so I wouldn't have any proof of my own, and I couldn't get in touch with Jen to have her verify my story.

I would be impressed with her forethought if it weren't so thoroughly messed up.

"I don't remember ever telling her, but I wouldn't be surprised if she does," I admitted. "She has access to my emails and my phone. She could have reset the password herself so she could access my account remotely."

"Do you know anything else about this woman?" Vicky asked. "Her last name? Her username?"

We never bothered with last names. I didn't think she knew mine either at the time, but she must have. And her username... I could almost remember, but not exactly. It had something about California in it? I hadn't looked at her profile since the very first time she contacted me, trying to avoid the temptation that her pictures presented.

I did, however, have one other idea. "The hotel we stayed at over the weekend will have her information because she checked in under her own name. I can get in touch with the owner there."

"Do it," Vicky advised. "The sooner, the better. It seems like your wife isn't above manipulating the records to suit her narrative."

Apparently not, but what Jen might or might not add to the story, I couldn't guess.

Chapter Ten

Celine's last text ran through my mind all that evening and the next morning. What did she mean that she had what she needed? She wanted to prove Gabe cheated and I told her the opposite, so why would she be satisfied? Unless he *confessed* to cheating? I wouldn't entirely put it past the sweet man, even though we only kissed, but surely, he would know what that kind of confession would mean and wouldn't let her get away with it.

I wished I knew what was going on inside his head.

However, I still hadn't heard a word from him. I sent one more message on Sunday evening, which went unanswered just as the others had. It started to feel like harassment the more I reached out to him without any sign from him that he wanted me to, so I didn't follow up again even though I desperately wanted to make sure he was doing okay.

On Monday, I forced myself back to work, though with none of my usual enthusiasm. Catching another guy willing to cheat only made me appreciate Gabe's loyalty more, misplaced though it may have been. The obvious, unsubtle flirting grated on me, leaving me wondering how any woman found these men attractive in the first place.

When my phone rang mid-afternoon from an unknown number, I answered, ready for a distraction from the dark cloud that had been hovering over me all day.

"Ms Bradshaw? It's Tara from the Four Winds hotel."

"Oh, hello." Instantly, my mind ran through the possible reasons for her call. Maybe I accidentally left something behind in my room? It shouldn't have been a problem with the payment, but strange things happened sometimes. Perhaps they just did a follow-up call with their new guests?

The reason she gave, however, was none of those. "This is a bit unusual, but I've had a call from Gabriel Carter. He's trying to get a hold of you. I told him I couldn't give out your number for privacy reasons, so he asked me to call you and give you his number instead. You can decide whether or not to get in touch with him. I hope that's okay."

None of that made much sense to me, but it relieved me all the same. Gabe *wanted* to talk to me, but if that were the case, why didn't he just message me as he always had before?

"That's fine," I assured her. "What's the number?"

I jotted down the number she gave me and as soon as we hung up, I called it, my heart racing with anticipation.

It went to voicemail.

"Hey, this is Gabe. Sorry I missed you, leave a message and I'll call you back."

The sound of his voice, warm and rich in my ear, made me yearn to talk to him even more. "Gabe, it's Jen. I just heard from the hotel and they said you called there to get my number. I'm not sure what's going on, but if you prefer to talk this way, it's fine with me. I still have some things I need to tell you, and I want to know how things are with you. Call me back anytime."

After leaving him my number, I hung up, hoping it wouldn't be too long before he would call.

When my phone rang again, an hour later, I pounced on it, answering without even checking the display. "Hello?"

"Is this Jen?" a woman's voice asked.

Definitely *not* Gabe.

My hope deflated, I tried not to sound too disappointed as I answered. "It's Jennifer Bradshaw, yes. Who am I speaking to?"

"My name is Victoria Fairbanks. I'm representing Mr Gabriel Carter and I have some questions for you. If you have the time, we could go through them now."

My ears perked up at the sound of Gabe's name. "Representing?" I repeated curiously, though I could guess what she meant based on the fact that Eda told me Gabe had been looking for a divorce lawyer.

She quickly confirmed I had it right. "Representing him in his divorce from Mrs Carter."

I exhaled as discreetly as possible, relieved to know Celine wouldn't be able to cause him any further pain. "I see. I'm happy to help however I can. Did Gabe give you my number?"

That explained why he would have wanted it, but not why he didn't just message me to ask for it.

"He did, and I'm glad you're willing to speak to me. Mr Carter wasn't at all sure that you would be."

Those words surprised me so much, I couldn't help blurting my immediate reaction out loud. "Why would he think that?"

She didn't answer my question, and I could hear papers rustling in the background as she dove into her questions instead. "Let's start at the beginning. When did Mrs Carter hire you to loyalty test her husband?"

My heart stuttered in my chest, ice freezing my veins. For a long moment, I couldn't form any kind of response. I couldn't seem to form any coherent thought at all other than the one echoing through my mind.

He knew.

I didn't get a chance to tell him but he already knew.

As my blood began to thaw, a million questions rushed in after it.

How did he know? How did he find out? Did he hate me? Was that why he hadn't been in touch?

Had I lost his trust forever?

"Ms Bradshaw?" The lawyer's voice sounded impatient as she prompted me for an answer. "Are you still there?"

"Yes, I'm..." I cleared my throat as the words came out choked and tight. "I'm here. I'm just checking my records to get the exact date for you."

My hand trembled as I pulled my laptop close and opened Gabe's file, trying to ignore the burning behind my eyes as I pulled up my initial conversation with Celine and read the date off to the woman on the other end of the phone.

Somehow, I made it through the rest of the call, answering the lawyer's questions as honestly as I could, though I left out Eda and Monica's role. I only said that I had become suspicious of Celine's motivations, not that I had any prior knowledge of the situation surrounding Gabe's inheritance.

"That's very helpful," she said when we were finished. "Depending on whether we can settle without the need for arbitration, it may be enough. If not, we may ask you to come and give a statement in person."

"Sure. That's fine." Before she could hang up, I asked one more question. "She's not going to get any of his inheritance, is she?"

"Not if I have anything to do with it," Ms Fairbanks said, which didn't sound like a full 'no' to me. "Have a good day, Ms Bradshaw."

The line went dead and I lowered the phone, my heart still aching over the idea of Gabe finding out about me from someone else. Why didn't I just tell him when I had the chance? Hindsight made it all seem so simple.

He must have been so angry with me that he didn't even bother to confront me. In my memory, I could see the bewilderment on his face as he realized Celine might be cheating on him, and I could picture that same anguished betrayal hitting him again when he figured out I lied to him. Lied from the beginning, and over and over again.

Hurting him had been the very last thing I wanted to do, but I'd done it anyway.

Winning his trust again wouldn't be easy, but somehow, I needed to try.

~Gabriel~

After struggling through two days at home, staring out the window and trying to salvage any part of my pride, I went back to work on Wednesday morning.

Monday had been the worst. After my appointment with the lawyer, I called the hotel to try to get Jen's contact information, and when she called me, I sat watching the phone ring before it went to voicemail, unable to face the prospect of speaking to her. It took ten minutes to force myself to listen to the message, and as soon as I hit play, the sound of her voice sent another painful stab of regret through my body.

She sounded so warm and concerned, as if she actually cared about me. As if everything between us hadn't been a complete fabrication.

How could I feel so betrayed by someone I barely knew?

I sent her details to my lawyer, and Vicky responded to me later that day to confirm that Jen had backed up everything I said and provided some additional details. She asked if I wanted to see the correspondence between her and Celine, but I declined. It wouldn't make me feel better but it could certainly make me feel worse, and at that moment, I was simply in survival mode. My focus was on getting through the next five minutes and I couldn't think any further ahead than that.

On Tuesday afternoon, after I took another unscheduled day off work, Monica showed up at my door, banging on it until I let her in.

"You look like shit," she announced, eyeing me up and down, her eyebrow arched. "Have you slept?"

"Not really."

"Well, it's time to stop wallowing. I'm here to celebrate. Now that Celine's on the way out, you can move on to greener pastures."

She pulled a bottle of champagne out of her handbag while I groaned. "I'm really not in a celebrating mood."

I also couldn't think about moving on, not with the memory of my attraction to Jen still hanging around the corners of my mind.

"You're better off without her," she answered firmly, ignoring my protests as she popped open the champagne and poured two tall glasses full, one for each of us. "I know so many great people I can set you up with. When you're ready."

She added the last sentence quickly when I opened my mouth to protest, and I couldn't even muster the energy to argue. Though I didn't feel like celebrating, a little alcohol-induced memory loss might be helpful.

While we gradually emptied the bottle between us, I told my little sister everything, about the distance Celine had begun to put between us, my suspicions about her, and about Jen. She couldn't hide her surprise when I explained how I kissed her.

"You must have really liked her," she mused.

"It doesn't matter." My words had started to come out slurred. I couldn't even remember how many glasses of champagne I'd had at that point. Were we even still drinking champagne? Maybe Monica had switched us to something else. The glass in my hand didn't have any bubbles in it. "The whole time, she worked for Celine."

"Did she, though?" Monica wondered. "Something doesn't add up."

Vicky had said the same thing, but to me, the facts were pretty clear. "She sent Celine screenshots of our conversations, even after we met in person and she helped me hire the private instigator... intra-skater... investigatator."

My mouth refused to form the word properly and Monica giggled into her glass. "You're drunk."

"It's your fault," I reminded her, and she couldn't disagree.

"But wait." Her face scrunched up as she thought about something, not too far behind me in the getting drunk department. "She deleted your messages."

That didn't sound right to me. "Jen didn't delete the messages."

"No, not Jen. The bitchy one."

"You mean my wife?"

Monica giggled again, everything seeming funnier to her than it should be. "That one. She deleted them, right?"

"Right." I had no idea what point she wanted to make, and it kept getting harder to concentrate on the conversation anyway.

"So that's it!" She raised her arms in the air triumphantly, though she hadn't explained anything.

"That's what?"

"The messages."

We were starting to go around in circles. "What about the messages?"

Monica put her glass down and took a deep breath, trying to organize her thoughts. "Celine deleted the messages, which means she could get into your account."

"Right." I followed her so far.

"That means she could have seen the messages herself before she deleted them. She said Jen sent them to her, but maybe she lied. She always lies. She's a lying liar who lies."

Even in my not-completely-coherent state, I could see she had a point. Maybe Jen didn't send those messages to Celine. Maybe Vicky had wanted me to see that. I could call her and ask to see the messages between Jen and Celine after all, but it would have to wait until the next day. Drunk me couldn't focus, and the law firm had probably closed for the day anyway.

"Even if that's true, she still lied to me from the start," I pointed out. "Jen, I mean. She's not who I thought she was."

"How do you know?" Monica asked. "She could be anyone."

I didn't want her to be anyone. I wanted her to be the woman I'd felt that connection with, the one I'd traded stories with for hours in her hotel room, laughing and feeling thoroughly comfortable and content in her presence.

It must have been an act. No one could be that perfectly matched to me.

After promising Monica I would check with my lawyer the next day, we moved on to other topics until the conversation literally made no sense anymore and I dragged myself back to the guest room. When my alarm went off the next morning, I still felt like shit, but at least I'd slept. Monica was fast asleep on the couch, and I let her sleep. Tired of feeling sorry for myself, I showered, got ready, left a note for my sister, and headed into work.

A chorus of greetings rang out as I walked in, most people coming over to see how I felt. Most, not all, because Isaac sat at his desk, studiously ignoring me. I ignored him right back, doing my best to behave as if nothing were bothering me, just in case he would be reporting back to Celine.

I spent the first hour catching up on things I'd missed over the past two days, but at ten o'clock, when the office opened to the public, the receptionist called my office.

"There's someone here to see you," she said over the phone. "She doesn't have an appointment, but she said she spoke to you about a trip recently."

"That's fine, send her in." My hangover had improved to the point where my head no longer pounded, and I could do with a distraction.

My eyes stayed on the computer screen in front of me, finishing my reply to another client's email when I saw someone at the door in my peripheral vision.

"Come on in, have a seat," I invited without looking over, reading over my words one last time before hitting send.

With that done, I forced a smile onto my face and pivoted to face the woman who had just closed the door behind her, and a cold wave of shock washed over me.

"Jen?"

~Jennifer~

After speaking to Gabe's lawyer, I knew I needed to talk to him and explain myself. Unfortunately, he seemed just as determined to ignore me as I was to get in touch.

First, I tried messaging him on Instagram, where we'd always communicated before, only to find that he'd blocked me. That stung, even though I couldn't really blame him for it. If I were in his shoes, I'd have blocked me too.

After psyching myself up for a while, I called instead, but the call went straight to voicemail, not even ringing that time like it had the time before. He must have turned his phone off. I sent a text instead, asking him if we could talk. That message went unread. For the first time, I started to get an inkling of what the men I flirted with as part of my job went through when I ghosted them.

At a loss, I went to bed Monday evening with a heavy ball of guilt in the pit of my stomach, and it hadn't gotten any lighter by the time I woke up. I tried calling again on Tuesday with the same result, and eventually, out of options and getting worried, I asked Eda to check in with Monica.

When she told me that Monica didn't reply either, I made up my mind.

He wouldn't be able to ignore me in person, but going to his house would be risky. Celine might still be there, Gabe might have moved out, or both. So, although I had his address from hiring the PI, using it didn't seem like the best idea.

His office address might work, however.

Ambushing him at work might be stalker-ish, but in my head, I didn't have any other options left. I would tell him my side of the story, answer any questions he might have, and if he wanted me to disappear after that and never contact him again, I would honour his wishes.

I just couldn't live with the idea of not even *trying* to make things right.

Using my favourite last-minute travel site, I booked a cheap flight to San Francisco for first thing in the morning on Wednesday. Not long after Gabe's office opened, I stood outside, staring up at the name above the windows and steeling myself to go in. The travel agency had a bright blue storefront in a mostly-residential neighbourhood, away from the more touristy parts of the city. A pretty, welcoming café with yellow-and-white striped awnings sat next to it, on the corner, and I could easily picture Gabe there, sipping his coffee and looking as casually handsome as he did at the market in Napa on the weekend.

With a deep breath, I forced myself to go in.

A bell chimed over the door as I pushed it open, and a pretty young woman with tight black curls and a bright smile looked up from a desk in the middle of the room. Colourful brochures of exotic destinations lined the walls, and a few more people sat at desks towards the rear of the room. Beyond them, I could see a hallway that appeared to lead to private offices.

Gabe was nowhere to be seen.

"Good morning. Can I help you?" the woman asked.

"I hope so. I'm looking for Gabriel Carter."

My fear that he wouldn't be there after I came all that way proved to be unfounded when she asked if I had an appointment.

"No, but we spoke last week about a trip I'm planning."

Accepting that answer, she picked up her phone and called Gabe. He must have said he'd see me because she pointed to the hallway after hanging up. "Second door on the left."

"Thank you."

As I walked past her, the other people in the room gave me warm smiles too. Two men sat at the desks, and with a jolt of surprise, I recognized one of them as Isaac, the man from the photos with Celine.

His eyes dropped to my chest as I walked by, which seemed about par for the course.

Once a cheat, always a cheat.

I caught my first glimpse of Gabe a moment before he saw me. Deep in concentration as he typed on his keyboard, he looked good, as always, but I could see the signs of strain too. Bags beneath his eyes hadn't been there over the weekend, his cheeks looked far paler than they had at the hotel, and his mouth, which had always seemed ready to break into a smile during our time together, pulled downwards instead.

With one more deep breath to try to steady my drumming heart, I stepped into the doorway and Gabe spoke. "Come on in, have a seat."

He didn't look at me as he said it, still focusing on his email, but I did as he said, stepping fully inside and closing the door behind me.

At last, Gabe's gaze moved from his screen to me, and instantly, any small amount of colour in his face drained away. "Jen?"

"Hi." I offered him a tight smile, trying to gauge his reaction to my unexpected presence in his office, but his face remained blank, showing nothing but shock. "I'm sorry to show up unannounced, but you haven't returned my calls. I owe you an explanation, and I wanted to make sure you're doing okay."

Two slow blinks were the only response I got, so I gestured towards the chair in front of his desk.

"Can I sit down?"

His deep inhale reminded me of the one I'd taken just before walking in. "I suppose, but I don't think we have much to say to each other."

"I understand why you feel that way," I said as I slid into the chair, placing my purse on the floor beside me, and finally, a bit of life flickered in Gabe's eyes.

"With all due respect, I don't think you have any idea how I feel."

Point to Gabe.

"That's probably true," I agreed, not looking to argue with him. "And you might not have anything to say to me, in which case, you don't need to say anything. I, however, do have some things to say to you."

He didn't reply, but he leaned back in his chair, effectively yielding the floor to me, and I did my best to stick to the script I'd been rehearsing for the past two days.

"My name is Jennifer Bradshaw, and for the past couple of years, I've worked as a loyalty tester. My clients, usually women, hire me to hit on their partners online because they have reason to suspect that partner is being unfaithful. Sometimes, men pass my test. More often, they don't, and I pass the evidence of their willingness to cheat to the person who hired me. It all takes place online, and I don't ever actually meet the men or sleep with them."

Gabe's lips parted for a second, and I paused, waiting to see if he wanted to say something. When he clamped them shut again, I kept going.

"A few weeks ago, Celine contacted me like any other client, and she told me she believed you were cheating. She mentioned business trips that you went on when you were out of contact with her, and she said you kept your phone locked and hidden from her."

"That's not true," Gabe muttered.

"Wait, Celine lied about something? I'm shocked." I offered him another small smile, trying to break the ice, but his cold front remained firmly in place. "She provided a bit of background information about you and your interests, along with links to your social media. Based on that, I latched onto travel as an interest that we have in common, and used it to approach you. It's better if I can find a legitimate connection rather than inventing a whole new person every time."

Gabe's eyes remained wary, but he asked a question. "So, you actually do like to travel?"

"Yes. Of course." The idea that he would think *everything* I said to him had been a lie made my heart hurt. "All the travel stories I told you were true. The only thing I lied about was going to Uzbekistan anytime soon. Matt wanted to go, so I knew a bit about the country, but I have no plans to go there myself."

His lips twisted into a tight grimace. "Matt is real?"

It felt like another punch to the gut with the insinuation that I would have invented Matt's life and tragic death. My next words came out sounding breathy as I struggled to take enough air in. "Yes. Everything I told you about him is real."

Forcing an inhale, I pushed ahead.

"After we texted for a while, and especially after we spoke for the first time, I told Celine I didn't see any signs that you would be interested in cheating. She insisted that I keep trying. Obviously, now I know why, but at the time I simply found it a bit strange. I tried again, that time we video chatted and I wore my bikini, but you not only made it clear you weren't interested, you told me that you thought Celine might be cheating on *you* instead of the other way around."

Obviously, he knew that part already, but I wanted to walk him through the whole timeline with me, to see things from my point of view.

"I hadn't quite decided what to do about all of it when I went to Napa, and I had no idea you would be at the hotel. None of that was planned, and I've never met someone from my loyalty tests in person before. I should have told you then about all of this, but I thought you would trust me more to help you with Celine if you didn't know. I made the wrong choice, and I see that now. I'm so sorry for betraying that trust, Gabe."

He thought that over for a long moment before shaking his head. "How am I supposed to believe anything you say?"

Even though he had every right to feel that way, disappointment stabbed at my stomach anyway. "You'll have to take my word for it, I suppose. I also sent a copy of all my correspondence with Celine to your lawyer."

His eyebrows lifted, just a touch. "You did?"

"Yes. Celine blocked me and deleted our chat on Instagram, just like you did, but I always take screenshots of everything. I have the whole conversation, which she might not realize. It might be an advantage for you."

He considered that for a while, and as the silence stretched out between us, I made him an offer.

"This is a lot for you to take in, especially since you weren't expecting to see me today. Why don't I give you some time to think about things, and if you want to talk more later, we can. I'm going to stay in the city overnight, so we have some time if you'd like to continue this conversation in person. You can also phone me. Or text me. It's up to you."

Gabe nodded slowly. "Alright."

I waited for more, but no more words came, and that same disappointment from before dug in deeper. At least he heard me out. I would have to be thankful for that for the time being.

I stood up to go, grabbing my purse off the floor and heading to the door, but when I placed my hand on the handle, Gabe's voice stopped me.

"I didn't block you."

"What?" I turned back to him, not sure I'd heard him correctly.

I had, though, since he repeated the same words. "I didn't block you. Celine did. She must have had access to my account."

His eyes didn't meet mine, but the disappointment inside me eased a little. He didn't want me to think he cut me off entirely, and maybe that meant he didn't completely hate me either.

It might not be much, but at that point, I would call it a win.

"Have a good day, Gabe."

Chapter Eleven

~Gabriel~

If I thought concentrating on work had been difficult before Jen's visit, it became almost impossible afterwards. Assuming she actually lived in Pasadena as she told me she did, and I couldn't really imagine why she would have lied about that part, she'd come a long way just to see me.

She seemed sincere, but then, I'd thought that before. Obviously, I wasn't the best judge of character, and I hated not being able to trust myself. It left me feeling completely off-balance and unsure which way to step next.

Desperate to do something concrete, I reached out to my lawyer and asked her to verify what Jen said. In response, she sent over the messages between Jen and Celine that Jen provided. Over my lunch break, I stayed hidden in my office and read through them all, juxtaposing them with the messages between me and Jen, which Jen had also provided since Celine had deleted them on my end.

Reading through our conversations through a new lens, it felt even more dishonest and underhanded to me, but I couldn't deny that what Jen told me seemed to be true: she *did* tell Celine that she didn't think I would cheat, and she tried to end the job a few different times. Celine kept pushing, and that would be when Jen turned more aggressive in her flirting. Before, I wondered if she had some kind of split personality. Now, I could see that it came down to Celine pulling the strings in the background.

Nothing she told me that morning seemed to be a lie, but did I want to put my faith in someone who literally lied to men for a living?

> Did you actually go to work today?

Monica's message, received mid-afternoon, made me smile, one of the few things that had all day.

> I did. Are you just waking up?

> I had the day off work, thankfully. How's it going?

> Not getting a lot of work done, but I'm here. Jen stopped by.

Rather than reply to that, Monica called me, the sound startling me as I sat with my phone still in my hand.

"She came to your office? In person? Tell me everything, now!"

Rising from my seat, I went to close my office door so I could speak without being overheard. I didn't want to take any chances, especially with Isaac lurking around. "Yes, she just showed up, out of the blue, because I hadn't returned her calls. A lot like you did, actually."

"It's a good strategy," Monica confirmed. "I can vouch for it, it works. Maybe you can learn from this and pick up the phone once in a while. But let's get to the point: what did she say?"

"She gave me her side of the story, I guess."

"Which is?"

As thoroughly as I could, I repeated what Jen told me and what I'd read in the screenshots. "According to the screenshots, she didn't send Celine any of the messages from the time we were at the hotel together. Celine must have gotten those through my account, just like you suggested when you were drunk yesterday."

"That's because drunk me is really rather brilliant at times," Monica said with a laugh. "But this is great news! It means Jen didn't betray you. She really *is* on your side, at least once she figured out something fishy was going on."

"But she didn't tell me the truth," I countered. "She had so many opportunities during that weekend, we spent so much time together. At any point, she could have told me about Celine hiring her, but she didn't."

Monica pondered that for a moment before asking a simple question. "Did you ask her why?"

I hadn't. I'd been too surprised by her appearance in my office to ask much of anything, and I didn't know whether to believe a word out of her mouth. After seeing the emails for myself, I'd become more inclined to believe her, but the 'why' question remained unanswered.

"No, I didn't, but she's staying in town tonight. She said I could call her if I wanted to talk."

"Then you should," Monica urged me. "Even better, go and see her and hash it all out in person. Get all the answers before you make up your mind. Personally, I think what this woman does helping other women is pretty badass."

"But..." I started to protest, but Monica cut me off before I could get another word out.

"Yeah, it sucks that you got caught up in it, but she seems to genuinely feel bad about that. I think you should give her a chance to explain herself in a real conversation. If nothing else, you'll get some closure. Besides, what's your alternative for tonight? Go back home and stare at the walls again?"

"You always know how to cheer me up."

My deadpan statement only made her laugh. "Trust me on this one, Gabe. You should talk to her."

"I'll think about it," I promised. "But I need to go now. I haven't done anything productive all day."

"Alright, but keep me updated. I love you. And if you need Celine roughed up a little bit, just say the word."

I groaned, rubbing my forehead with my hand. "Please don't say things like that in front of other people. Someone will think you're serious."

"Who says I'm not?" I could hear the smile in her voice even though I couldn't see her. "Call me tomorrow."

"I will. I love you too."

For the first time in days, something close to a smile lingered on my face after I hung up. I had a feeling that Monica would like Jen if she got to know her, or at least, the version of her that I knew. How close was that to the actual woman? And why had she kept lying to me, even after she began to suspect Celine?

Those answers would only be found if I took Monica's advice and spoke to Jen, and as Monica suggested, in person would be better. Half an hour should be more than enough time to get the answers I needed to satisfy my curiosity and move on. Not to mention, as Monica said, I had no other plans anyway.

Making up my mind, I sent Jen a text.

> I have some questions. Where are you staying? I can meet you for coffee nearby.

~Jennifer~

Gabriel's text made me frown. Not because of its content; on the contrary, it thrilled me that he wanted to talk, but after he told me that Celine had access to his accounts, communicating by text seemed like a bad idea.

With that in mind, I called the travel agency and asked to speak to him. The receptionist put me through on his office line, which Celine shouldn't be able to trace.

"You need to get a new phone," I told him as soon as he said hello. "Without knowing exactly what Celine has access to, it's risky to keep using it. You should change all your passwords too, for anything that she might be able to get into."

Gabe sighed. "Shit. You're right, but that's a lot of work."

"We can make a list of what needs to be done," I offered. "I've been through this process with a few of my clients."

He didn't say anything, and I grimaced at my tactlessness in bringing up my business when it remained a sore spot between us.

As briskly as possible, I moved on. "Anyway, coffee would be great. I'm near Fisherman's Wharf. There's a place called the Hyacinth Café right across the street that looks pretty casual."

"Fisherman's Wharf?" he repeated, sounding bemused. "I didn't expect you to choose somewhere quite so touristy."

"Last-minute trip," I reminded him, my lips curling into a smile. His gentle teasing seemed to be returning, which felt like an even better sign than agreeing to meet me for coffee. "I didn't have time to ask for recommendations. Where would you have stayed?"

Almost as if he remembered he should be angry with me, he paused, and when he spoke again, his voice had turned cooler again. *And* he ignored my question. "I'll meet you at the café at 5:30."

"See you then."

Work kept me busy until the time came to meet Gabe. I gave myself a quick check in the mirror, not wanting to look like I'd made too much of an effort but not wanting to be a complete mess either. A quick touch-up of my makeup and a brush through my hair would do the trick.

Naturally, as soon as I stepped outside, the brisk wind coming off the bay blew my hair into a tangly mess anyway, making my earlier efforts pointless. Sitting at the outdoor tables would only make it worse, so I headed inside instead and grabbed a table near the window so I could see Gabe when he arrived.

He showed up just a couple of minutes later, right on time. With his hands in the pockets of his wool overcoat, he looked both professional and casual at the same time, turning a few heads as he walked down the street, his gaze fixed on the pavement, oblivious to everyone around him.

When he looked up, his blue eyes scanned the sign above the door to make sure he had the right place before looking down into the window and connecting with my gaze. Even with the window between us, a little jolt of electricity passed through me, reminding me that while he might hate me at the moment, my attraction to him hadn't died off at all.

"Sorry I'm late," he apologized as he walked up to the table, shucking his coat and placing it on the back of the chair across from me. "Have you ordered?"

"No, not yet, and you're not late. I'm early. Please, sit down. I'll get it. Black coffee?"

He looked about to argue, his natural chivalry fighting against his resentment, but eventually, he gave in. "Yes. Thanks."

After placing the order at the counter, the woman there told me she'd bring the cups over when they were ready, so I sat back down, putting on a smile that I hoped felt inviting but not too familiar. "So, you said you have questions. What do you want to know?"

Glancing around to make sure no one paid any attention to us, Gabe leaned forward, his elbows on the table and his hands clasped in front of him. He'd taken his wedding ring off, I noticed. A thin pale band of skin on his fourth finger betrayed where it had sat for more than two years.

"When we were at the hotel in Napa, you helped me arrange the PI and deal with the fact that Celine might be cheating, or at least lying. You must have been fairly convinced that she'd done something wrong."

I didn't hear a question in there, but I nodded anyway. "Yes. By that time, I felt pretty certain."

"Why didn't you tell me then that she hired you? Why keep up the pretense if you weren't working with her anymore?"

Damn. He didn't waste any time in getting straight to the heart of the matter. Thankfully, the waitress arrived with our drinks at that moment, giving me a few seconds to gather my thoughts and try to decide how to respond. On the flight that morning, I promised myself to be as truthful as possible, since withholding the truth from him got me in trouble in the first place. Too afraid of losing his friendship, I'd lost his trust instead, so even if the truth was a little embarrassing, it seemed like the safest option.

"I was afraid you wouldn't accept my help if you knew," I said after we both took a sip of our hot coffee. "I thought you might not want anything to do with me, and selfishly, I didn't want that to be the case."

"Selfishly?" His brow drew down as he repeated the word, as if it didn't make sense to him in that context.

My stomach clenched with nerves, but I forced myself to answer fully. "Yes, selfishly, because I enjoyed talking with you and getting to know you. I felt... well, I felt drawn to you, and that doesn't happen to me very often. I didn't want to lose that connection before we really had a chance to get to know each other, but I should have realized that we couldn't *truly* get to know each other as long as we had that deception between us. It was a very awkward situation for us both to be in, and I wish I'd been honest with you once I had an inkling what Celine was up to. I wish that we could have met under entirely different circumstances, to be honest, but there's nothing I can do about that. Continuing to keep you in the dark is something I did have control over, and I made the wrong choice. I'm sorry."

Gabe took a few seconds to process all of that, his fingers sliding along the handle of his coffee cup as he thought over my words. "So, you lied to me because you liked me?"

"It sounds stupid when you say it that way." I threw him a sheepish smile. "But basically, yes. You're nothing like the men I usually meet through my work, and I lost sight of the line between the job and my personal life. Even so, I almost told you several times. The last time right before we..."

I trailed off, my eyes dropping to his lips as the memory of their warm press against mine flooded my body, sending a delicious tingle through me.

Gabe seemed to know exactly which moment I meant, even though I hadn't said the words. "You said you had something to tell me," he remembered, his voice lower than before as his eyes dipped down to my mouth and back up again.

Clearing my throat, I forced my eyes to return to his and stay there. "I went to your room the next morning to tell you then, but you'd already checked out."

His lips parted as he blew out a long breath. "It would have been nice to know before Celine told me."

"I'm so sorry about that. I know I can't turn back time, but I wish I could make it up to you."

Though I hadn't meant that to sound sensual in any way, the words sounded provocative as soon as I said them and Gabe swallowed another mouthful of coffee before answering.

"You sent the screenshots to my lawyer," he reminded me. "That's going to be a big help."

"She doesn't think there's any chance Celine will get your inheritance, does she?"

He shrugged. "She's not making any promises, but with you backing up my side of the story, I have a much better chance."

"I'm glad. Really."

We both took another drink, the tension between us growing stronger by the moment, but it didn't feel like resentment from his side anymore. It had morphed into something else, something that had me squirming in my seat.

Gabe spoke first. "You make it pretty difficult to stay mad at you."

"You're a very understanding person," I countered. If he could forgive me, he deserved the credit for that, not me.

"You, uh, you mentioned you could help me make a list of things I need to change so Celine can't access them anymore?"

"Yes," I answered too quickly. "I actually have a template, believe it or not. I should have put it on my phone so I could show you, but I can send it to you at work once I get back to my room. You'll have to adjust it a little based on what accounts you have, but it'll give you a place to start."

Gabe glanced out the window, over at the hotel across the street where I had a room. "You've got it on your computer?"

"Mm-hmm." Not trusting myself to speak again, I took another drink instead.

"I wouldn't mind talking it through with you," he admitted. "Would you have time to look through it tonight?"

That sounded an awful lot like he'd just invited himself to my hotel room, and butterflies launched in my stomach at the idea, even though there couldn't be any way his thoughts were heading in the same direction mine were.

"I don't have any plans tonight. The only reason I'm staying over is that I couldn't get a cheap flight home until the morning. If you want to come over to my room, we can look at it together. That's fine with me."

I took another sip of my drink, trying to ignore the way my heart had begun to pound. Gabe and I had been alone together in a hotel room a couple of times before and I'd never felt so wound up. But then, he'd still been hanging onto his marriage at the time and I knew deep down that nothing would happen.

His new separation made him a lot more dangerous, but neither of us seemed to want to resist that danger, as he made clear when he accepted my invitation.

"I would appreciate that. Are you ready to go now?"

Downing the remainder of my coffee, I licked a few stray drops off my lips. "Ready as I'll ever be."

~Gabriel~

The logical part of my brain screamed at me as Jen and I walked across the street, through the lobby of the hotel and into the elevator that would take us to her room.

This woman lied to you. She pretends to be attracted to men for a living. Nothing about this is real. Walk away before it's too late.

Unfortunately for my self-control, other thoughts and instincts drowned out those perfectly reasonable objections. The thoughts brought on by watching her tongue run across her lips back at the café, for example, or the way our bodies seemed to drift together as we walked down the hall towards her room.

"I didn't expect company," she explained apologetically, waving a hand towards the room as we walked in. She had nothing to apologize for, though. Aside from her small carry-on bag by the door and a laptop which sat on the dark brown desk next to a notepad, the room seemed pretty neat. From her pocket, Jen pulled out her phone and placed it down next to the computer. Its screen lit up as she did so, a new message popping onto the screen.

"Do you need to answer that?"

I took off my coat and hung it on the hook by the door while Jen slipped her shoes off. The hotel room had none of the individuality and charm of the room at the Four Winds, but it sufficed for a night's stay. Two queen-sized beds with slate-grey comforters faced the wall-mounted TV, a night stand between them, and heavy curtains covered half of the windows that faced the bay. Alcatraz Island could be seen in the glistening water in the distance.

"No, it's just something for work. It can wait." Dropping her purse on the desk, Jen picked up the laptop and took it to one of the beds. "Let me pull up that spreadsheet for you."

I sat on the other bed, keeping my distance, but my eyes returned to the phone that she'd left behind, which lit up again. "Are you sure you don't need to deal with that? I don't mind waiting."

"I have no idea how long it would take," she said, her shoulders raising in a sheepish shrug as she navigated around the computer screen. "It'll be one of the men I'm engaging with right now, and it could go several different ways."

The idea of another man hitting on her didn't thrill me, but logically, I understood it was her job, and knowing that she'd chosen to spend her time that evening with me instead, curiosity won out over jealousy. "What exactly do you say to them?"

Her hazel eyes met mine hesitantly, but when she saw I meant the question genuinely and not with any kind of accusation, the tightness in her expression eased. "Do you want me to show you?"

Surprisingly, I did. After everything with Celine, I didn't want there to be any secrets or hiding, and I appreciated her willingness to be open about it. "I'm interested to see how it works on someone that isn't me."

"Okay." Springing back to her feet, she grabbed the phone off the desk and returned to the bed, with the laptop open in front of her and the phone next to it. With an inviting smile, she patted the bed next to her. "Come here, I'll walk you through it."

I shuffled over and sat down next to her, keeping my feet on the ground, my body turned towards the screen.

"Obviously, this is all confidential," she began as she pulled up a document with screenshots of an Instagram chat. "Ignore any names you see, or any other identifying information."

"Got it," I promised. "This is the initial email you received?"

"From my client, yes. She told me that she's been seeing this guy for a year, she just found out she's pregnant, and the same day, she found out that he hooked up with her cousin over the weekend."

"Ouch." I winced as I read through the woman's hurt-filled message. "And she has doubts about whether she should leave?"

Jen shrugged again. "Everyone's situation is different. I never judge what they decide to do, I just help them gather the information they need. In this case, she wants to know if it's likely to happen again. That's where I come in."

She switched programs, bringing up a Facebook profile instead.

"He works as a DJ, so his profile is public. Do you notice anything about it?"

I leaned forward as Jen scrolled down the man's page. "Lots of pictures of him with women at his gigs, but none with the woman he's dating."

"Exactly. That's the most common red flag I see: no public acknowledgement of the relationship. Yours is one of the exceptions."

The reminder that she'd analyzed me the same way she did this man helped to cool off some of the heat caused by our close proximity on the bed. "What else do you look for?"

"Shirtless pictures, workout pics, anything suggesting they're open and looking. And from a practical standpoint, I look for information on where they've been recently so I can come up with a reason to contact them."

The initial message that Jen sent me commenting on my recent travel pictures flashed across my memory. So far, everything lined up with how she approached me.

"In this guy's case, he DJ'd at a club last weekend, so I sent him this message."

She returned to her document of screenshots where it showed her initial communication.

> Hey! I know this is random, but I saw you spin a couple of weeks ago and I thought you were super hot. I was too shy to say anything, but one of my friends gave me your name and I looked you up. Hope it's okay to say hi. ;)

His response came pretty quickly, a mix of flattery and wariness.

> You got nothing to be shy about. Damn, girl. You in NY? Your profile says California.

> I live in Cali but I go to New York all the time for work. I'll be there again this weekend. Any chance you'll be working again?

> I might be. What type of music are you into?

They chatted about music for a while before he said he had to go, still without answering her question about whether or not he'd be DJing the next weekend.

"That all looks pretty harmless to me," I pointed out. Sure, he complimented her appearance, but she *was* gorgeous. Pointing it out didn't make a guy a cheater.

"It's pretty tame," she agreed. "Except he told me he had to go exactly when his girlfriend came home."

"Maybe he wanted to give her his full attention," I suggested, playing devil's advocate. "Doesn't mean he hid it from her."

"Well, according to her schedule, she just went to work her night shift today and now he's messaging me again. You want to see how this plays out?"

She held up her phone with the new messages on it, and I nodded in agreement. "Sure."

Pulling up their chat, she held the phone out so we could both see it.

> I listened to that track you suggested, think I might include it in my set on Saturday.

> You could come and hear it for yourself if you're still planning to be in town.

Eyebrows raised, Jen looked over at me. "Still thinking it's all innocent?"

"It's not looking so good," I had to admit. "But he hasn't actually done anything wrong."

"Not yet, but let's see."

Her thumbs flew across the on-screen keyboard as she typed out a reply.

> I would love that. What club?

Bump, in the Village.

After each message, she immediately took a screenshot, just in case he deleted it.

I don't think I know where that is.

West 10th. I can send you a map.

Jen looked over at me with a smirk. "You ready?"

"For what?" I asked, but instead of answering me, she typed out another message.

I'm SO bad with directions. Any chance you could meet up with me before and show me the way? I promise I'll make it worth your while.

I blew out a long breath. "That's going in pretty strong."

"He's ready for it," she assured me. "I've got a sixth sense with this stuff. Trust me."

His reply popped up a moment later.

You better send me a picture so I know who to look for.

"He wants to make sure he's not getting catfished," Jen explained. "I always do them one better and send a video."

Smacking her lips together to refresh her lipstick, she pulled her shirt down a little more to show more of her cleavage before starting the video.

"This is me, begging for help to find the club." She giggled in a way that sounded nothing like her usual laugh. I'd never heard her laugh that way before. "Please?"

After pressing stop, she sent the video, and unsurprisingly, he responded very quickly. His tone also shifted.

I can help you find anything you need. Where you staying in town?

"Almost there," Jen said as she typed out her response.

> I haven't decided yet, but now that I know the club, I'll get a hotel nearby. Sometimes, I get too drunk to take the subway.

I groaned as she sent the message. "Really?"

"It works. Sad, but true."

At first, his reply seemed chivalrous.

> I'll make sure you get back safe.

She pushed a little harder.

> Is that all you'll do? ;)

> What would you like me to do?

Yeah, it definitely felt a lot less innocent by that point, and Jen went in for the kill.

> I'd like to see if those hands feel as good as they looked on the mixer.

> These hands can take good care of you, don't worry.

> Show me.

A pause followed with nothing to indicate typing, but Jen didn't seem worried. "He's about to spectacularly fail," she predicted.

Sure enough, a moment later, a video popped up in the chat, and when she opened it, we were both treated to a view of one of the hands in question as he stroked it along his exposed dick.

"Fuck." I winced as Jen matter-of-factly downloaded the video and swiped to a different chat, sending the video and a record of the conversation to the guy's unfortunate girlfriend. It only took a minute to get the expletive-laden reply, and with the woman's permission, Jen blocked the guy and threw the phone down on the bed.

"That's the way it usually goes," she said, turning to face me fully for the first time since I sat down beside her. "You can see why your case took me by surprise."

I could only shake my head. "How have you not lost faith in the entire male gender?"

She laughed softly, her eyes locked on mine. "It's touch-and-go sometimes, but I know that there are good ones out there. It makes it even more special when I come across one."

Her eyes dropped to my lips again, just like they did at the restaurant when we skirted around the memory of our kiss, and this time, nothing stood between us except my uncertainty about whether or not I could trust her.

The interaction I'd just witnessed didn't feel anything like the woman I spent time with in Napa, or even the woman who video chatted with me about travel when we were first getting to know each other. Maybe it hadn't been entirely an act after all?

I couldn't be certain, but at that moment, it seemed like a risk worth taking.

For the second time ever, but the first time as a free man, I leaned over and pressed my lips to hers.

Chapter Twelve

~Jennifer~

Of all the things that made people behave irrationally, lust had to be one of the most powerful.

What I felt when Gabe kissed me definitely fell into that category: a primal, primitive need as my body responded to his invitation, wanting nothing more than to give in to the dizzying, throbbing desire inside me, a longing I hadn't felt so strongly in many years.

His lips, firm and demanding against mine. His hands caressing my face, holding me as if he didn't want to ever let go. The spicy, fresh scent of his cologne and the sound of his contented sigh as we kissed.

All of it beckoned me to let go and give in to the connection I'd felt with him since the beginning. That connection grew stronger the more we got to know each other, and had been strong enough that even the revelation of my deception had only slowed it rather than stopping it altogether.

However, in the back of my head, a little voice tried to get my attention, nagging at me with all the reasons why abandoning reason entirely wouldn't be smart, at least not that night.

"Gabe." I whispered his name against his lips as I pulled back, only enough to speak but not far enough that he removed his hands from my face. "I don't know if this is a good idea."

"It feels pretty damn good to me," he murmured, his thumb gently stroking my cheek.

"That's not at all what I mean." With a shaky laugh, I pulled back further, taking his hands and bringing them to rest between us. Large and warm, they cradled mine perfectly. "You're just getting out of a very long relationship. Technically, you're not even out of it yet."

He shook his head, his blue eyes staying fixed to mine. "My marriage is over. Maybe not on paper yet, but in my heart, where it matters. Nothing can fix the way Celine broke us. I'm not ever going back, so why shouldn't we move forward?"

He had a point, but I still had more concerns. "You're vulnerable right now. You're still hurting, even if you want to move on, and I don't want to be just a rebound to you. You mean more to me than that."

"You mean more than that to me too, and if we both want this, what's the point of denying it? Celine took years from me, years that I thought we were building a relationship and maybe even a family, and I don't want to waste any more time. Not when what I want is perfectly clear to me."

A soft groan rumbled in my throat. "You're making an awful lot of sense."

He reached up to my face again, tucking the windswept strands of my hair behind my ear. "Because *this* makes sense. You feel it too, you just said you do. You came all this way to see me and you're going home in the morning. I don't know for sure what comes next, but I know that I don't want to walk away right now."

I *did* make the trip to see him, but not once did I imagine it would take this turn. If luck was on my side, I thought we might agree to remain friends. Worst case, he might have thrown me out of his office and never spoken to me again. But sitting in my hotel room with him, his incredible eyes looking at me with all the desire he'd been holding back before? That never crossed my mind as a possibility.

"You might have the wrong idea about me because of my job and the way I flirt with those men," I said next, still determined to voice all my objections before making a decision. "That's not me. The Jennifer you see online is all talk. Some people are fine with casual sex, and that's great, but it's not how I'm built."

"And you think I am?" he probed gently. "You already know I take commitment seriously, and even outside of a relationship, random partners have never been my style. I want this tonight, yes, but it doesn't mean I *only* want tonight."

He made it really hard to remember why I thought we should slow down.

"If you want me to go, I will," he added, the back of his hand running down my cheek with a feather-light touch. "It's up to you."

"I... I don't think we should have sex tonight," I managed to breathe out despite my body screaming in frustration. "On a practical level, do you even have a condom with you?"

Gabe's eyes widened before he shook his head sheepishly. "I can't remember the last time I bought any."

I had a feeling that might be the case. "Probably best not to go down that path, then. I'm not on birth control since I don't need to be, and if I end up pregnant with your baby, it might strengthen Celine's argument that we were having an affair."

A laugh burst through Gabe's lips as the ridiculousness of the entire situation hit him anew, and his laughter proved contagious. Soon, we were both almost in tears, feeding off each other as the tension between us shifted, still there but a little less visceral.

When we finally got ourselves back under control, Gabe reached over to pull me into a hug. "Fuck, that really shouldn't be so funny."

"You have to laugh or you'll go crazy. Trust me, dark humour has gotten me through a lot of tough times."

He nodded before letting me go. "Have you eaten? Why don't we order food and go through that spreadsheet?"

Despite me being the one to pull the brakes, a strong wave of disappointment washed over me as I realized how effective I'd been in killing the mood.

I put on my best poker face, determined not to let my frustration show. "Sure. Any requests?"

The hotel's room service arrived half an hour later, and by the time we finished the meal, we had a viable plan for Gabe to follow to sever all his ties with Celine and limit her ability to interfere in his life. He let out a long sigh as I emailed a copy of the completed spreadsheet to his work email.

"That sucked, but having your help made it a lot easier. Thank you."

"What are friends for?"

As soon as the word left my mouth, I heard how wrong it sounded, and Gabe cocked his head. "Friends? Is that what you want?"

"Yes."

I let him sit in his disappointment for a few seconds before I added a few more words.

"And hopefully more."

His eyes narrowed, trying to look angry but barely concealing his relief. "You have a bit of a mean streak."

"What are you going to do about it?"

My laughter was cut short as Gabe picked me up, squealing and squirming, and tossed me onto the other bed, away from our dirty dishes and the laptop. In no time at all, his body covered mine, his hands holding my wrists above my head as he stared down into my eyes. Desire flamed through my body again, as if it had never been extinguished but only temporarily dimmed.

"There's plenty I'd like to do about it," he said, his voice deeper than before.

My heart thumped heavily, mimicking the rhythmic pulsing that started up between my legs. "We said..." I tried to remind him, my voice coming out breathy and weak.

He said the words for me. "No sex." His eyes roamed across my face and downwards, over my collarbone to the top of my breasts which were pressed against his chest. "But there are other things I could do to you, things that'll make you want to be a lot nicer to me."

My teeth tugged at my bottom lip as my mind raced, trying to remember all the reasons I'd articulated before about why we should wait, but it came up blank.

Lust charged back in, and as it did, reason went out the door.

"Let's see what you've got."

~Gabriel~

The more time I spent with Jen, the more convinced I became that the woman I had gotten to know in Napa was the real version of her. Online, she played the seductress, and she played it very well, but in person, her natural empathy, intelligence and sincerity shone through. It showed in the way she helped me try to pick up the pieces of my life in the wake of my marriage falling apart, and I felt it even more in the reasons she gave for not wanting to get too physical that evening.

That she felt *something* for me didn't seem to be in doubt, both from the things she said and the fact that she came all that way to see me in the first place. Combined with the chemistry in our kiss, I already knew that no matter how unusual the circumstances under which we met had been, the connection between us was real.

It might have been the realest thing I ever felt.

Even so, I did my best to respect the distance she wanted to keep between us.

I succeeded all the way up until she teased me, nearly stopping my heart by saying she only wanted to be friends.

I couldn't let that go, and as she lay beneath me, looking up at me with those deep, gorgeous hazel eyes, her words broke my last shred of restraint.

"Let's see what you've got," she said, like a matador waving a red flag at a bull.

She wanted a taste of what this spark between us could turn into, and I wanted it too, so fucking badly.

"Before I leave tonight, you're going to promise to give this thing between us a chance," I told her as my hand slid beneath her shirt, stroking the soft skin of her stomach. "That's all I need for now: a chance."

Jen shivered beneath me, my touch sending goosebumps down her arm. "Am I? What if I don't?"

My lips curled into a smile, knowing she didn't mean it. She tested me with her challenge, trying to establish what the dynamic between us would be when things got more physical, and luckily for both of us, we seemed to be on the same page. I liked a woman who pushed back, and I would bet anything from the way she reacted to me that she liked a man who kept pushing. We would be a perfect match.

"If you don't..." I let the words hang in the air for a moment as I pulled her shirt up further, lowering my lips to brush along her stomach where my fingers had just been. "I'm going to get you all worked up and leave you unsatisfied."

She huffed in disapproval. "That sounds sadistic."

"It would be *masochistic* in this case because the choice is yours. All you need to do is say the words and we'll both be happy."

Gently, I lifted her shirt even higher, giving me my first glimpse of her beautiful breasts in the pastel pink bra she wore. Honestly, I'd seen more of her when she wore the bikini top on our video chat, but being so close to her chest, within breathing distance, affected me completely differently. I couldn't tear my eyes away from the full swell of her breasts, and when I brought my mouth down onto the fabric, teasing at her nipple with my teeth through her bra, Jen let out a sigh that sent blood rushing straight to my cock.

"How would this 'chance' of yours work?" she asked, her voice a lot breathier than it had been a few moments earlier. The last word cut off in a choke as I pulled the top of her bra down, exposing more of her smooth flesh, and sucked her nipple fully into my mouth without the fabric in the way.

Letting the question linger, my tongue ran across the tightening bud, working it into a firm peak while her body shifted under me, unable to contain her arousal.

"We... um... we live in different... cities," she gasped out when I released her in a temporary reprieve. Moving to the other breast, I gave it the same attention, sucking and licking her until she moaned.

"I have an awful lot of air miles saved up," I said, finally answering her question as I raised my head. My hands, which had been holding her shirt up, moved lower, drifting to the waist of her pants. "We could see each other regularly. If you're talking long-term, I'm probably going to be looking for a new job and don't need to stay in San Francisco. You work from home. We'd have options."

The sound of the zipper on her pants lowering sent another shiver down her spine, and my cock began to throb. Even though *I* knew it wouldn't be getting anywhere near her pussy that night, my dick must have missed the memo.

Ignoring the strain in my pants, I slid my hand into the newly-created opening on Jen's, over her underwear and down between her legs, groaning as my fingers pressed against the warm, damp fabric. She was just as turned on as I could have hoped, and feeling it for myself made the blood rush through my body so fast, I almost missed her answer through the pounding in my ears.

"Long-term?"

Pressing against her through the fabric, I swirled my tongue around her nipple again before answering. "I told you: I'm not thinking about just one night. We don't need to jump too far ahead, but that much needs to be clear. Are you ready to give me your answer now?"

Her hips tilted upwards as I stroked her through her panties. "What... uh... what was the question again?"

With a chuckle, I hooked my fingers around the edge of her underwear, pulling it to the side so I could feel her wetness directly against my skin. Her smooth pussy, so warm and wet, made me lose track of the conversation too. "Fuck, Jen. You feel incredible."

"How did you know?" she breathed. "I *do* feel incredible."

Laughing again, I began to explore her more thoroughly. Dipping just my fingertip inside her to coat it, I slid it up to her clit, circling and stroking and paying careful attention to her response to see what she liked. Her hands reached for me, her fingers threading through my hair as she gazed down at me from beneath her half-closed eyelids.

"A little harder," she whispered.

I pressed harder as my finger circled her, waiting until her eyes fluttered closed before I moved back down again, sinking one finger deep inside her. Her back arched and my cock pulsed, protesting against its confinement.

After being with one woman for so long, I'd never imagined having this kind of intimacy with someone else, and I certainly never thought it would feel as natural as this did. Even though each sensation was new and exciting, it felt completely right.

It felt... inevitable.

After adding a second finger to her pussy and my thumb on her clit, watching as Jen's body began to writhe against me, I figured she had to be close but she still hadn't given me what I wanted.

"You're going to give this a chance, right?" I grunted, the movements of my hand steady and driving.

She whimpered, looking absolutely gorgeous laid out on the bed beneath me, still fully dressed except for her exposed breasts and the opening in her pants filled by my hand. "What?"

"You owe me a promise," I reminded her. "Say you'll give this a chance and I'll make you come."

"Gabe..."

"Say it."

Celine used to say I got too aggressive in the bedroom sometimes. She preferred to be the one in charge. But even though Jen teased and pushed against me, she also shuddered at the hard edge to my voice, confirming what I already suspected.

She liked this rougher side of me, the side that only came out in bed.

When she didn't immediately answer me, I lifted my thumb off her clit and slowed the movement of my fingers. "Say it, Jen."

Groaning, she pulled my head against her chest, her hips pushing against me impatiently. "Yes. We'll give it a chance. Just don't stop, please."

With her promise secured, I gave her exactly what she needed. My fingers thrust into her hard as my thumb rubbed her clit and my mouth covered her nipple again, sucking her into my mouth.

"Oh, God, fuck, yes." After another thirty seconds, and with a shuddering jolt, Jen came. Her pussy contracted around my fingers as her hands tugged my hair, and a deep wave of satisfaction filled me.

I'd imagined it would be good with her, but she'd already exceeded my expectations and I couldn't wait to learn her body even better.

However, I knew that we'd already pushed things enough for one night. Gently pulling out of her, I brought my fingers to my lips and sucked on the two that had just been inside her. Fuck, she tasted good. I would be dreaming about tasting her directly until we had a chance to be together again.

We both got cleaned up in the bathroom before Jen pushed me towards the door.

"I don't need to leave right away," I tried to tell her, but she shook her head, opening the door for me.

"You stay any longer and I can't guarantee things won't get heated again. I think we've gone far enough for one night."

Something in her voice made me pause, and I stopped halfway out the door. "You don't regret it, do you?" My eyes searched hers, looking for any hint of unhappiness, but she smiled back at me.

"I think I got a lot more out of it than you did, and no, I don't regret it. Call me when you get your new phone, okay?"

"I will. And somehow or other, I'll see you soon."

I gave her one last, lingering kiss before heading back downstairs and out of the hotel. Unable to hold back my smile as the last couple of hours repeated in my head, I gave into it, grinning like an idiot as I walked down the street. A drugstore sat on the corner, so I ducked inside and picked up a box of condoms while I had it on my mind. It wouldn't hurt to be prepared next time I saw her, just in case.

My smile even wider than before, I headed back home.

~Jennifer~

The sun felt a little brighter than usual the next afternoon as I lay outside in my backyard, enjoying the warmth as I worked.

Everything felt a little brighter, to be honest, and that had a lot to do with Gabe.

His text came through just after noon, not long after I arrived home from my morning flight back from San Francisco.

> This is my new number. Should we avoid using our names, just in case? I won't tell you who I am, but I will say that I haven't been able to stop thinking about how good you felt on my fingers last night. Hope you had a good night's sleep and a safe flight home.

His words sent a shot of lust straight to my centre, my pussy clenching at the memory of his hand there and the wonderful orgasm he gave me. Although I hadn't meant to let things get that far, I couldn't bring myself to be upset about it either, not when he felt so damn good inside me. Seeing him let go had been almost as hot as his actions, and his dominant edge came as a very welcome surprise. The idea of exploring even more with him kept the smile on my face as I teased him in my response.

> Hmmm, you might have to be more specific. I'm not sure who this is.

> Very funny. How many orgasms will it take until you remember me?

> Maybe we can find out this weekend. How does a trip to Pasadena sound?

> Better than you can imagine. Let's put those air miles to work.

Ten minutes later, he sent a screenshot of his flight confirmation, arriving at LAX the next evening. My body began to thrum in anticipation despite the arrival time being more than thirty hours away.

> I'll arrange a ride for you. Can't wait to see you.

> The feeling is more than mutual. Better get back to work for now.

> Me too. We'll talk later.

After that, my flirting with other men felt even less sexy than usual, but the guys didn't seem to notice. I bagged two more fails that afternoon until I got an unexpected message in my work profile inbox.

> Hi Jen, you probably don't remember me but you helped me expose my scumbag husband last year. I'm seeing someone new now and things are so much better.

I *loved* hearing things like that. There were still good men out there, as I'd recently found out for myself.

Her message went on.

Anyway, I'm in a chat with some other women you've helped, and we get new people joining us sometimes to ask if they should use you. We always tell them you're totally worth it.

My cheeks flushed at the compliment. I had no idea such a group existed, and it thrilled me to know that these women were out there supporting each other long after my involvement, and that my service had helped to bring them together.

Normally, it's all positive, good vibes, but today, this woman came in and started talking shit about you. She said she hired you and you stole her husband and no one should trust you. She had a bunch of receipts, which I'm sure she faked. I know you'd never do something like that, but I thought you should know that she's out there saying this shit. It's probably not just our group either, she seemed really crazy and determined to ruin your reputation. Sorry to dump this on you, but I thought you should know.

The woman didn't sign her name, but she did attach several screenshots of what had been shared in the chat. I recognized Celine's handiwork immediately.

"Son of a bitch," I muttered as I scrolled through the images. There were screenshots of my conversations with Gabe and my conversations with her. The names had been blacked out, but I recognized the rest of it easily enough. The texts, I already knew she had, but the other photos took me completely by surprise, and all the light, happy excitement that had been bubbling inside me all day immediately withered.

There were images that must have come from security cameras at the Four Winds, showing me and Gabe at the check-in desk, having dinner together at the restaurant, and going into my room together. Put together, it looked really bad. How the fuck did she have those?

As if that weren't enough, more photos followed.

Me coming out of Gabe's office the day before. The two of us at the Hyacinth Café in San Francisco and walking into my hotel afterwards. A photo of Gabe at a drugstore, buying a box of condoms.

Okay, the last one made me smile, but only for a second. Overall, it painted a picture of two people engaged in a very active affair.

Shit. *Shit.*

What her trash-talking would mean for my business, I couldn't be sure yet, but it didn't matter as much as the other thing I knew for sure: she didn't have those photos just to destroy my reputation. That would be the icing on her poison-laced cake, but the cake itself would be using them to build her case for Gabe's inheritance.

She must have paid a PI to follow him, just as we'd done to her, but the photos her investigator got were even more damning than what we turned up.

By Gabe and I spending time together, we were reinforcing her argument that he had, in fact, cheated on her. Technically, anything we did after he filed for divorce no longer counted, but it gave the impression that things between us had started before then, and as in so many things in life, perception counted for a lot in this situation.

Not wanting to upset Gabe at work, I called his lawyer directly instead. In a meeting at the time, she returned my call an hour later.

"This isn't great," she understated once she reviewed all the screenshots I sent her. "Ideally, these photos wouldn't exist, but since they do, she messed up by posting them. At least we know she has them and we can prepare a defense in time. If we'd been blindsided with them, things could have been a lot worse."

"So, we should be grateful that she's so vindictive?" I asked, and Victoria laughed.

"If I had a dollar for every time someone would have been better off by keeping their mouth shut, I'd be able to give Mr Carter his inheritance myself and be done with it. Needless to say, my advice to you and to Mr Carter is to say nothing in response. Don't let her know that we know about the screenshots, and don't give her any more ammunition."

I nodded along with her right up until the last sentence. "What do you mean by ammunition? Gabe and I can't spend time together?"

"It would be better if you didn't until after the hearing. I'm not going to tell you what to do in your personal life, but if you want Mr Carter to win, staying away from him is the best thing you could do."

Although I understood her reasoning, it still left a pit in the bottom of my stomach. If Celine had someone following Gabe, they could follow him to the airport and find out the flight he got on. Would that be enough time to arrange for someone to follow him once he arrived in Los Angeles?

Would it be worth the risk to find out?

Chapter Thirteen

~Gabriel~

Going through all the steps of cutting my ties with Celine made me a little paranoid about staying at my own house. What if she had a way of watching me? If I called Jen, would she be able to listen in? The idea of her spying on me made my skin crawl, so I texted my sister in the afternoon.

> Can I crash at your place tonight?

Her answer came back nearly instantly.

> Of course. As long as you need to. I'm actually heading out of town this weekend, so it's all yours if you want it.

I would be heading out of town too, but she didn't know that yet. No matter what, my sister had my back, and I'd never appreciated it more than during this confusing time in my life.

I picked up Vietnamese food on the way over, Monica's favourite, and we ate in front of the TV in her apartment while I filled her in on what happened the day before with Jen. Most of it, anyway. I didn't go into detail about what happened in Jen's hotel room, but I said enough that Monica understood we'd gone a little further than just kissing.

"Maybe you need to slow things down a bit," she suggested gently, taking a long slurp of her noodles. "Your marriage isn't even cold in the ground yet. Don't get me wrong: I'm the first person in line to cheer for you moving on from Celine, but this thing with Jen seems pretty fast."

"I know," I assured her. "If I take a step back, it looks like a terrible idea, but when I'm with her, it doesn't feel that way. It feels right. I can't explain it."

At that moment, my phone buzzed with a text from Jen, sending a rush of warmth through my chest and a smile spreading across my face.

Monica rolled her eyes and teased me, "Can't guess who that is."

Ignoring her, I read the text, my smile fading as I took in the words.

> This weekend might not be such a good idea. Call me when you can.

"Excuse me a second," I mumbled to my sister before pressing the call button next to Jen's name. Before she could even say hi, I blurted out my question. "What's going on?"

"Hello to you too." Her warm chuckle helped to ease my worry, making it clear I hadn't done anything wrong to make her rescind her earlier invitation. "Are you free to talk? It's about Celine."

"My sister's here, but she knows all about you and all about Celine, so she'll probably end up dragging it all out of me later anyway."

Ducking, I narrowly avoided the pillow Monica tossed at my head before muting the TV. "Put it on speaker," she whispered, and I did. Since I would probably tell her all about it anyway, she might as well hear it straight from the source.

With the phone held in my hand in front of me, I repeated my earlier question. "What's going on?"

Without mincing words, Jen shared the message she received that afternoon, the additional 'evidence' that Celine had, and her conversation with my lawyer. "I went to her because you were at work and I didn't want it to wait until tomorrow," Jen explained. "I hope that's okay."

"It's fine." If anything, I appreciated her taking the initiative. Now that we'd heard her news, I turned off my phone speaker and left the room to continue our conversation, ignoring Monica's mimed protests. In the kitchen, I looked out the window at the street below, watching other people go about their lives which had to be less complicated than mine at the moment. "So, you want to cancel this weekend?"

Jen sighed, and I could almost feel the soft rush of her breath against my skin, the memory of holding her close to me so vivid. "I don't *want* to, but I'm not sure it's worth the risk to go ahead. We can say that I went to San Francisco yesterday to share information with you for the divorce proceedings, which has some truth to it, but I'm not sure how we could spin you coming here for a whole weekend. If Celine managed to get security footage from the Four Winds, I don't know how far she'll go."

Neither did I, and where did she get the money for all this investigating, anyway? If Jen hadn't paid for the PI, I would have struggled to afford it. I could only buy the plane ticket to LA because of the air miles I used. We hadn't had extra money in ages, so where did all Celine's disposable income come from?

"As much as I hate to say it, maybe you should cancel the flight." Jen's voice pulled me out of my questions and back to the more immediate matter. "Save your air miles for another time?"

Despite her being the one to suggest it, I could hear the disappointment underpinning her words, the same disappointment that lodged itself in the pit of my stomach. I had really been looking forward to spending time with her and getting to know her better without Celine being the main topic of conversation. Somehow, my wife managed to insert herself right back into the thick of things.

Ex-wife. I'd have to start thinking about her that way, since in every way that mattered to me, she'd earned that title.

"Yeah, I guess I should," I agreed, my voice sounding hollow. "Thank you for letting me know about all of this. Is this campaign of hers going to affect your business?"

"I'm not sure yet. For now, I'll stay out of it and see how things play out."

"That's probably smart." She seemed to be taking the whole thing pretty well, her concern much more for me than for herself, which only reinforced the impression I already had of her. "I better get back to my sister before she gets a crowd together with pitchforks to track Celine down."

Jen's laugh helped to ease a tiny bit of my disappointment. "I think I'd like your sister."

"I think you would too. I'll talk to you tomorrow. Have a good night."

We hung up and I returned to the living room to find Monica tapping away on her phone, her thumbs flying across the keyboard.

"What are you doing?" I asked with some trepidation as I sat back down beside her.

"Saving your weekend," she replied airily. "I planned to leave tomorrow morning, but now, I'll wait until you're done with work. I let my friend know that I'll be arriving a little later."

She'd completely lost me. "Back up several steps. What are you talking about?"

With an exasperated sigh, she lowered her phone. "I told you I'm going away this weekend. I've recently made friends with this woman down in LA and she invited me to visit."

"LA?" I perked up immediately, starting to get on board her train of thought.

"Uh-huh." She grinned at me before continuing. "I'm going to drive down and I've got room for a passenger."

Tentatively, I ran through the scenario in my head. "How does that help, though? If Celine's having me followed, they can follow your car as well as they can track my flight."

Monica's eyebrows raised in mock offense. "Really? You don't think I can lose a tail?"

"Alright there, James Bond, calm down." She threw another pillow at me, but I caught that one in mid-air. "How are you going to lose them?"

"I'll take a diversion or two along the way, down quiet roads. If someone's following us, we'll know. Way easier to spot someone on a deserted back road than in a busy airport."

That actually made some sense, or maybe I was just desperate. Either way, I found myself agreeing. "I'm willing to give it a shot, but I'm not going to tell Jen I'm coming until I get there, just in case it doesn't work out."

Monica shrugged. "That's your call. My only request is that if I'm going to all this trouble, I get to meet her."

That seemed fair, and I really did think Monica and Jen would get along. "Deal. I can't wait to see your spy skills in action."

"You'll be blown away," she predicted with a laugh as we settled back in to finish the show we'd been watching, the disappointment I'd felt after Jen's call vanishing into a steady drum of anticipation.

~Jennifer~

After spending way too much of my time on Thursday and Friday dealing with questions from clients and potential clients who saw Celine's posts about me and wanted reassurances that I wouldn't *actually* be attempting to seduce their partners, I went to bed early on Friday night.

At least I tried to. Just after midnight, a phone call woke me up.

"What's going on?" I mumbled into the phone after seeing Eda's name on the screen. "Are you okay?"

"Physically, yes," she reassured me, knowing that after Matt's death, I still had a fear of out-of-the-blue phone calls that no amount of time would ever truly erase. "You still haven't told Gabe about me getting dirt on his marriage through Monica, right?"

"You called me at midnight to ask me that?" I groaned, rubbing my eyes with my free hand as I tried to focus. "No, I haven't told him, but only because there hasn't been a natural opportunity. I will."

"Well, I think it's gonna have to happen sooner rather than later," she said in a hushed whisper. "He's currently in my living room."

"What?" The remains of my sleepiness drained away as I sat up, pinching the skin on my wrist to make sure I wasn't dreaming. Since it stung, I figured I must be awake. "What are you talking about?"

Her voice still low, she offered an explanation. "My roommates are both out of town, so I invited Monica down for the weekend to see a show that we've both heard good things about. She texted me yesterday to say she'd be arriving late because she needed to give someone a ride. Fifteen minutes ago, she showed up with her brother."

"You've actually seen him? Spoken to him?"

"I have," she assured me. "And I've got to say: *nice*, Jen."

Her appreciation of Gabe at a time like that made me giggle despite the tenuous nature of the situation. "What is he doing there?"

"Apparently, he came to town to see someone. I assume that 'someone' is you. They got here later than planned because they took some long-ass detour, so Monica asked if he could crash in my living room tonight, probably because showing up at your door in the middle of the night would be creepy as hell."

I couldn't find any flaws in her logic, and the idea that Gabe would have endured a six-hour car ride after we both agreed flying to see me would be too risky made my heart melt. How could Celine not return the love of a man who would go to so much effort for someone he cared about?

Now, I just needed to figure out how to explain to him how Eda and Monica knew each other.

"Alright. Here's what we're going to do: first thing in the morning, I'll come down there and I can explain everything in person."

"Are you sure? It's going to be awkward." I could picture Eda biting her lip like she did ever since we were little, whenever she got caught doing something she shouldn't have. "Monica might be really pissed off at me."

"And Gabe might be upset with me too," I admitted. "We kind of crossed a line, both of us. It makes sense to own up to it together. If they storm out, at least we'll have each other."

Although I tried to keep my tone light, another confrontation with Gabe wasn't at all the way I wanted to spend the weekend when I invited him to come visit in the first place.

Hopefully, it would be the last thing I had to apologize for keeping something from him.

"It'll be a big ol' family reunion." Eda gave a half-sigh, half-laugh that perfectly encapsulated the way I felt. "Okay. I'll keep him from leaving until you get here. Go back to sleep. See you tomorrow."

"See you then."

After hanging up, I looked around my darkened bedroom, knowing the chances of getting back to sleep after that conversation were pretty slim. Not quite sure what to do with myself, I started scrolling through my texts with Gabe from earlier in the day, looking for any hints that he might have dropped about coming to see me. Try as I might, I couldn't find any.

Seemed I wasn't the only one good at keeping a secret.

> Are you still up?

The text notification startled me, and I scrolled back down to the bottom of the conversation to find the new message from Gabe waiting there.

> I am. Why are you awake?

> You don't get to ask me that when you're up too.

I could practically feel the warmth of his smile in the words on the screen before he sent me a real answer.

> I'm not at home and I don't have the most comfortable bed.

Having slept on Eda's pull-out couch before, I could sympathize. Curious about how he would answer if I questioned him about it directly, I asked the obvious follow-up question.

> Where are you?

> With my sister.

Technically, he didn't lie, but he left out a few details too, I noticed.

> Thinking about you, though.

The warm feeling returned to my chest with his sweet, simple statement, and I grinned as I teased him.

> Well, I would hope you're not thinking about your sister.

> Is that the razor-sharp wit all the guys fall for?

> Usually. Is it making you swoon?

> Not as much as the thought of having you in this bed with me.

> That's not a nice thing to say when you just told me how uncomfortable it is.

> I'd let you lie on top of me.

> Oh, yeah? Would that make it softer?

> Nothing about me is soft when you're around.

Fuck. My body had begun to ache, a combination of his words and knowing only a short drive separated us. Would he be in this bed with me the following night? Would I be able to resist the chemistry between us when we were together again in person?

Did I even want to?

The flirting and teasing went on for another half hour before I told him I needed to get some sleep, knowing that I had an early morning ahead of me.

Even with one more awkward conversation ahead of us, I held out hope that the next day would be the first day of our new start, one less about his past and much more about the future I was beginning to see for the two of us.

~Gabriel~

As soon as the California sun began to light up the living room of Monica's friend's apartment, I got up and put the sofa bed away, staying as quiet as I could while I had a quick shower. Logically, I knew it made sense for me to stay there when we arrived so late the night before, but after texting with Jen and realizing she was still awake, I wished I'd made the trip to see her. I couldn't wait to head out that morning and surprise her.

Monica had been as good as her word on the drive down, and sure enough, the first time she pulled off the interstate for a restroom break, several cars followed us to the gas station we'd seen from the road. Unable to tell if any of those might be Celine's investigator, she took us on a long detour down one of the secondary highways. One car stayed resolutely with us, sending a chill down my spine the longer it followed us.

How far *was* Celine willing to go to get her way, and how had I never known before just how ruthless she could be?

"Hold onto something," Monica muttered, pressing the gas pedal to the floor as the two-lane highway stretched ahead of us. "This is where we lose him."

"Don't do anything stupid," I warned, but she only grinned as she accelerated until we could no longer see the car in the rear-view mirror.

"Sharp turn!" she called out.

As we rounded the next bend in the road, I saw what she'd already noticed on her GPS: a side road that led into Pinnacles National Park. She pulled a sharp right off the main road, and as soon as we were out of sight of the highway, she slowed right down and pulled over on the side of the road.

For several tense moments, we waited, anticipating the car passing us at any moment, but no one else came.

"You are insane," I breathed out, finally releasing my grip on the door handle. I couldn't even remember grabbing it.

"But I lost him," she crowed triumphantly before returning to the highway and turning back the way we came until we could reconnect with the I-5 interstate.

After literally putting my life in my sister's hands, I was more determined than ever to make this weekend with Jen count, and that meant not wasting a second more than necessary before going to see her.

However, just as I'd located a piece of paper and a pen to write a short thank you note to my hostess, the woman herself appeared from her bedroom.

"Good morning, Gabe." Eda gave me a warm smile before her eyes swept the room, taking in the folded sheets and my packed bag and her smile faded into concern. "You're not leaving already, are you?"

"I am. I don't want to intrude any longer than necessary. You and Monica have plans, and so do I, but I really appreciate you letting me stay here last night. Thank you for your hospitality."

Assuming that would be the end of it, I picked up my bag and turned towards the door, but Eda rushed over, nearly tripping over the rug in the middle of the floor, and blocked my path.

"You can't leave," she blurted out, staring up at me with wide hazel eyes that, in the early morning light, reminded me of Jennifer's. It had been dark when we arrived the night before, the apartment lit only by some floor lamps, and I hadn't gotten a very good look at her then.

"I... can't leave?" I repeated, my eyebrows drawing together in confusion.

"Not yet, I mean," she said, letting out a nervous-sounding laugh. "I'm going to make breakfast."

"That's kind of you, but I'm okay. I'll pick something up on my way."

I tried to step around her but she moved again, straight into me. "Coffee, at least?"

How much clearer could I make it? "Not necessary. Have a good day, Eda."

"Wait!" She grabbed my arm when I went around her, and I started to get concerned. How well did Monica know this woman? With her strange behaviour, I didn't know if I felt comfortable leaving my sister alone with her.

Before either of us could say anything else, someone knocked on the apartment door, and Eda sighed in relief. "Finally."

What the fuck?

She dropped my arm and headed to the door while I glanced around the room, looking for something I might be able to defend myself with in case the person on the other side of the door had some kind of unfriendly intentions. Had we been lured there so we could be robbed, or worse?

I managed to get my hand on a heavy candlestick holder just as Eda turned the knob, making me feel like some kind of Clue villain, but all thoughts of self-defense flew out the door when the woman on the other side walked through it.

"Jen?"

I blinked a few times in rapid succession, sure that my mind must be playing tricks on me, but each time they opened again, she still stood there, looking casually elegant in a pink blouse and cream capris with strappy sandals that showed off her pretty pink-painted toenails, her honey-blonde hair hanging over her shoulders.

What in the world was she doing there? *How* could she be there?

"Hi." She offered me a soft smile before turning to Eda and embracing her. "I got here as early as I could."

"You were almost too late," Eda admonished her. "I thought I would have to tie him to a chair to keep him from leaving."

My eyes darted back and forth between the two of them, trying to make *any* sense of the situation as Jen's gaze returned to me.

"I know you've got questions. You look like you've seen a ghost."

"I'm afraid there's a hidden camera somewhere and someone's going to jump out and yell 'surprise'," I told her bluntly. "What are you doing here? How do you know Eda?"

She answered my second question first. "Eda's my sister."

As soon as the words left her lips, I could see it. Aside from the similarities in their eyes, which I'd already noticed, they had the same full lips and narrow nose, but that still barely scratched the surface of the explanation I needed.

"What's all the commotion?" Monica grumbled as she walked out of the guest room, still in her pajamas. "And where's the coffee?"

"Coming right up," Eda proclaimed as she stepped into the corner kitchen to turn on the machine.

Never one to be shy, Monica walked over and gave Jen a once-over, looking her up and down curiously. "Who are you?"

"Let's start from the beginning," Jen suggested. "Everyone take a seat. Please."

She turned a puppy-dog look on me that I couldn't resist, even though her sudden appearance there unnerved me more with each passing second. Just when I thought she'd been totally honest with me, more 'coincidences' occurred.

Monica and I sat down on the couch where I'd spent the night and Jen sat across from us, looking so ridiculously beautiful that even if she did turn out to be a complete psychopath, part of me thought I could find a way to accept it.

She turned to my sister first. "I'm Jennifer Bradshaw. I'm the woman Celine hired to try to tempt Gabe into cheating. You must be Monica."

For once, my sister seemed to be too stunned to speak. Her head swivelled slowly between Jen and me, as if I might be able to offer some kind of explanation, but I had nothing to add. We were as lost as each other.

"Eda, whose apartment we're in, is my sister," Jen continued. "And it's because of me that Eda and Monica know each other in the first place."

"What?" Monica managed to squeak out one word just as Eda returned with two cups of coffee. Greedily, my sister took it from her and took a long sip while Eda sat on one of the other chairs with her own cup.

"You already know how Celine hired me, right?" Jen asked her. "I don't want to repeat things you already know."

"I do," Monica confirmed.

"So, after I started getting suspicious about Celine's refusal to accept Gabe's pass, I told Eda the whole story. It didn't make sense to me, but I couldn't understand what her motive would be for the whole charade. Eda offered to get in touch with some San Francisco friends and see if she could dig up any dirt on Celine, on the off-chance anyone knew her. Obviously, she hit the jackpot."

Monica gave Eda a shrewd look. "You wanted advice about your sister-in-law."

Eda shrugged sheepishly. "She doesn't exist. I made her up so you would talk about yours. I didn't think it would go this far, I thought we'd just talk that one time and that would be it."

"What did you tell her?" I asked Monica, chagrined to know that my sister would have divulged any personal information to a complete stranger.

It was Monica's turn to look repentant. "I may have mentioned that I thought she married you for your inheritance."

Pieces of the puzzle began to slot into place as I turned back to Jen. "You knew about the inheritance before Napa?"

"I did," she admitted. "You asked me the other day if I was convinced Celine was cheating on you by the time we hired the PI, and I said yes. This is *why* I thought so. Nothing else made sense given the information I had. Everything else I told you is true; I just didn't mention getting this information because I didn't want to get Eda in trouble."

"*Am* I in trouble?" Eda blurted out, her attention focused on Monica rather than me. "I know I lied, but I only wanted to help my sister. I could tell as soon as we talked that you cared about your brother too. You might have done the same thing for him if the situations were reversed."

Remembering how my sister risked both our lives and a speeding ticket the day before just to get me down to LA, I had to agree with that, and Monica conceded it too. "I probably would have. You're a damn convincing liar."

She sounded almost impressed, and I shook my head in disbelief. It seemed our sisters had a lot in common, but the fact remained that Jen hid this from me. Even when we cleared the air a few days earlier at the café, she held this information back. How many other things hadn't she told me?

If Celine managed to fool me so thoroughly, maybe I was truly a terrible judge of character. In which case: how could I trust Jen at all?

Chapter Fourteen

~Jennifer~

I could feel Gabe pulling away from me.

As Eda and Monica quickly found common ground despite the initial lie that brought them together, Gabe began to withdraw. Even though his position on the couch next to his sister stayed the same, I recognized the look of confused disappointment in his eyes, the same look as when he realized his marriage was over.

Not quite to the same extent, perhaps, but similar all the same, and the idea of him lumping me and Celine together in his mind as being cut from the same backstabbing cloth sent a sharp pang of regret and pain straight to my heart.

"Can we talk in private?" I asked him quietly, glancing towards Eda's balcony. The words were barely audible above our sisters' chatter, but his gaze followed mine, lingering there for a second as if he were picturing the two of us standing out there, the whole scene playing out in his mind.

"I don't think that's a good idea," he replied, the distance between us growing greater with each passing second. "I think I should go."

Eda picked up on the word despite being in mid-sentence herself and stopped abruptly. "Go? Go where?"

Both of our sisters turned curious eyes towards Gabe and his face tightened beneath the scrutiny.

"Coming here was a mistake." He nodded to himself, and I couldn't tell if he wanted to convince himself or the rest of us of that fact. "I'll find a hotel and you can let me know when you're ready to go back."

He directed the last part at Monica, and her eyebrows drew together in a way that I'd seen Gabe's do several times before. "Don't you want to…"

She didn't get a chance to finish before Gabe got to his feet, grabbed the bag he'd dropped on the floor earlier, and headed out the door without another word. He didn't slam it behind him but he might as well have, considering the dramatic stillness that descended over Eda's living room after he'd gone.

For a long moment, none of us spoke. After our flirting the night before, I'd convinced myself on the drive to LA that morning that things would be okay. Awkward, yes, but ultimately, we'd move past it, just like we did in San Francisco a few days earlier.

Now, I felt a lot less certain.

Eda broke the silence first. "Is he always that much of a drama queen?"

Her gaze moved between me and Monica, and though Monica tensed, her chest rising to say something, I blurted out an answer before she could.

"He's not being dramatic. He's trying to trust me after his wife broke his trust in the worst way possible, and I'm not making it easy on him."

Monica blew out the breath she'd inhaled. "Yeah. That."

Eda's mouth opened beside me, ready to jump to my defense, but I placed my hand on her arm, holding her back. I could accept when I made a mistake, and besides, it seemed Monica had more to say.

"It's not just you," she added a moment later, a grimace pulling at the corners of her lips. "He thinks I can't keep a secret, and apparently, I just proved him right. He'll forgive me eventually because he knows I love him, but I get why he's feeling alone in the world right now."

"Jen cares for him too," Eda stated firmly. "I haven't seen her this interested in a man for years."

Monica's eyebrows raised as she looked over at me, and I let out a half-frustrated, half-affectionate sigh. "You two really *do* have a lot in common. You see, Monica? My sister can't keep her mouth shut either."

Eda gave me a playful shove away from her before wrapping her arm around me and pulling me into a sideways hug. "It sucks seeing someone you love get shit on by life," she said softly, her tone softening her coarse words. "I think we both know what that feels like. Matt dying sucked. A nice guy like Gabe marrying a bitch like Celine sucked. The two of you together? That *doesn't* suck, and we won't rest until Gabe sees that."

Monica didn't disagree with that, but she did tilt her head at me curiously. "Who's Matt?"

Leaving Eda to tell that story, I excused myself and went out onto the balcony alone, staring out over the sprawling city below us. Gabe could be anywhere in the mass of people and buildings, and if he chose not to get in touch with me that weekend, I didn't know when I'd have a chance to see him again in person, not with Celine watching his every step.

Moments we'd spent together flashed across my mind as I stared out at the city, seeing Gabe's face in front of me rather than the view. In just a matter of weeks, he'd gotten past the wall I put up around myself after Matt's death, a wall I hadn't even fully realized existed until he breached it. I told myself that dating didn't fit into my life, that it felt too much like work after spending all day flirting with strangers online, but with the right person, it shouldn't.

With Gabe, it didn't feel like work at all.

Despite all the external complications, it felt right, and I kept screwing it up.

When my phone buzzed, I almost ignored it, thinking it would probably be one of my current jobs and I definitely wasn't in a flirting mood. Something made me slip my hand into my pocket anyway, though, and when I pulled it out, Gabe's name immediately caught my eye.

> Why is it that I can't stay mad at you?

Hope flared inside me, sparking into an immediate flame.

Rather than answering his question directly, I tried teasing him, wanting to gauge his openness.

> Did Monica steal your phone? Are you being held hostage? Send me two winky faces if yes.

> I wouldn't put it past her, but no. It's me. Isn't she there with you? I waited downstairs to see if she would storm out too, but I guess she has more self-control than I do. Either that, or she's killed you and stolen *your* phone.

A warm wave of affection filled my chest at his gentle self-deprecation.

> Your self-control is fine. I owe you yet another apology. You must be so tired of me saying I'm sorry.

> Probably about as tired as you are of me shutting down. I don't want to keep pushing you away, so tell me: is there *anything* else I need to know? This is the time to get it off your chest, Jen.

He didn't say it, but I heard the warning anyway: this would be my last chance.

Luckily, I'd run out of things to confess.

> That's it. There's nothing else, and I was going to tell you about this too. I know that means nothing after the fact, but I planned to tell you today.

When he didn't immediately reply, I sent another message.

> Now that you've met Eda, you only need to ask her and she'll spill any secrets anyway.

> Wonder what that's like.

My smile almost split my cheeks, and tentatively, I asked the question I wanted answered most at that moment.

Where are you?

On the street outside Eda's building. I didn't get far.

Grabbing the rail, I peered over the side of the balcony, and sure enough, I could see him on the sidewalk ten floors below me, staring down at his phone.

Look up.

His head raised and I waved. Even with that distance between us, I could see the smile on his face and feel the connection between us, the one that neither of us seemed to be able to resist.

Want to get out of here and go back to my place?

Fuck yes.

We shared another smile before I pulled back from the edge and sent one last text.

I'll be right there.

~Gabriel~

Maybe I needed to have my head examined, but as I sat next to Jen in her car, chatting about our sisters while we made our way to Pasadena, I couldn't bring myself to regret my choice to trust her.

Things made a lot more sense knowing that Jen already had some background information about my grandparents' will before she suggested sending an investigator after Celine. Rather than telling me what she suspected, she helped me put the pieces together for myself. It might not have been the most straightforward way to approach things, but I couldn't see any proof that she'd ever had anything other than my best interests at heart.

Those thoughts had already been in the back of my head, and the text from Monica gave me the final push I needed.

> I should have kept my mouth shut and I'm sorry. For what it's worth, I like Jen so far. And I was right about Celine, so maybe I'm right about this too.

Monica had always been picky about the women I dated, so for her to say she liked Jen already seemed significant. Maybe my instincts weren't entirely broken after all.

I let out a low whistle as Jen pulled into the driveway of her house. The craftsman-style house had a large porch, a landscaped, well-kept lawn, and more windows than walls, it seemed. "This is really nice. Are there that many cheating men out there to pay for it all?"

She laughed good-naturedly. "Unfortunately, there are, but the down payment actually came from my portion of Matt's life insurance policy. We'd been looking at this neighbourhood to buy a house after we got married, so when this one came on the market right after I got the payout, it felt like a sign."

With all the drama in my life, I'd almost forgotten the story she told me about her fiancé leaving her money when he died and the schism it caused between her and his family. "I'm sure he'd be happy to know you were taken care of."

"I think he would." She smiled her agreement before opening her car door, making it clear she wanted to move on. Just like I didn't want to dwell on my marriage this weekend, she didn't seem to want to linger too long over her past either. We only had about twenty-four hours together before I would need to return to San Francisco, and that time should be about us.

Inside, the interior had been immaculately decorated. Wood paneling provided plenty of warmth while the windows gave the illusion of being part of the outdoors. Although elegant and undoubtedly expensive, it also felt natural rather than pretentious.

In other words, it felt like her.

"Would you like a tour?" she asked, taking my bag from my hand and placing it on a bench by the door.

"Absolutely."

Each room impressed me more. The fireplace in the family room, the large island in the middle of the well-equipped kitchen, and the tranquil pool in the backyard, each place seemed design to provide peace and comfort, and yet, I couldn't stop my mind from wandering to all the places I might have her body pressed against mine. Despite all the windows, the space surrounding the house gave the illusion of privacy. My fingers itched to reach out and wrap around Jen's waist as she led me towards the bedrooms.

"This is my room," she announced, looking almost nervous as she gestured for me to go in.

Just like the rest of the house, it had a comfortable, lived-in feel. We stepped inside, stopping a few feet from the door as I took a look around at the king-sized bed and the large windows overlooking the backyard and pool. I could easily picture her lounging on the bed in soft, silky pajamas, or slipping out of those pajamas as she stepped into the large ensuite bathroom. My body began to react to the mental images, and her next words didn't help.

"There are a couple of guest rooms down the hall. You're welcome to sleep anywhere you like."

I turned back to her, one eyebrow raised in a teasing challenge. "Anywhere?"

She'd been the one who wanted to take things slow while we were at the hotel, and even though she'd invited me to come and spend the weekend, she hadn't said whether or not she wanted to move forward with our physical relationship.

For my part, I wanted to be close to her in every way possible. Sure, it was fast, especially coming out of a very long-term relationship, but when Jen and I were together, it felt completely right and natural that we should take the next step.

Nothing had ever felt so right.

Although she tried, Jen couldn't hold back her smile. "Why do I get the feeling you're not thinking about sleeping right now?"

"Because you're incredibly good at reading people. That's what makes you so good at your job."

"False flattery won't get you anywhere," she laughed.

"It's not false, it's absolutely true." I took a step closer to her, the room seeming to narrow around us as our bodies came into closer proximity. "I bet you can read my mind right now."

Jen's smile faded, her eyes staying locked on mine as her hand came up to rest against my chest.

"I think you're still very much on the rebound and don't know what you want," she told me gently. "An hour ago, you walked out of my sister's apartment rather than talk to me. I'm not blaming you for that, but I think it shows that your emotions are heightened."

"I walked out, but I came back. I came back because something keeps pulling me to you. I think you feel it too."

I stepped even closer, so only her hand on my chest separated us. My hips were close enough to hers that she had to notice how hard I'd been ever since we walked into her room and I started imagining her there in her most private, intimate moments.

"I feel... something."

Her eyes dropped, letting me know exactly what she meant, and we both laughed before I reached out to brush her hair behind her ear, resting my fingers on the side of her face so she couldn't look away. "I won't rush you if you're not ready, but I am. I trust you. In spite of everything, I do. I really like you, and I want you. That much is painfully obvious."

My hips pushed against her again, just enough that she felt it, and she looked up at me from beneath her lashes. Desire filled her hazel eyes, the same desire I saw in them that night at the hotel when I made her come.

She seemed to be thinking about that night too, if her next words were any indication. "We never talked about the fact that you went to go buy condoms after leaving my hotel."

I choked out a laugh, remembering the photo among the others Celine's investigator took. "No, we didn't. I didn't plan on telling you, but I wanted to be prepared."

"Well, I don't think we need one right now," she said. A sharp stab of disappointment hit me, I couldn't deny that, but I nodded anyway.

"Of course. It's up to you. Maybe we could just sit in the living room and talk for a while, or we could…"

Jen raised her hand to press a finger to my lips. "Hold on. I didn't say we have to leave this room, only that a condom won't be required."

Blood raced to my cock as I tried to decipher her meaning. "You want me to touch you? I would love to, Jen. I'd love to touch all of you, to taste you…"

Her whole hand replaced her finger, covering my mouth entirely. "That's not what I meant. You're the one with the *painful* problem, and you've already seen me come. I haven't seen how you look when you do yet. Maybe it's time we change that."

~Jennifer~

Part of me still wanted to take things slow with Gabe, especially after the awkwardness between us that morning when he found out about

Eda and Monica's involvement in the whole situation. However, when he looked at me with the kind of desire and determination I could see shining in his eyes in my bedroom, it made it hard to remember *why* we should wait.

He wanted me. I wanted him. We were both consenting adults, he'd left his wife and had no intention of going back to her. Seen from that viewpoint, nothing stood in our way.

So, what did?

The more I thought about it, the more I realized that *I* did.

As I told him in San Francisco, I didn't want to be a rebound for him. I didn't want him to rush when his whole life had been turned around.

I thought I had his best interests at heart, but maybe fear played a part as well. With my rather unusual job, I'd gotten very good at erecting a wall between sexual advances and real emotion. Letting someone past those walls didn't come naturally anymore. Being vulnerable and opening myself up to the possibility of being hurt by someone I actually cared about felt completely foreign.

Not since Matt had I truly cared about being rejected, and for that reason, I held back from diving all the way in the way that Gabe seemed ready to.

Gabe took a chance on me by giving me the benefit of the doubt when I lied to him, by coming back and giving me another shot.

He'd been brave.

I could try to be too.

When I slid my hand down the front of his pants, pressing my palm over the erection starting to grow against me, he let out a stifled groan beneath my other hand that covered his mouth.

"I want to make you feel good," he pleaded, the words muffled against my fingers.

"You already did that at the hotel," I reminded him. "It's my turn."

"You don't have to do that."

Longing and hesitation warred in his eyes, and I softened my voice and lowered my hand from his lips before asking the next question.

"Didn't Celine take care of you sometimes, just for fun?"

I didn't *want* to bring her up, didn't want her there in that room with us, but I needed to understand the reason for the concern darkening his gorgeous blue eyes.

Embarrassment twisted his lips but he answered honestly, holding my gaze. "Usually only when she wanted something."

From his reaction, I figured as much. Despite our brief acquaintance, I expected that Gabe would prove to be a giving, unselfish lover, the same as in every other aspect of his life, and the idea of anyone, *especially* Celine, taking advantage of that made my blood boil.

Rather than letting my anger simmer, though, I redirected that heat into something much more productive. "Well, what *I* want is for you to enjoy yourself. You're here as my guest, and I take good care of my guests."

Giving him a wink, I let my other hand slide down his body to join the one still lightly stroking the front of his pants. Together, they undid his belt buckle in no time, popped the button of his jeans open, and pulled down the zipper almost before he had time to breathe.

"Jen." My name came out of his mouth as a groan, and I tilted my head up to press my lips to his at the same time my hand slid into his pants, feeling his stiff cock with only his underwear between it and my fingers.

Gabe's sharp inhale satisfied me almost as much as feeling his hands on me did. This act might be focused on him, but I would definitely be getting my own enjoyment out of it too.

My fingers hooked into the waist of his jeans and underwear, pulling them both down over his ass while I kissed him deeper. His hands cupped the back of my head, holding onto me for dear life as I reached back between us to free his cock fully and ran my palm down the bare length of him.

"Fuck."

Gabe mumbled the word into my mouth as my hand wrapped around him and squeezed. His cock already had a decent girth to it, growing thicker almost by the second within my grip. Anticipation began to pool deep in my centre as I broke our kiss and slid down his body, sinking to my knees on the bedroom floor.

"Oh, fuck."

He seemed to have forgotten any other words. Glassy blue eyes stared down at me, and I held his gaze as I lifted his cock to my lips. Watching his lips part and his body shudder as my tongue darted out to lick his head, I couldn't remember the last time I felt so powerfully sexy.

Men told me every day they found me sexy. They flirted, seduced, even cheated on their significant others, at least over text, because they couldn't resist me. But none of it mattered, none of it felt important, because those men meant nothing to me. Their words of admiration meant nothing because they came from men with no character to back them up. A compliment from Gabe equalled a thousand from those other men put together, and the way he looked down at me when I took him into my mouth, the awe and desperation in his gaze, was the very best compliment I could ask for.

Dropping my eyes, I focused entirely on the task at hand... or in my mouth, as it were. Veins lined the stiff length of him, and my tongue slipped over them as I took him in deeper and deeper with each bob of my head. For a full minute, I sucked on him, one hand wrapped around the base of his shaft and the other cupping his balls. The thick head of his cock pressed against the back of my throat as I swallowed around him, drawing out another groan from above my head.

"I'm... shit." He mumbled the words as his hands gently brushed the hair back from my face. "This is embarrassing. I'm close, Jen."

I pulled back, releasing his cock with a satisfied slurp. "I take it as a compliment. Means I'm doing a good job."

"You are," he confirmed, tilting my chin up so my eyes met his. "It feels so fucking good, but I want you to feel good too. Let me..."

"No."

I cut him off decisively before turning back to the cock in front of me, licking my lips at the sight of it. A perfect length for me, not too long but long enough I would definitely feel it when I had it inside me later, and I'd already decided I *would* have him later.

First, though, I planned to finish what I'd started. "Let *me*."

Before he could protest any further, I took him in again, all the way in so that my nose pressed against his abdomen, and any other words Gabe might have intended to say disappeared in a strangled moan.

My hand began to stroke his base, pumping in harmony with my mouth, savouring every inch of him and the symphony of guttural sounds coming from deep in his throat. With my other hand still on his balls, I felt the moment they began to tighten. His breathing shortened, coming in quick gasps, and his warm release soon followed, his hands tightening in my hair and his cock pumping hard in my mouth while I swallowed every drop.

Slowly, I pulled back, letting his cock fall from my lips before placing a soft kiss against his hip. He groaned once more, his hand caressing the back of my head before I stood back up and placed one more kiss at the side of his mouth.

"I'm glad you're here," I whispered.

A warm puff of air curled over my skin with his breathy laugh. "I am too. That was incredible."

"Good. Let's go have some lunch."

With that, I turned and walked out of the room, my grin spreading wider at the thought of the almost limitless possibilities the rest of the day held.

Chapter Fifteen

~Gabriel~

It took me a minute or two to collect myself after one of the most incredible blowjobs of my life, but eventually, I shoved my cock back into my pants and found my way back to the kitchen. By that time, Jen had already pulled out various ingredients for our lunch, everything lined up neatly on her large countertop as she placed a pan on the stove and turned on the gas burner.

"What are we having?" I asked, stepping forward until my body pressed into her back, my lips finding the side of her neck as I placed gentle kisses along the delicate curve.

A satisfied sigh hummed in her throat and she leaned back against me for just a moment before straightening up again. "Crab cakes. Do you want to make a side salad?"

"Sure. All this stuff here?"

Reluctantly, I pulled myself away from her and stepped over to where she had laid out some spinach, strawberries, feta cheese, honey and balsamic vinegar. My mouth started to water at the sight of it, reminding me that I never did eat breakfast that morning.

"Yeah." She turned back to her other ingredients, confidently tossing things in a mixing bowl. "Can you figure it out?"

She threw me a teasing grin over her shoulder, but it felt like a test too, to see whether I knew my way around the kitchen or not.

Luckily, I did. "I think I can manage. Do you cook a lot?"

"No one else is going to do it for me," she answered matter-of-factly. "But yes, I enjoy it most of the time. What about you?"

"I enjoy it too."

Other words sat on the tip of my tongue, about how Celine had a long list of food she disliked so the variety of meals I prepared had been pretty limited in recent years, or how she never enjoyed cooking together, but I didn't want to keep bringing her up. If I wanted this new relationship to grow, and I really did, we had to move past the initial thing that we had in common: my wife.

Reading my mind, Jen turned to me, temporarily stopping her mixing. "You don't have to hold back if you want to talk about her. She was a huge part of your life for a long time. I don't expect you to pretend she didn't exist."

I could have told her my reasons for holding back: how Celine always hated when I mentioned anyone I'd dated before so I'd taught myself not to, or how Jen herself had expressed concern that I might not be ready to move on, and I worried that mentioning Celine too much would prove her right.

I could have told her any of that, but I kept it simple and straightforward instead. "I would rather be thinking about you."

The honest answer drew a mischievous smile on her lips. "After I just sucked your cock, I would hope so."

My laugh nearly choked me, and the grin stayed on her face as she turned back to her work.

After preparing the salad, I followed Jen's instructions to find some dishes for our lunch, and when the crab cakes were ready, we took everything outside to her back porch where a small circular table had two chairs set up, one on either side, perfect for a cozy meal. Jen ducked back into the house to get a bottle of white wine from the fridge, one of the bottles she picked up in Napa, and we talked and ate together in the warm afternoon air, the conversation flowing between us just as easily as it always had. Now that we'd met each other's sisters, we talked more about our families and about our lives growing up, getting to know each other better just as I hoped we would when she first suggested I come and spend the weekend with her.

"You have quite a lot of privacy back here," I commented after we'd finished eating and were sitting back with another glass of wine, enjoying the California afternoon. From where we sat, I couldn't see any spot where anyone else could see into her yard.

"I really like how deep the house goes from the street," Jen agreed. "It means the backyard is smaller than the surrounding yards, but more secluded. The house almost completely blocks my neighbours' view into the yard."

That sounded like a good trade-off to me, especially since I'd been dying to reciprocate the incredible pleasure she gave me before lunch. "So, no one could see us if I do this?"

In one fluid motion, I placed my wine on the table, got to my feet and made the two steps around the table to her chair. Knees bent, one hand slipped around the back of her neck, tilting her head upwards so I could claim her mouth in a deep, slow kiss.

She didn't waste a second in indecision, kissing me back just as eagerly as if she'd been waiting the whole meal for me to do it.

Maybe she had been.

Slowly, I lowered down onto my knees at the side of her chair before grabbing the chair's arms and tilting it back just enough that I could pivot it towards me. Jen gasped in surprise before letting out a surprised chuckle and spreading her legs to let me settle between them.

"Lunch was really good," I murmured. "But you taste even better."

My fingers slid up the length of her capris, my thumb running up her inner thigh until it rested just below the juncture between her legs. I'd had just a teaser the other night when I licked my fingers that had been inside her, but it made a poor substitute for the full experience.

"I'd love to taste more of you."

A shiver worked its way through her body, leaving her trembling under my touch. "Out here?"

"You just said no one can see us," I reminded her. "And I don't think I can wait."

An exaggeration, obviously. I could if I had to, but I really didn't want to, and when my fingers found the button of her pants, Jen made no move to stop me.

Despite having fingered her in the hotel in San Francisco, feeling the delicious heat of her on my hand, I still hadn't actually seen her yet. The mere idea of it made my mouth water even more than the sight of food had earlier, and when she lifted her hips from the chair to allow me to pull down the white capris and the white underwear beneath it, I got my first look at her pretty pussy as I spread her legs even wider. With the care she took about her whole appearance, it didn't surprise me to find her waxed and smooth, and I swallowed hard to stop myself from drooling as I leaned in and inhaled.

"God, you smell good."

My cock had completely forgotten its earlier satisfaction, stiffening uncomfortably in my pants, but I ignored it as I dipped my head to get my first real taste of her.

"Gabe."

Jen gasped my name as my tongue connected with her clit, tracing around it and over it as I learned the topography of her body. From there, I moved lower, drawing a line down to her entrance, wet and ready for me. A happy hum vibrated in my chest as I dipped my tongue inside her, echoed by the sweet sound of her moan above me.

No description I could think of would do justice to the taste of her, simply because it tasted of *her*. I only knew that I loved it and craved it, wanting more even with her still on my tongue. Already, I knew that I'd miss her flavour when we were apart.

Wanting to get deeper, I brought her legs up and hooked them over my shoulders, pulling her ass towards me and tilting her up so I could bury my face more fully. Jen's hands tightened around the arms of the chair as she writhed against every swipe of my tongue and gentle scrape of my teeth.

"Stay still," I directed from between her legs, my eyes flicking up to find her stare locked on me, her lips parted and her cheeks flushed with the heat of her impending orgasm. "Stay still and hold on tight."

Two fingers pressed inside her as my mouth returned to her clit, and Jen let out an involuntary cry, a plea and a curse that begged me not to let her down. I had no intention of it. Pumping into her with my hand, curling my fingers to drag against her skin, I sucked her clit into my mouth, pushing her harder and harder until she came. Her thighs trembled around my head while my tongue went back to her pussy to lick up every drop, and just as I predicted, almost as soon as I pulled back, I wanted to do it again.

"You are... really... good at that," she eventually managed to breathe once her chest stopped heaving.

"I guess we're evenly matched, then, because you're damn good too."

I pushed myself back to my feet, giving her a clear view of the straining erection inside my pants that she had taken care of for me earlier, but which had returned in full. Jen swallowed again, her eyes on my groin for a long moment before she looked back up at me.

"I suppose we better move this inside because I don't think we're done quite yet."

~Jennifer~

Gabe didn't even wait to let me pick up my pants and underwear before lifting me off the chair, one arm around my back and the other beneath my knees, cradling me against his chest. His mouth melded into mine, kissing me long and deep with the taste of my orgasm still fresh on his tongue, the same way the evidence of it remained slick between my legs.

"Which way is your bedroom again?" he mumbled as he stepped back into the house, kicking the door closed behind him. His eyes had opened so he didn't run into anything, but his lips stayed close to mine, like he couldn't bear to let go.

"Down the hall to the left," I instructed, snuggling my face into the crook of his neck so he could see which way to go and I could inhale his clean, masculine scent. Even though he just made me come, my desire hadn't dampened at all. If anything, the thought of having him inside me made me want him even more, and there didn't seem to be any doubt that we were heading towards that intimacy in the next few minutes.

Everything between us felt easy, and right, and inevitable. Just how it should be when you met someone suited for you. That it should happen to be with someone I met through my job, I never would have predicted, not in a million years.

Life threw up surprises, both good and bad. I'd had the bad. The very worst. I dealt with it because I had no choice, but now that the good had come, I got to choose, and I would make the choice to embrace it.

As soon as my back hit the mattress, Gabe laying me down gently but with undeniable intent, his fingers went to the buttons of my blouse, eager to remove the remaining clothes I still wore. He pulled the un-buttoned fabric open, his eyes lingering on my breasts for a moment before he dipped his head, scraping his teeth over my nipples through the fabric of my bra.

"Yes," I moaned, my back arching up to try and deepen the contact. My thighs rubbed together, the aching need already returning between them, and I reached behind my back to undo my bra before Gabe had a chance. Maybe if I got fully naked more quickly, he wouldn't be far behind.

A sound somewhere between a groan and a growl rumbled against me as the bra loosened. With a firm yank, he pulled it down, revealing my breasts and the puckered nipple he'd just been teasing. When his mouth returned, sucking hard over my bare skin, my stomach clenched with desire.

"You have a condom, right?" I gasped, grabbing him by the hair and pulling his head up to make it clear no further foreplay would be needed. I wanted him and I didn't want to wait any longer.

With an almost sheepish smile, he reached into his pocket and pulled one out. "Fresh from the store. I have photographic proof."

No further words were necessary as I tossed the rest of my clothes aside and he shed his, both of us naked together for the first time. I knew how his cock looked and how it tasted, but I didn't know how it felt inside me, and I wanted so badly to know. I *needed* it. If a photographer had shown up in the middle of my bedroom at that moment, I didn't know if I could stop.

Gabe's eyes roamed over my body for a few seconds before he tore the condom wrapper open with his teeth and rolled the latex over his stiff cock, fingers almost slipping in his haste. Every action proclaimed his impatience, his need to be inside me just as strong as my wish to have him there.

At last, after what felt like minutes but probably took no more than twenty seconds, he climbed onto the bed with me, spreading my legs around him in that firm, possessive, surprisingly dominant manner that aroused me so much in San Francisco.

"This is the first time I'll fuck you," he said, his hand reaching between my legs and two fingers pressing inside, checking I was still ready for him. Of course I was. "But it won't be the last, Jen. This is just the beginning."

"Just the beginning," I agreed, my legs wrapping around him to draw him closer, letting him know just how much I wanted him. "What are you waiting for?"

Obviously not one to back down from a challenge, Gabe thrust into me so hard and fast that my hands slapped against the mattress, the sudden sensation of being completely filled by him straddling the line between pleasure and pain.

"Fucking hell," he muttered above me, pausing there to savour the moment. "Even better... than I imagined."

The breath he had to take in the middle of the sentence brought a smile to my lips, and any lingering pain fell away immediately when he began to move. Slowly at first, his hips rolled against me, pulling out and thrusting back in, each time feeling a little deeper than the one before, even though I knew that couldn't be possible. Maybe it just felt that way because with each stroke, he claimed a little more space in my memory, branding himself in me in a way that would never leave me.

My hands moved on their own, tugging on his hair, down his neck, my nails scraping his shoulders while my heels dug into his ass that tightened with each push of his cock into me. His thrusts sped up, coming harder as I called out his name.

"Don't go easy on me, Gabe."

"I won't," he grunted, his blue eyes staring down at me with a possessiveness I didn't expect. "You're going to be feeling me all week, Jen. When we're apart, you need to remember this."

I would, I had no doubt. When his fingers slid between us to find my clit, my brain refused to form any more words. Gasps and cries, yes, but nothing that could be called language. It didn't matter; he got the message anyway, rubbing and fucking me until my orgasm crested and pulled me under.

Gabe's body stuttered as I shuddered, his orgasm coming hard and fast on the heels of mine. He pulsed inside me while I contracted around him, our bodies having one final wordless conversation, one last give and take before he pulled out of me and rolled over onto the bed next to me, out of breath, a little sweaty, and just as utterly satisfied as me.

Only after I rolled over to cuddle up next to him, my head on his shoulder and my hand on his chest, did I realize that everything else had faded away during those intense moments of physical connection. Not once did I think about Celine or Matt or loyalty tests or private investigators, and that, more than anything else had so far, reassured me that we were both exactly where we were meant to be.

~Gabriel~

Despite the stumbling start to the day with the shock of seeing Jen at Eda's apartment, the rest of the day couldn't have gone any better. Everything between us felt easy. Effortless.

Perfect.

After having sex in Jen's bedroom, we went for a swim in her pool and took a shower together afterwards, fucking again in her shower. We barbecued chicken kebabs for supper and ate out on the patio, trading more travel stories, and when we came back inside to clean up after our meal, we ended up naked again, her perched on top of the counter as I drove into her.

I should have bought more condoms.

Back in her bed, we fucked one more time before getting ready to sleep, both of us exhausted in the best possible way.

"You didn't do any work today," I said, only realizing it when she checked her phone before laying it face-down on the bedside table and flipping off the light before climbing into bed next to me. "Do you usually take the weekends off?"

She shook her head before laying it down on my shoulder, her body curling against mine like it belonged there. "Weekends are usually the busiest days for me, actually, but I can take time off when I need to. I just have to plan ahead."

"Today counted as a 'need to' occasion?"

"What do you think?" I could hear the smile in her voice as she snuggled in deeper beside me. "I had a wonderful time today, Gabe."

"Me too." If I dwelled too long on just how wonderful it had been, my cock would get too hard to go to sleep, so I forced my thoughts in a different direction instead. "Can I ask you something personal?"

"After everything we've done today, I think we're past the point of needing to ask permission."

Her teasing tone, warm and affectionate, landed on my skin like an embrace, putting me at ease.

"You're amazing."

She lifted her head to peer at me in the darkened room. "That's not a question."

"You didn't let me finish." My hand on the side of her head pushed her back down onto my shoulder, eliciting a soft giggle from her.

"You're amazing," I repeated. "Men fall for you in a matter of minutes all the time. Why aren't you in a relationship?"

I suspected it had something to do with her former fiancé, but I didn't want to put words in her mouth, preferring to hear her perspective on it instead.

A soft sigh blew against my chest, and somehow, that exhale told me her answer would be the truth. "I wasn't ready for a long time. It's not that I think we only get one love in our lives or anything like that, but the idea of opening myself up again to someone new, of letting them see the real me and not just the me that I pretend to be online, scared me."

"I can understand that." My fingers gently trailed up and down her soft arm, keeping us connected physically as well as emotionally through this conversation. "Have you dated?"

"Yes. I try to, at least, every now and then, but I never figured out how to stop myself from comparing the men I go out with to Matt. It always feels like he's there in the room, at least in the back of my mind. It's not fair to them, so it never goes very far."

I knew very well how a person could haunt your thoughts, even when they were still alive. "Is he in the room with us right now?"

I phrased it as a joke, hoping she'd laugh, and she did, her chest vibrating against my side in a low, sexy chuckle. "No. That's how I knew you were different. When we were first together in person, Matt kept his distance. It felt like a sign to me."

Warmth bloomed in my chest, my heart taking that as the compliment she obviously meant it to be.

"I think I know what you mean. At lunch, you told me that I could talk about Celine if I want to, but since then, she really hasn't been on my mind at all. I think I needed to hear from you that she wouldn't be an issue between us, and that freed me from worrying about it."

Her nails scratched lightly across my chest. "I know you can't just forget about her. You loved her."

"I did. I wouldn't have married her otherwise. But I think..."

I trailed off as all the emotions of the past ten days washed over me: the disbelief at her betrayal of our vows, the shock at her cold dismissal when I confronted her about it, the helplessness when she lied and manipulated the situation with Jen, and one more thing, something I'd barely allowed myself to admit that I felt.

Relief.

Relief that I didn't have to carry the marriage for both of us anymore. Relief that I could move on and possibly find more happiness than I ever had with her.

"I think that maybe I loved the idea of her more than I actually loved *her*. That sounds terrible, doesn't it?"

"I don't think so." Jen's voice sounded lower in the darkness, when I couldn't see the brightness of her eyes. "I think we can all be guilty of seeing what we want to see sometimes. With Matt gone, it's easy to forget that we ever fought or that he had imperfect qualities. Some days, I worry that I've forgotten the reality of him and only remember the fantasy I built up in my head."

"That's exactly it. I think I had that fantasy even though Celine isn't gone. She was right there with me, but I still saw everything through the lens of who I wanted her to be rather than accept the clues she gave me about her true character."

We lapsed into silence, both of us absorbing that and pondering the implications of what I said.

Jen spoke her thoughts out loud first. "How do you know you won't do the same with me? See me as who you want me to be, I mean, instead of who I am?"

Luckily, I'd just been thinking about the same thing, so I had an answer for her. "Well, for one thing, I never had a conversation like this with Celine. I can't imagine how it would have gone if I tried. And more than that, I think that even though we've only known each other for a few weeks, I understand you in a way I never fully understood her. I think you understand me better too. Is that crazy?"

"I don't think so." She pressed a kiss into my chest, her lips warm against my skin. "I feel that way with you too. We see the world in a similar way. Not exactly the same, because that would be boring, but close enough that things feel comfortable with you. We can be open without having to worry about misjudging the fundamentals. I think this could be something real, Gabe."

"I think so too." I hooked her chin with one finger, tilting her head up so I could place a soft kiss on her lips. "If it doesn't freak you out too much, I'd like to start looking for jobs around here."

"Is that smart?"

Even in the dark, she seemed to sense my frown, and she quickly clarified further.

"I mean, until things are settled with Celine, we're supposed to be staying away from each other."

Right. I'd almost forgotten about that, and as fatigue set in, I didn't want to worry about it too much that night.

"There's no harm in looking. I'll have to give notice and make moving arrangements, so it won't happen right away, but at least I can get the process started."

"That sounds good." The sigh she released sounded pleased, and relieved, and tired, so I stopped talking to let her get some rest. Before long, we both drifted off to sleep.

Chapter Sixteen

~Jennifer~

By the time Eda and Monica arrived at my house the next day, Gabe and I had lunch ready and waiting for them. It felt strangely familiar and comfortable for us to act as hosts together, and the more time I spent with Monica, the more I liked her. She seemed to have inherited the impulsive, extroverted genes in the family while Gabe tended to be more introspective, but they balanced each other out well, a lot like Eda and I did.

The conversation centred mostly around work. Monica had a lot of questions about my job, and I learned about her career while Eda and Gabe filled each other in on their day-to-day lives. Neither of the other women asked Gabe or I anything about our time together or our relationship in general, which felt out of character. They must have decided between themselves not to push us on the subject while we were all together, so I fully expected to be grilled by Eda once Gabe left.

The Carter siblings had to leave by mid-afternoon to get back to San Francisco at a reasonable hour, and Gabe and I shared an awkward moment on the front steps to say goodbye, knowing both our sisters were watching.

"I'm going to start looking for work here," he reminded me, his fingers brushing lightly along my cheek. "And I'll speak to my lawyer tomorrow and try to get a better timeline of when everything might be settled. I hate the idea of being away from you for very long."

I hated it too, but I could also appreciate that a little distance might be a good thing. In his presence, everything else fell away. Time apart might give us more perspective to examine our feelings and make sure that we weren't rushing into anything.

"Let me know when you're home safely."

Our lips brushed together softly, not at all the kind of earth-shattering, tongue-devouring kisses we'd shared over the past 24 hours, but enough to send a trail of goosebumps down my arms anyway. The feel of him, the smell of him, the sight of him, even while walking away... I loved it all.

"Oh, yeah. You've got it bad." Eda snorted once the car drove out of sight and the two of us walked back into my house. "The way you were looking at him? The only one more lovesick than you is him."

"I'm not lovesick," I argued, flopping down onto the sofa with a dreamy sigh that undercut my words. "I'm just happy. Is that a bad thing?"

"It's not a bad thing at all." My sister sat next to me, taking my hand in hers. "I'm happy *for* you. From all the things Monica told me this weekend, he sounds great."

"You probably know him better than I do now," I teased.

A wicked grin lit up her face. "I'm not so sure about that. I'm guessing you know him pretty well after this weekend, with that freshly-fucked look you have going on."

I almost choked on thin air. "What? I do not."

Her cackle filled the air between us as my cheeks heated.

"*If* I had a freshly-fucked look, which I don't, how would you even remember what it looks like?" I demanded, trying to keep some control over the conversation.

Almost instantly, the laughter stopped and the smile fled her face, replaced by a sympathetic purse of her lips. "It's been a long time, I know. Monica and I talked about it, and I'm worried I haven't been very helpful."

My head pressed into the back of the couch as I let out a groan. "You talked about my dry spell with Gabe's sister?"

Eda shrugged. "Neither of us have much of a filter. You don't want to know all the stuff we talked about."

No, I probably didn't.

"You know that I loved Matt," Eda continued, "but Monica suggested that I put him on too much of a pedestal, making you feel like no one else would ever be good enough."

"You didn't do that. But maybe I did? Or maybe I just wasn't truly ready to move on before now. Gabe and I actually talked about something similar."

"It's good that you feel comfortable talking to him about Matt," Eda ventured, and I had to agree.

"Yeah. There isn't much that doesn't feel comfortable with him."

"And what about Celine?" Eda asked, addressing the elephant in the otherwise cozy room. "What's going on with your business?"

That part, I actually *didn't* share with Gabe, since I didn't want him to feel bad. When he asked about me not working the day before, I said I arranged to take the time off. The other part, the part I didn't tell him, was that I'd had far fewer enquiries than usual over the past two days.

The situation didn't call for full-blown panic yet, but letting it go without issuing some kind of response might not be possible after all. If I didn't want the rumours and speculation to grow, I'd probably have to address them.

"Gabe said he's going to talk to his lawyer tomorrow, and I might try to talk to her too to find out exactly what I can say about the situation without affecting the divorce proceedings. Celine is succeeding at causing trouble if nothing else. I still can't believe they drove down here to avoid her spies. Did Monica tell you about their car chase?"

"Of course! I'm jealous. If you ever get a stalker, you better ask me for help."

We shared a laugh before Eda brought the conversation back to Celine.

"She's not really going to get half of his inheritance, is she?"

She grimaced at the thought, and so did I. "I really hope not. He's going to do everything he can to fight it, and I'll do everything I can to help."

We chatted for another hour before Eda left to get ready for her upcoming week and I settled in with my work laptop and phone for the first time in two days. Unfortunately, my inbox had more scathing messages in it than anything else, angry rants from women accusing me of abusing my position and betraying the women I claimed to help.

This had to stop.

My blood simmering in my veins, I drafted a detailed post to explain the situation from my point of view. In the morning, I would try to run through it with Gabe's lawyer and get her approval before I posted it. It might not convince everyone, but at the moment, everyone only heard Celine's side. I had to at least give them a choice of whom to believe.

As much as I wanted to believe everything could be as easy and comfortable as the weekend with Gabe had been, I knew that we still had a few hurdles to get over first, and restoring my reputation would be the first one to cross off the list.

~Gabriel~

By the time Monica dropped me off at my house, we'd worked everything out between us. She promised not to share intimate details of my life with complete strangers going forward and I shared how things went with Jen over the weekend. *Not* the intimate details, obviously, but the more general ones, and my sister couldn't have been more thrilled.

"I'm going to miss you if you move to Pasadena," she pouted, but a twinkle in her eye gave her away.

"What are you up to?"

"What?" She tried to fake innocence, but I knew her too well for that.

"You're up to something. What is it?"

It didn't take her long to crack. "Eda introduced me to some of her friends in the LA theatre scene this weekend. I might be able to get some work there, and she said I could move in temporarily while I figure out if I want to make the move."

"That's moving pretty fast," I couldn't help pointing out.

"As opposed to you, Mr I-broke-up-with-my-wife-a-week-ago-and-already-have-a-girl-friend?"

Point taken, but I tried to defend myself anyway. "Jen and I haven't defined a relationship yet."

The lift of her eyebrows said more than a hundred words could. "Don't bullshit me. You like her a lot, and I like her too."

With that endorsement still ringing in my ears, I let myself into the house Celine and I had shared for the past two years, and nearly dropped my bag in surprise when I found her sitting at the kitchen table.

"What are you doing here?" I managed to gulp out between rushed intakes of breath.

"Last I checked, my name is still on the deed." She didn't offer even a smug smile, her expression set and serious. "Sit down, Gabe."

Figuring it would be better to get whatever she had in mind over with, I took a seat across from her. "What do you want?"

"You know what I want. I have the paperwork all drawn up." She tapped a stack of papers on the table next to her that I hadn't even registered yet. "Sign this agreement and I'll get out of your life for good."

Looking at the hard lines of her face, such a contrast to Jen's soft, warm smile, I struggled to remember why I ever found her attractive. "That's between our lawyers now. I'm not talking to you about this."

"I had a feeling you'd say that, but this has to be dealt with tonight."

My eyebrows shot up in disbelief. "I'm not signing anything tonight. Why would I..."

My words died off as she pulled a photo out from beneath the pile of papers and slid it across the table to me.

A photo of me and Jen kissing each other goodbye on the front porch of her house earlier that day, Monica standing by the car and Eda on the porch next to us. My blood ran cold for a second before heating in my veins and I raised my eyes back to her with thinly-veiled fury. "How did you get this?"

She couldn't have had us followed, not after Monica lost the guy tailing us.

The first sign of a smirk showed on her face, a tug on her lips that only made her look crueller. "The hotel you two shacked up at in Napa had a lot of interesting information."

The rest remained unsaid but I filled in the blanks easily enough: she got Jen's address from the hotel's reservation system. Obviously, she had a way of accessing their security footage to get the photos of us there, so it shouldn't have surprised me that she'd gotten into their computer system too, but even after all her scheming, I still couldn't quite comprehend the lengths she seemed willing to go to.

"I bet there are a lot of people who would be interested in knowing where she lives. A lot of men whose lives she ruined. It would be a shame if it somehow got posted online."

The heat that had been building inside me vanished in an instant, replaced with ice-cold fear. Jen didn't ruin anyone's lives; the men ruined their relationships all by themselves by cheating in the first place, but I would bet a lot of them didn't see it that way. What if someone with a grudge took things too far? "You can't post her address. Doxxing is illegal. It's..."

"Very difficult to prove," she interrupted, sounding almost bored as she threatened to expose Jen to dangers I could barely begin to imagine. "Do you think I haven't figured out how to post it so that no one could trace it back to me? It'd be your word against mine."

My eyes bore into her, trying to find some scrap of empathy or decency, and came up empty. "Why are you trying to ruin her? You're the one who hired her! She did exactly what you asked her to, so why do you have it out for her?"

"What I hired her for?" Celine scoffed. "I hired her to prove you're a cheater, not to actually cheat with you. She crossed the line."

That answer made no sense to me. "She told me that you pushed her to meet me in person but she refused."

"And then she did it anyway. She hooked you for herself."

"Why do you care?" I exploded, slamming the palms of my hands down on the table so hard that she jumped. "You wanted to get rid of me, and you did."

"I didn't want you to fall in love with her!"

The words hung heavy in the air between us, ringing with sincerity. They might have been the first true thing she said all night.

Through parted lips, Celine drew in a deep breath, trying to regain her composure, but I pushed harder while I saw the crack in her armour.

"Why does it matter to you if I love her?"

I used the words even though I hadn't said them to Jen yet, hadn't even said them to myself. A declaration of love seemed premature, but I couldn't deny we were heading towards it. It certainly felt possible in the near future.

I thought Celine might ignore the question or turn it back on me somehow, but she didn't. The crack in her carefully constructed facade widened a little more as she replied, "Because you never loved me. Not like that."

"Of course I loved you." I told Jen the same thing the night before when we were talking about Celine and I meant it both times.

"Not like that," she repeated. "I know how passionate you can be about the things you love. About travel and food and stupid stuff like that."

'Stupid stuff'. The fact that she would refer to my interests that way exemplified everything wrong in our relationship.

"You were never like that about me. You tried to be, I'll give you that, but it never came naturally. Not like it does with her."

That was... surprisingly insightful, and not completely incorrect. Things with Celine had never been like they were with Jen. I thought they were good between us, but maybe only because I didn't know how good they could truly be with the right person.

"I realized it just before you proposed," she carried on, dropping all her defenses as her shoulders slumped. "I almost broke up with you then because you didn't seem to realize it the same way I did."

I remembered the way she had started to pull away then, and how I thought I wouldn't have even been that upset if it had been the end. "But then you found out I had all this money coming and you decided you could stick it out long enough to get your hands on it?"

Bitterness seeped into my words and Celine's posture stiffened. "You were using me. It seemed like a fair trade."

"Those two things are not equal. I tried to love you, Celine. I wanted to."

"You shouldn't have had to *try*."

No, I shouldn't have. I could see that now in a way I didn't at the time. It didn't excuse what she'd done, what she still wanted to do, but I had to accept it as an explanation.

"Things are different with Jen," I admitted softly. "She didn't plan it to be that way and neither did I. Nothing would have ever happened between us if you hadn't pushed us together. Why did you do it? Why not wait another year and avoid all of this?"

Once again, I didn't know whether or not to expect an answer, but again, she surprised me by giving me one. "I fell in love. It's different with him too. I guess now you know how that feels."

Well, we'd certainly made a mess of things. Her more than me, certainly, but maybe I should have picked up on the signs too. Maybe I should have realized that when I didn't fall apart at the idea of losing her, I shouldn't have proposed to her when she pressured me to.

Maybe I should have trusted that the right woman for me was out there somewhere. I just had to find her.

"I'm sure we can reach a reasonable settlement," I offered as gently as I could, but as soon as the words were out of my mouth, all traces of vulnerability in Celine fell away. The cold, hard lines framed her face once more.

"I need the whole amount. There are debts I need to pay. You'll sign *this* agreement or I'll release Jen's address. It's not a negotiation, Gabe. It's an ultimatum."

"What debts?" I asked, momentarily distracted by her admission.

She shrugged defensively. "I got a few credit cards to pay for some of the things your salary didn't cover. I knew I could pay it off when your inheritance came through."

Well, that explained where she got the money to hire Celine and whatever investigator had been following us. The idea that she'd been accumulating credit card debt while I rode the bus to work and took a packed lunch every day should have made my blood boil, but at that point, I'd become almost numb to her deception. I could have asked how much money we were talking about, but I probably didn't want to know.

"I can't sign anything without even reading it," I tried to reason with her instead. "Give me until tomorrow."

I didn't know what good one more day would do, but at least I could try to come up with a plan that didn't involve destroying Jen's security or signing away half of a fortune.

Her brown eyes searched mine, eyes I once looked into and pledged myself to, eyes which now felt completely foreign to me, and eventually, she nodded.

"I'll come to your office tomorrow morning and you can give me your answer then. You want to move on, obviously, and I do too."

She pushed the papers towards me, pushing the picture of me and Jen onto the floor in the process, and left the house without another word.

What the fuck was I supposed to do now?

~Jennifer~

Worn out from the high of Gabe's visit and the comedown after he left, I planned on an early night, but a phone call interrupted my bedtime routine. I had already showered and put on my robe while I went through my skincare regime, but seeing Gabe's name on the screen, I accepted the video chat and flashed him a warm smile.

"Hey. Are you home?"

I hadn't seen much of the inside of his house yet, but he sat on a sofa, not in the car, so it seemed like a good guess.

"Yeah, I'm here."

The flatness in his tone and the tightness around his lips instantly alerted me that something had changed. The man who left my house earlier that day had been replaced by a defeated, worried version of him. "What's wrong?"

With a deep sigh, Gabe ran a hand over his face. "Celine just left."

"She has some nerve showing her face." The words slipped out before I even realized I meant to say them and they earned me a small smile, but only for a second.

"She's got a lot more nerve than that. She has more than nerve. She has your address, Jen. Someone took pictures of us at your house today."

Immediately, my eyes darted to the open windows overlooking my backyard, and I pulled my robe a little tighter around my body. "That's concerning. How did she get it?"

"From the Four Winds' computer system, apparently. I'm so sorry." He let out another deep breath, looking down at something I couldn't see before he got to the worst part. "She threatened to post it online if I don't agree to give her half the money."

My whole body froze, my mind leaping to the worst-case scenarios that Gabe had no doubt already considered. Men I'd exposed looking for revenge. Men who simply thought they had a right to me because of the pictures I posted online. People who might track me down for the sick pleasure of scaring me and those who might actually hurt me.

"Jen? You okay?"

Gabe's concerned question cut through my dark thoughts and I forced a smile onto my face that I didn't feel at all. "Yeah. I mean, I'm not great, but I'm okay. She knows that's against the law, right?"

"She does, and she doesn't care," he confirmed with a grimace. "She said we'd have no way to prove it came from her."

That sounded plausible, unfortunately. "I don't suppose you happened to record her saying that?"

"I'm afraid not." Gabe's blue eyes held my gaze through the phone screen, trying to read my mind. "I won't let her do that to you. If I have to sign these papers, I will."

"No." My head shook in determination as I pushed my fears down. "That would just be rewarding this psychotic behaviour. She can't get away with this."

"If it's between the money and your safety, then I choose you. It's no contest."

His fierce protectiveness warmed my heart, but I didn't agree with his conclusion. "I'll move. If she puts my address out there, I'll find somewhere else to live. At the end of the day, it's just a house."

"A house that you love."

I did love it, but I turned his own words back on him. "If it's between the house and justice for you, I choose you."

Before either of us could make any other suggestions, his doorbell rang.

With a frown, Gabe looked over his shoulder. "I'm not sure who that would be. Let me go check."

Rather than putting the phone down, he took me with him, dropping the screen to his side so I had a view of his jeans while he opened the door with his other hand.

"Allie?" His surprised tone came through loud and clear, but the name didn't mean anything to me.

"Hi, Gabe. Can I come in?"

"If you're here on behalf of your sister, then no. I don't think so."

"I'm not," Allie insisted. "I'm here because of her, but not *for* her."

Gabe didn't sound convinced. "I'm actually on a call." He raised the phone and the world on my screen tilted until I could see a pretty woman standing outside the door. She bore enough of a resemblance to Celine that I put the pieces together pretty quickly, guessing whose sister she must be.

I racked my brain, trying to remember anything Gabe had told me about Celine's sister. I thought I could recall him mentioning that he believed she covered for Celine during her affair, so she must have known about it. What she would want with him now, I couldn't imagine, and clearly, he couldn't either.

"Is that Jen?" Allie's gaze darted between me on the screen and Gabe off of it. "This concerns her too, so we can talk in front of her."

With my curiosity thoroughly piqued, I gave my agreement. "That's fine with me."

Outnumbered, Gabe gave in. "Alright. Come in."

The two of them walked back to the living room where Gabe had been sitting before, and he set the phone down in a holder on a piece of furniture in front of the sofa so that I had a view of both of them and he could look at Allie.

"If you know about Jen, you must know the whole story," Gabe started. "I'm guessing you knew about it all before I did."

Allie's lips pursed but she didn't deny it. Instead, she chose to make a confession. "You know that Brad travels a lot for work. A couple of years ago, I got involved with someone else during one of his trips. Celine helped me realize that I didn't love the other guy, I was just feeling unappreciated, and she covered for me. I thought her situation might be similar, that she needed some excitement but that she'd eventually come back to you and I felt I owed it to her to repay the favour. So, yes, I knew about Isaac and I didn't tell you."

I stayed quiet, watching Gabe for his reaction since I assumed he knew Allie's husband and this all had more relevance to him than it did for me.

His body remained tight, everything about him on edge. "Why are you telling me this?"

"Because when Celine got Jen involved, I realized she didn't just want a distraction, she wanted a way out, and I made her tell me why."

"You know about the inheritance?" I asked, wanting to be sure we were all on the same page.

Allie nodded. "I do, and I know the lengths she's gone to in order to make her case. However, I also know something else, something she's too blind to see."

"What's that?" Gabe asked warily.

"Isaac's only with her because of the promise of the money. He's not in love with her."

Gabe and I exchanged a look through the phone screen, and I had a feeling his thoughts mirrored mine: it would serve Celine right, quite honestly.

"How do you know?" I asked.

"She's been staying with him since leaving this house. I went over there to see her a couple of days ago and met him for the first time. During my visit, he got a phone call and left the room. I needed to use the restroom, and when I came out, I could hear him talking to someone in another room down the hall. He promised someone he'd have a whole lot of money soon thanks to the 'dumb bitch' he'd hooked. I would bet anything he's pushing her to seal the deal with you as soon as possible."

"Did you tell Celine?" I wondered.

"Yes, but she didn't believe me. She's wrapped up in her own narrative, and when she told me today that she planned to expose you, Jen, I couldn't take it anymore. This is all getting out of hand. I had to say something to you."

She addressed the last part to Gabe, whose frown had deepened. "I appreciate your concern, Allie, but I'm not sure what I'm supposed to do with that information or how it helps me."

"Actually, it *might* help."

Both of them turned to look at me as I gave a grim nod of determination. Remembering my brief interaction with Isaac at the travel agency when I went to see Gabe, an idea had started to form in my head.

"I need as much information as you can get me on Isaac, including all of his social media accounts."

"What are you thinking?" Gabe asked.

"He had no problem cheating *with* her, and in my experience, cheaters never change. Maybe it's time to give him a little loyalty test."

Chapter Seventeen

~Jennifer~

It took almost an hour to get all the information I needed. Allie searched through Celine's social media accounts to find any links to Isaac while Gabe checked his work group chats and Googled for anything else he could find. As they fed me information, I built up a picture of the man and what would tempt him.

"Won't he recognize you?" Gabe wondered as we worked. "Celine might have shared everything with him."

"She could have, and he definitely saw me visit you in your office last week. I recognized him when we made eye contact."

His eyebrows drew down in a look of concern. "How is this going to work, then? He'll know who you are."

"I won't approach him under my regular account. I have a backup account for just this purpose."

Allie looked up from her phone, her eyebrows raised skeptically. "How often does this exact scenario happen to you?"

Gabe and I both laughed, appreciating the moment of levity in the midst of so much stress. "Alright, maybe not for this *specific* purpose. I use the backup account when my first approach doesn't go well, not because they pass but because I did something wrong. Even the best flirters in the world make mistakes."

I gave Gabe a wink that made him grin.

"Sometimes, I'll say something that's a turn-off to them that I didn't realize would be. If I think it's worth trying again, I let a few days go by and I approach them from my back-up account instead. The profile pictures belong to a friend of mine who gave me permission to use them. It's harder because I can't video chat if they get suspicious, but often, it's still enough to get through."

As my methods became more honed with experience, I needed that account less and less, but I kept it updated anyway, just in case. Isaac definitely counted as a 'just in case'.

Allie's phone dinged after a few more minutes and she grimaced. "That's Brad, I need to get home. Good luck, guys. And I'm sorry, Gabe, for the part I played in all of this."

"Thank you for coming over tonight." He stood to give her a quick hug, as forgiving and understanding as always. "We probably won't see each other again."

"Probably not," she agreed with a regretful smile. "Take care of yourself. Bye, Jen."

"Bye." I waved through the screen and went back to my work while Gabe walked Allie to the door. I'd almost finalized my plan of action, but I wanted to suggest one more thing to Gabe first. When he returned to the living room on his own, I dove into my idea. "I think you should go to a hotel. I'll get in touch with Sarah, the private investigator, and see if she can stake out there with a camera."

Gabe didn't need me to explain any further, already on the same page with me. "You're going to invite him to meet you there."

"Exactly. I'll have records of the screenshots and we'll have pictures of him arriving. You'll need to give him the ultimatum when he gets there."

Gabe let out a small huff. "That's the same word Celine used tonight: ultimatum."

"Well, she had one thing right: this has to end. The sooner, the better."

He nodded, his jaw firmly set. "What options am I giving him?"

We still needed to talk about that. "Here's how I see the situation based on what Allie said. Celine loves Isaac but Isaac is using her for the money they're hoping to get from you. We're going to bank on the fact that Celine cares more about Isaac than she does about the money."

Another breath left Gabe's lips, slower and longer than before. "That's a gamble. I'm not sure she's ever loved anyone but herself."

"That's your bruised ego talking," I suggested gently. "She said she loves him, so for now, let's assume that's true. We get Isaac to tell her to take the settlement you offer her or he'll break up with her. If she really does love him, she'll take the deal."

"And Isaac will go along with that if he doesn't want us to reveal to Celine that he almost cheated?"

"Exactly." It felt like he read my mind sometimes, we were so in tune. "Now, we just need to decide what to offer her. It has to be significant enough to make Isaac want to stay on her good side. If he's with her for the money, there has to *be* some money."

"She might not accept the promise of a future payout," he warned me. "She might not trust it, assuming that I'll try to find a way out of it, and she has debts she wants to pay off now."

I'd already reached the same conclusion. "I agree, and it would be much better for you to get it all taken care of for good rather than having it hanging over you."

"I don't have anything to offer her now, though."

"No, but I do."

Gabe's eyes went wide as he stared down at me through the phone screen. "Jen, I can't take your money. This isn't your issue."

"How is it not my issue? She's threatening to expose my address and I'll have to move if she does. Paying her off would spare me that hassle. I have some money invested from what Matt gave me. It's not nearly as much as half your inheritance, but if it can end this madness tonight, I'd consider it money well spent."

Gabe turned away, staring out his window at the setting sun as he considered my offer. My fingers twitched to get back to my work, knowing we didn't have a lot of time, but I held back, waiting for him to make up his mind.

At last, he turned back to me. "I'll pay you back. When I get my inheritance, I'll repay every penny."

"Alright." I had no intention of holding him to that, but it obviously made him feel better to make the offer, so I let it slide. "You find a hotel and book a room. I'll get in touch with Sarah, and then we'll go after Isaac."

Another half-hour later, Gabe and Sarah were both on their way to the hotel and I typed out my first DM to Isaac. My heart beat so fast, it almost felt like my very first job.

Instagram looked like my best bet to make contact. His profile couldn't be more textbook for the type of men I usually dealt with: shirtless pics, mostly in the gym, along with travel pictures showing him looking sophisticated and wealthy. Comments from friends about the fun they had on nights out. A few comments here and there from Isaac himself about liking a direct woman who made the first move. Showing off his car and his expensive clothes. More than enough for me to take an educated guess at what would hook him.

Just like I had with Gabe, I started with a shared interest in travel.

> Hey. You don't know me, but your travel pics are incredible! You're so lucky to travel so much.

He didn't reply right away. They never did. They always took a couple of minutes to check out my profile and decide if talking to me would be worth their time, based purely on the way I looked. In this case, he'd be looking at my friend who, from my point of view, had the advantage over me in the looks department anyway. Isaac stared at my chest when I went to the travel agency office, and a few of the first pics on my fake profile showed off my friend's very shapely breasts in a way I knew deep in my gut would appeal to him.

I could have tried to distract myself while I waited, but it wouldn't have been any use. All my attention remained focused on the phone in my hand. When the notification for a message popped up, I nearly jumped in my seat.

> Thanks. I'm a travel agent, so I get paid to do it. Living the dream. ;)

The message itself didn't give much away, but the winky-face at the end opened the door to a more flirtatious tone, and I jumped straight through it.

> Sounds amazing. Looking for an assistant? I don't take up much room.

> In my suitcase?

> Or your bed. ;)

I threw in a wink of my own as I cranked the heat a little higher.

> Your profile says you live in SF. Are you here now or are you somewhere exotic?

> I'm home. You in SF?

> Just for tonight, leaving in the morning. I'm alone in my hotel and bored.

> So you're scrolling IG for a hook-up? Girl, you heard of Tinder?

I sent a few laughing emojis, as if it were the funniest thing I'd ever heard.

> Not specifically looking, but your pics have me thinking all kinds of things I shouldn't. If you like taking trips, maybe you should take one over to my hotel.

The phone went quiet for a minute and my stomach sank. Did I push too hard, too fast? Had we actually misjudged him? A dozen worst-case scenarios raced through my mind before another message eventually came through.

> I'm in the middle of something but I could head out in about an hour. Send me a pic so I know what you're wearing tonight.

He wanted to check my identity, but luckily, I'd anticipated that. From my cache of photos of my friend, I pulled out one of her in a teasing pose sitting on a hotel room bed, her chest pushed out and a wolfish grin on her face. Using an app built for that purpose, I adjusted the embedded info to make it look like the picture had been taken that night and sent it with a short message.

> Don't make me wait too long.

His reply came a lot faster that time.

> What hotel are you at?

If this were a normal case, I'd screenshot that message and consider this a fail, but that night, I sent him the address before sending Gabe a separate message.

> He says he's coming. Over to you now.

~Gabriel~

Along with the investigator waiting with a camera outside, I set up my phone inside the hotel room to record our conversation, hidden behind my bag so it wouldn't be seen. Doing anything undercover or underhanded or sneaky had never been in my comfort zone, but faced with Celine's scheming, I didn't hesitate. As soon as the message from Jen came through to say that Isaac took the bait, I set up my phone and sat back to wait for his arrival.

While I waited, my thoughts drifted over the past month of my life and the crazy turns it had taken. If someone had told me at the beginning of the year that my marriage would be over and I'd be happy about it, and that I'd be eagerly looking forward to building something with someone new, I would have suggested they get their head examined. Everything I knew about myself and my relationship had been flipped around, giving me an entirely new perspective, and even though the way it came about was hardly ideal, I would always be a little grateful to Celine for hiring Jen.

If she hadn't, we might have never met.

The knock on the door came almost ninety minutes after Jen's message, just after midnight. Had Isaac left Celine sleeping in his bed while he came over for a booty call with a stranger? He'd always seemed like a nice enough guy in the office, but now, I knew the truth. *What a piece of shit.*

I went over and pressed 'record' on my phone before going to the door.

Knowing he might try to bolt when he saw me standing there instead of the beautiful woman he expected to see, I didn't give him the chance. In one fluid motion, I swung the door open wide, grabbed him by the shirt and yanked him inside the room, slamming the door shut behind us.

"What the fuck? Gabe?"

Wearing a baseball cap, he gaped at me, a mixture of confusion, guilt and fear dancing across his face.

"You remember I exist? That's a good start." I shoved him away from me but kept my back to the door, blocking his exit. "We need to talk."

His dark eyes looked back over his shoulder, scanning the room to see if anyone else lingered in the dark recesses, but he missed the phone peering out from behind my bag, recording every word. A nervous hand ran over his beard while his brain caught up with the situation.

"You set me up?" he demanded when he seemed satisfied we were alone.

"Bingo. You were texting Jen, the same woman Celine hired to try to set me up. She used someone else's account."

His nostrils flared. "Fuck."

"Exactly: you're fucked. We've got the screenshots of your conversation and someone outside who took pictures of you arriving here. Celine will get a copy of all of that first thing in the morning unless..."

I let the last word linger in the air, giving the implications of his actions a chance to set in before I made my demands.

"Unless what?" he eventually asked, his eyes still wary but curiosity getting the better of him.

"Unless Celine agrees to my settlement terms."

He let out an unimpressed huff. "You should talk about that with her."

"I tried. She refused. Now, I'm going to explain to you why you're going to convince her otherwise. Take a seat."

My hand waved at the two chairs I'd set up at a perfect angle for the phone to capture everything. Mistrust lingered in Isaac's expression but he took a seat as I suggested and I did the same, now that I felt fairly certain he wouldn't bolt before hearing me out.

"Since you've been having an affair with my wife for a while now, I'm going to assume you know about the money I'm due to inherit."

Greed flashed through his eyes before he could rein it in. "Celine mentioned it."

"Her having any right to that money hinges on her proving that I cheated on her, which is why she tried to set me up. Even after all the trouble she went to, she must know her case has holes in it or she wouldn't be blackmailing me by threatening to release Jen's personal information online. I've spoken to Jen and she's prepared to deal with the consequences if Celine goes ahead. There's a very good chance Celine will get nothing from my inheritance, and if my lawyer really wanted to play dirty, I could probably make a case for me keeping the house too, since I've been the only one paying for it and she cheated on me with you."

His jaw tightened as I laid it all out. "Why are you telling me all of this? Why did you bring me here?"

"Because apparently, she cares about you, although I'm not sure why given that you ran over here to cheat on her tonight." He didn't bother to look guilty about that or show any degree of shame so I moved on. "I think you're the only one who can convince her not to doxx Jen. If you tell her not to, she might actually listen. She sure as hell won't listen to me."

"And if I don't stop her, you'll tell her about this," he guessed, gesturing at the room around us.

"Right. If she has any sense, she'll dump you and you'll get nothing."

"You just said she won't get anything anyway," he reminded me grumpily.

"No, I said she won't get my inheritance money. However, if she doesn't expose Jen and she signs the agreement my lawyer will put together, I'm willing to give her the house and $250,000 right away, without needing to wait for the inheritance to come through."

Jen had decided on the figure. She said it needed to be significant enough to make it worth Isaac's while, and from his reaction, I could tell I had his full attention. It might not be fair to me given what Celine had put me through, but I still had my inheritance coming to me, and if it put this whole mess behind us, it would be worth it.

"The whole thing can be over tomorrow, you guys can move on with your life and I'll move on with mine. But there will be a clause in the agreement that if Jen's personal information *ever* comes out online, you have to repay every cent."

"That's not fair," he immediately protested. "What if someone else releases it?"

"She's been doing this job for years and Celine's the only one who's been crazy enough to stalk and threaten her. I'm not worried about anyone else. If it comes out, I'm blaming Celine."

His lips pressed tightly together and he looked to the side, thinking it all over. "It's a lot less than she expected to get."

"It's also a lot more than nothing. The inheritance isn't an option. You just need to decide between the deal I'm offering or having your cheating ass exposed."

His jaw tightened, clenching hard as he ground his teeth, but eventually, he nodded. "Alright. I'll talk to her and try to get her to agree."

I should have let it go there but I couldn't help asking one more question. "Did you ever love her?"

"Celine?" The fact that he even had to clarify would have answered my question enough, but he gave me a further explanation. "It's nothing personal, Gabe. She came onto me first, when you were out of town. I thought it would be a one-time thing, but she kept coming back. Then she told me about the money and..."

He spread his hands, like that explained everything.

"You know the rest."

I knew enough. "Go home, Isaac."

He didn't wait to be asked twice. He disappeared out the door and I went over to stop the recording, sending a copy to Jen as a backup before I packed up and headed back to my own house. One way or another, this would all be coming to a head the next day so I needed to try to get some rest while I could.

~Jennifer~

I hadn't left my home so often in years, but early Monday morning, I sat on another plane, heading back to San Francisco. Gabe had an appointment with his lawyer at nine o'clock, before he headed to work, and I wanted to be there for it.

At almost one o'clock that morning, he sent me the recording from his meeting with Isaac, and though I usually maintained that nothing good happened over text after midnight, that might have been the exception. It provided everything we could have asked for: he didn't deny that he'd been looking for a hook-up and he all but admitted he only wanted Celine for the payday she promised.

In spite of everything, I actually felt sorry for her. Men could be awful, and Isaac certainly fell in that category. To think that she threw away someone like Gabe to be with him filled me with pity.

Gabe met me outside the office building downtown, giving me a nod of greeting like he might give to any acquaintance. We couldn't be sure if Celine still had a tail on him, so he didn't touch me at all until we got in the elevator to go to his lawyer's office and, finding ourselves alone, he leaned down to press a hard, needy kiss on my lips that stole my breath away.

"I missed you."

"We were apart for one night," I tried to tease, but my voice came out too breathy for it to have any sting.

"One night too long." His hand fisted my hair, pulling my head back so he could kiss me again. "I'm going to give my notice today at the office and take the rest of my vacation time. I'm coming to Pasadena with you when you go back. I'll find a cheap place to stay until I get a new job. I'll sleep in the park if I have to, as long as I can see you every day."

This possessive, dominant side of him never failed to weaken my knees, and I leaned into him, kissing him again until the elevator computer announced our floor. We broke apart just before the doors opened.

Victoria welcomed us into her office right on time. "It's nice to meet you in person, Ms Bradshaw, though I'm curious about what made this meeting so urgent since we last spoke."

I let Gabe handle the conversation as he brought her up-to-speed on his visit to Pasadena, Celine's threats, and his covert operation the night before. I chimed in at the end only to bring up the ongoing damage being done by Celine's posts about me online.

"I want to get something together for her to sign, quickly, that'll be legally binding," Gabe explained once we'd put everything on the table.

"Are you sure?" Victoria asked point-blank. "If she makes good on her threat, we could get the police involved. Even if she doesn't, I feel pretty confident that we can win this and leave her with next to nothing. This kind of unhinged behaviour doesn't go over well with the courts."

"I don't want to take the chance." Gabe glanced over at me, his hand finding mine under the table. "I'd rather protect Jen and get Celine out of our lives as soon as possible, even if it costs me."

"If that's your decision, then we'll put together an agreement." She typed something into her phone before looking over at me. "If Celine agrees to the terms, there'll be nothing stopping you from defending yourself online. You'll just need to be careful not to post anything that could identify her."

"I've actually drafted a response already, if you wouldn't mind taking a look at it?"

I handed over my phone and she read through it, making a few suggestions before returning the device to me. "I have to say: this is one of the more interesting situations I've dealt with. Just when I thought I'd seen it all, I get loyalty tests, surveillance and gold-digging new boyfriends."

"Trust me, none of it was my idea," Gabe told her drily, and we all shared a smile before shaking hands and parting ways.

Outside, Gabe called a cab and we made the trip to his office together. The café on the corner I'd noticed the first time I visited him there seemed like a perfect place for me to spend the day, working from my phone while I waited for Gabe.

"Celine said she'd come to my office today to get my answer," he reminded me. "I'm going to text her and ask her to meet me at the café instead. Hopefully, Isaac has spoken to her and I get the agreement from the lawyer in time, and we can get this all settled relatively easily."

"I hope so." Although I would have liked to give him a quick kiss to say goodbye, I settled for squeezing his hand instead, hoping it wouldn't be much longer before we could show affection publicly without worrying someone might be watching. How did famous people deal with it? I would much rather enjoy my quiet life behind my phone than deal with that every day.

The rest of the morning passed quickly as I got into a rhythm with work. Most of my tests took place later in the evening, but that day, I had a job that involved a man whose wife worried he might be messing around on her while at work. I messaged him directly through his office number and he quickly moved from the professional to casual flirting, leading me to believe she had cause for concern.

We were in the middle of an exchange when the text from Gabe came through.

> She'll be here in ten minutes.

I kept up the exchange with the other man for five more minutes before telling him I had an appointment and turned on the recording app on my phone, placing it face-down on the table. It might not fool Celine, but at least we'd have a record of whatever happened.

With my eyes trained on the door, I saw them the moment they came in, Gabe holding the door for her like the gentleman he couldn't help being.

After her playing such a large part in my life for the past few weeks, it felt strange to finally see her in person. Celine looked like I remembered her from Gabe's social media posts: tanned and confident, blonde streaks running through her brown hair and big brown eyes behind false lashes. Her pretty dress showed off her long legs in her high heels, making me feel underdressed in the slacks and blouse I wore to be comfortable on the plane.

Gabe led her straight over to my table, and when her eyes landed on me, they widened for a second before narrowing, disdain and dislike settling into the purse of her lips and the set of her jaw. Apparently, she hadn't had Gabe followed that morning after all. My presence came as a complete surprise, and it wouldn't be the only one she got during this meeting.

"Hello, Celine." I gave her a tight smile of my own, trying not to give anything away. "Thank you for joining us."

Her gaze flickered between me and Gabe as she sank into the seat he pulled out for her. "Why are you here? What's going on?"

Gabe sat down next to me, his shoulder brushing against mine in a clear demonstration of intimacy, and the flare of her nostrils intrigued me. She actually seemed jealous.

"I've had some time to think over your ultimatum," Gabe started. "And I'm not going to sign the papers. Instead, you can accept *my* offer or we can let this all play out in court."

Again, her gaze darted between the two of us, her mind obviously racing as she tried to figure out what she'd missed. "If you don't sign, then I won't hold up my end of the bargain either."

Apparently, she didn't plan to state her threat out loud again, not in public and not in front of me. Reckless, she might be, but not quite *that* foolish.

Neither was I.

"In all your scheming, you made one big miscalculation: you didn't get to know anything about me. When I start working with a new client, I find out everything I can about them. I do research, I ask questions. But you pulled me into your game without knowing the first thing about me."

She huffed, leaning back in her chair and crossing her long legs. "What's there to know? You seduce men for a living. I'm pretty sure there's a word for that."

If she couldn't do better than that for an insult, I felt even more sorry for her than before. Ignoring the comment, I continued my explanation. "If you'd checked into me, you might have figured out that, like Gabe, someone left me a large sum of money when they died. I don't *need* to work. I enjoy what I do, but if I had to stop doing it today, I'd be okay. If I need to move because you leak my address, I'd survive. What I *won't* put up with is you stealing from a man who would have never cheated on you if you hadn't set up this ridiculous charade in the first place."

From the corner of my eye, I could see Gabe's eyes on me. We hadn't discussed that I would say any of this. I hadn't planned to, but seeing her in person, seeing the consideration that he still showed to her thanks to his basic decency, snapped something inside of me.

"Gabe's offer is incredibly generous, and if you actually care about the money and not just causing as much destruction as possible, you'll take it and be grateful."

With that, I turned back to him, giving him a nod to tell him to go ahead. A smile played on the corners of his lips as he cleared his throat.

"Here's the offer: I'll give you the house and $250,000 if you agree today. You'll promise not to release any of Jen's information and to delete and retract everything you posted about her online. If her details *ever* come out, I'm holding you responsible and you would owe me the entire amount back. It's legally binding."

He pulled the papers out of his courier bag and pushed them across the table to her.

"This is only 10% of what I'm entitled to," she sniffed, and my hands clenched into fists under the table. Gabe took my hand in his to help calm me.

"If you include my half of the house, it's almost 20%," Gabe pointed out. "And you're not entitled to anything after cheating on me. It's a hell of a lot more than you deserve."

Although I hadn't said anything that time, her eyes flashed up at me, full of anger, before returning to the papers. "I can't sign anything without having my lawyer look at it."

"But you wanted me to sign your papers last night. Seems like a double standard to me."

Pride flowed through my veins as he stood up for himself, his hand never leaving mine. Celine grumbled a little more under her breath, but I could tell the offer tempted her. It seemed Isaac had done his job of convincing her to take the money and run.

When she pulled out a pen and signed the agreement, it almost felt anticlimactic. After everything she'd put Gabe through, it felt like there should have been a fanfare, something to mark the moment that she agreed to the divorce and removed herself from his life.

No trumpets blared, though. Only Gabe's hand squeezing mine marked the moment.

I'd take it.

When she stood up to go, however, I stopped her. "There's one more thing you should know."

Again, Gabe and I hadn't discussed what I would say, but in spite of everything, I still didn't think that anyone deserved to be cheated on.

Not even Celine.

"I did a loyalty test on Isaac. Do you want to know how he did?"

A spark of fear and doubt bloomed in her eyes, but she shook her head. "You're lying. I don't believe you."

Turning on her heel, she walked away, and Gabe and I both exhaled in unison.

"Would you really have told her?" he asked me. "We told Isaac we wouldn't."

"I'll always stick up for the person who's been wronged, so yeah, I would have told her. But I didn't have to. She knows, she just wants to pretend for a while. Maybe she thinks once she has the money, she'll be able to keep him. You can't help someone who doesn't want to be helped."

With that sobering thought, Gabe gave me a gentle kiss. "I have to get back to the office and finish wrapping things up. Do you have your return flight booked?"

"Not yet."

I had an idea why he asked, and when he confirmed it, I couldn't stop the grin that spread across my face. "Make it for two. I'm coming with you."

It would be our first flight together, but not our last. We were just getting started.

~Gabriel~

When I left the café with Celine's signature on the agreement, it felt like everything had fallen into place.

In reality, it didn't turn out to be quite that simple.

Two days after leaving San Francisco, two days in which I stayed at Jen's house, enjoying her company while I began applying for new jobs, we spent the afternoon at the kitchen table, both of us focused on our respective computers. I'd applied to several jobs and just opened an email from Manuel at the Four Winds hotel, telling me they'd figured out who Celine had bribed to access their records and security footage, when Jen let out a long breath from the other side of the table.

"Shit."

My head raised from my laptop, shooting her a concerned look. "What is it?"

"She posted it. My address. One of my clients just forwarded it to me."

My stomach sank as I leapt to my feet, taking the few steps over to her to see it for myself. Posted anonymously, it repeated the previous claims made about Jen stealing me for herself and, clear as day, listed her home address, the house we were sitting in at that very moment.

"Fuck," I muttered, smacking my hand against the table top in frustration. "Why would she do that?"

"I'm not sure, but people don't always act in their best interests. At least the money hasn't left my account yet."

My lawyer had been finalizing things with Celine's lawyer and I planned to sign over the house to her and send the payment next week. At that point, nothing had actually been completed. The whole process could be stopped, so Celine completely shot herself in the foot. For what? Revenge on Jen? To spite me? It didn't make any sense.

While I got on the phone to my lawyer, Jen made some calls of her own, making temporary arrangements for somewhere else to stay while she decided what to do in the long run.

By the time I hung up, I had several messages from Celine, asking me to call her urgently.

Gritting my teeth, I dialled. "I've got nothing to say to you," I spit out as soon as she answered. "You know what you did and you know what the consequences are."

"Gabe, please." She sounded close to tears if not actually crying already. "I didn't do it."

"*That's* what you're going with? Really?"

"It's the truth," she sniffled. "Isaac posted it."

That made even less sense. "Why would he do that?"

"Because I broke up with him after I searched his phone and found out he's been screwing around on me." Bitterness joined the despair in her voice, and I closed my eyes, shaking my head. It seemed Jen had been right: she didn't need to show Celine the results of her loyalty test. Planting the thought in her head had been enough, and when curiosity got the better of her, Celine figured out the truth for herself. "He got so angry, he posted the draft I'd saved out of spite."

Normally, I wouldn't take any pleasure in someone else's misfortune, but when that misfortune had been caused by the consequences of her own actions, I couldn't muster up a lot of sympathy. "You know what the agreement says: if the address gets out in *any* way, you're responsible for it."

"That's not fair, I didn't..."

I had no interest in hearing the rest of that sentence. "Are you really going to whine to me about what's fair? He never would have had access to the address if not for you, and he wouldn't have had access to your phone if you hadn't cheated on me with him. I'd say you reaped what you sowed here, Celine. My lawyer will be in touch. Don't call me again."

With that, I hung up and blocked her number, feeling a weight lift off me for just a moment before the reality of the situation crept back in.

"Any luck?" I asked Jen, who had finished her own call and caught at least the tail end of my conversation.

Her eyebrows were raised in curiosity but she answered my question. "One of Matt's sisters has an AirBnB that's empty at the moment. She says we can stay there for a while."

"I thought you weren't in touch with his family anymore." It had been clear when she told me the story how much she regretted that fact.

"I haven't been, but I thought it might be time to reach out. She sounded happy to hear from me. What did Celine have to say?"

I filled her in on our conversation while we both packed up our things for an extended stay in another house. My things were easy enough, since I only had the two suitcases I brought with me from San Francisco.

Jen sighed when I finished my explanation. "Usually, I say that men who cheat are the worst, but in this case, I think they're equally as bad as each other. I almost wish that they'd stay paired off so no one else has to put up with them."

My laugh came out as a snort as I pressed my lips together. "At least I won't have to borrow money from you anymore, but it means so much to me that you were willing to do it. I'm so sorry that your information got leaked."

"It's okay." When I cocked an eyebrow in disbelief, Jen smiled. "Honestly, it is. This house, this neighbourhood... this is the life Matt and I wanted. Maybe it's time to think about what makes sense for me without him. We could look at new places together if you want."

My body froze in place as I tried to interpret her words, wondering if I'd misunderstood or taken them a leap too far. "You want to get a place together?"

"It makes sense since we're both looking at the same time." She shrugged as she folded another shirt into her suitcase. "I'm not playing games here, Gabe, and I don't think you are either. They say that you see a person's true character under pressure. Over the past month, I've seen you under a hell of a lot of pressure, and I like the man I've seen. It seems silly to put off something we both want because of anyone else's expectations. I can buy it and you can be my tenant, or we can buy it together, whatever makes you comfortable. I only have one condition."

"What's that?" I asked, even though I couldn't think of much that she would say that would make me *not* want to move in with her.

"If you realize it's not working for you anymore, you have to be honest with me. Tell me the truth up front."

"I can definitely do that." Stepping up behind her as she folded more clothes for her bag, I wrapped my arms around her waist and pressed a soft kiss to her cheek before resting my head on her shoulder. "I want the same from you. Obviously, I'm clueless when someone isn't into me anymore, so if you don't tell me directly, I'll never figure it out."

Her giggle filled the room with warmth and I spun her around, grabbing the clothes from her hands and tossing them aside as I lowered my mouth to hers in a deep, hungry kiss.

I couldn't imagine ever getting tired of this.

Epilogue

One year later

~Jennifer~

Gabe's arms wrapped around me from behind, his body firm and warm against my back. "So? Is it what you imagined?"

In front of me, three massive, intricately tiled buildings with domed tops and columns faced each other across a wide square. People bustled around us, exclaiming to each other in various languages, taking photos and buying souvenirs. The strong sun warmed my arms and face and a hint of spice still lingered in the air from the market we'd walked through. More than 7000 miles from Pasadena, everything exotic and new, I felt completely at home in Gabe's embrace.

"You know I only said I wanted to go to Uzbekistan as a way to hit on you, right?" I teased, tearing my eyes away from Samarkand's majestic Registan Square to look over my shoulder at the equally stunning sight of the handsome man behind me.

Gabe's blue eyes were mere inches from mine as he placed a soft kiss on my cheek. "You can pretend all you want but I saw that sparkle of excitement in your eyes when we talked about it for an hour."

"An hour in which you ignored every single innuendo I made."

"Because I had a wife." His arms tightened around me, his relief at the past tense as obvious to me as if he'd stated it out loud. With the six-month waiting period and all the various stages of paperback in California, his divorce had only gone through a month ago. "I think I've made up for it, though."

"You definitely have. You catch all my innuendos now *and* you brought me here. I'll let it go."

Hand-in-hand, we explored the centuries-old madrasas, old Islamic schools with beautiful tile mosaics and stunning architecture. Together, we picked out a hand-painted plate from one of the stalls to hang in our new house back in Pasadena. The jewellery tempted me and I spent a long time debating over a gorgeous but expensive ring before deciding I didn't really need it.

We strolled through the garden alongside the square and spent the rest of the afternoon getting lost in the old city and Jewish quarter of the city, far from the sanitized tourist track. Without speaking a word of English, a man showed us how he baked the city's distinctive round loaves of bread in a large clay oven, sticking them to the rounded dome of the oven while they cooked and peeling them down with a long pole when they were perfectly baked.

In the evening, we had a reservation at the restaurant in our hotel, a place Gabe needed to vet before recommending it to the clients of the travel agency he started working for within a month of moving to Pasadena. In just a few weeks, the inheritance from his grandparents would come through, all five million dollars of it, but he intended to keep working for a while.

"The only thing I would want to use it on is travelling," he told me. "And my job lets me do that. For now, I'll put it away until it's needed."

That worked for me. I already had everything I truly wanted anyway.

When we reached the beautiful internal courtyard of our hotel, the garden providing a haven from the busy, warm streets of the city, Gabe pulled us to a stop and kissed my hand. "There's something else I need to check on for work. Why don't you have a rest and get changed for supper and I'll meet you back here in an hour?"

My head cocked to the side curiously. He hadn't mentioned any other places he needed to go. "What is it? I'm happy to go with you."

"It's a barber shop," he replied with a laugh. "Men only. I won't be long."

With a shrug, I let him go and climbed the outside stairs to our room. Each guest suite had its own staircase leading to an outside sitting area that faced the internal garden. Inside, the double bed lay beneath a painted fresco resembling the desert sky at sunset. Each morning, the staff brought breakfast to where we sat on the rectangular platform that surrounded the table, pillows at our backs and our legs stretched out in front of us, laying out enough food to feed an army in front of us. Thankfully, all the walking we'd done that day helped me to work up enough of an appetite that I could eat again that night.

I sat on the bench with a book for half an hour before having a quick shower to wash the dust of the day away and to put on a light dress for dinner, as Gabe suggested. Returning to the courtyard garden, I didn't see him immediately, so I took a seat on one of the benches, inhaling the rich, floral scent of roses and jasmine from the flowers around me. Another couple walked by, nodding hello to me on their way to the restaurant, but otherwise, I had only the chirp of birds for company. My eyes closed as I inhaled again, enjoying the quiet after all the excitement of the day.

When I opened my eyes again, Gabe had appeared, standing a few feet away from me with a soft smile on his face. His dark hair had been cut short, his face clean-shaven, and he'd changed too, wearing pants and shoes instead of the shorts and sandals that he'd had on earlier.

"What?" My lips curled and my cheeks flushed under his attention, staring at me as if I might disappear if he looked away.

His voice sounded husky as he took a step closer. "All the men you flirt with have no idea how amazing you truly are. I'm so lucky that I figured it out."

"I figured out how amazing you are first," I teased him, getting to my feet and taking the arm he offered me. "You're just lucky I made the first move."

Rather than teasing me back, as he normally would, he readily agreed. "I *am* lucky. So damn lucky."

His lips pressed gently against mine before we turned towards the restaurant, but after only a couple of steps, something fell out of his pocket.

"Sorry, hang on."

He crouched down to retrieve the item, and by the time I turned back to see what happened, he'd gotten to one knee.

The air flew out of my lungs and everything seemed to go into slow motion as he held out a beautiful ring to me, the same one I'd been admiring earlier that day.

We'd never talked about marriage in any concrete way. Until his divorce went through, there hadn't been any point, and I didn't want him to feel we had to rush into anything.

It seemed he had other plans.

"I told myself I wouldn't ever marry anyone again without travelling with them first." His eyes shone with humour, affection and love. "This has already been the best trip of my life, and I want a lifetime more of them. Will you take this adventure with me?"

"I will," I agreed, beaming as he got back to his feet and slipped the ring onto my finger. Before he could kiss me, though, I placed my index finger against his lips. "On one condition."

His eyebrows lifted in curious amusement. "What's that?"

"We sign a prenup to state that your inheritance is yours, no matter what."

He knew he didn't have to worry about me trying to manipulate him, but I wanted it to be clear anyway. I didn't want money to ever come between us, or between me and his family the way it had with Matt's parents. Matt's sisters and I had reconnected after one of them rented her house to me and Gabe last year, but his parents might never come around.

"I'll sign anything you put in front of me, as long as you're mine."

Wrapping his fingers around mine, he pulled my hand away and kissed me. As it sank in that we were actually engaged, happiness and excitement bubbled up between us, heat growing in every touch, and Gabe pulled back just enough to look into my eyes.

"You know, this restaurant will still be here tomorrow. How hungry are you?"

"Room service sounds pretty good right now."

With a growl of approval, he pulled me back towards the stairs and up to our room. The dress I just put on hit the floor as Gabe's firm hands undressed me in no time at all. He fumbled with his pants for a second while I pulled off his polo shirt, and as soon as we were both naked, we tumbled onto the bed, my laugh turning into a gasp as his body covered mine and his lips found the spot on my neck that always made me weak. He sucked and nibbled on it until I squirmed beneath him, my legs rubbing together in a desperate bid for the friction my body craved.

His knee slid between my legs, spreading them open, and his hard cock pressed against my pussy as he continued to kiss me.

"We need to keep a list of countries we make love in," he murmured against my skin. "This is number one."

He thrust in just deep enough that I wanted more and my legs wrapped around him, pulling him closer.

"Number two," I corrected. "We have to count the US too."

His second thrust went fully in, burying him inside of me as I moaned.

"Two," he agreed. "Only 190 to go, give or take."

With each roll of his hips against me, he went in deeper, the base of his shaft rubbing against my clit. My nails scratched at his back as he began to move faster. Flush with the excitement of our new engagement, it didn't take long for me to come, and he followed soon after.

"Two," he stated again as the high of my orgasm faded and his lips pressed softly against mine. "But the first as my fiancée."

For just a second, Matt flashed through my mind, but without the usual sadness. I only saw his smile as he waved in a gesture of farewell.

I always told the women I helped that there were good men out there, and somehow, I'd been lucky enough to find *two* of them.

Gabe's arms wrapped around me again as he pulled me into his side, pressing his lips to the new ring on my finger.

Neither of us were where we once thought we'd end up, but as long as we were together, we were exactly where we wanted to be.

~~The End~~

Keep in Touch

Thank you for reading!
If you enjoyed Gabe and Jen's story, please take a moment to leave a review.

For more about my other books and to keep up-to-date with new releases, find all the links here:
https://linktr.ee/melodytyden